THE
EDUCATION
OF
PATIENCE
GOODSPEED

HEATHER VOGEL FREDERICK

Simon & Schuster Books for Young Readers
New York   London   Toronto   Sydney

SIMON & SCHUSTER BOOKS FOR YOUNG READERS
An imprint of Simon & Schuster Children's Publishing Division
1230 Avenue of the Americas, New York, New York 10020
This book is a work of fiction. Any references to historical events, real people,
or real locales are used fictitiously. Other names, characters, places, and
incidents are the product of the author's imagination and any resemblance to
actual events or locales or persons, living or dead, is entirely coincidental.
Copyright © 2004 by Heather Vogel Frederick
All rights reserved, including the right of reproduction in
whole or in part in any form.
SIMON & SCHUSTER BOOKS FOR YOUNG READERS
is a trademark of Simon & Schuster, Inc.
Book design by Lucy Ruth Cummins
The text for this book is set in Minister.
Manufactured in the United States of America
2 4 6 8 10 9 7 5 3 1
CIP data for this book is available from the Library of Congress.
ISBN 0-689-86411-6

EDITOR'S NOTE: Please refer to the author's note, Patience's delicious
recipes, and a glossary of Hawaiian language terms on pages 301-314.

For my father

One

Although the rules laid down in these pages will not absolutely make a lady, an adherence to them will at all times prevent any glaring impropriety of conduct.

—*Etiquette for Ladies, or The Principles of True Politeness*

Aunt Anne was the last person on earth I expected to see at the wharf in Lahaina that morning.

The day began much as all our days had begun since our arrival in the Sandwich Islands two weeks earlier, smack in the middle of July. Papa pushed back from the breakfast table, thanked Mrs. Wiggins politely for the meal, and headed out the door for the harbor to oversee the refitting and reprovisioning of our ship, the *Morning Star*.

And just as I had on every other morning for the past two weeks, I trailed after him into the dooryard, pleading for release from my imprisonment.

"Can't Sprigg and Glum look after Thaddeus and me?" I begged. As crotchety a pair as were Pardon Sprigg, our ship's elderly steward, and Obadiah Glumly, our dour, scrawny cook, even their company would be preferable to that of the Reverend Titus Wiggins and his family.

"They've too much to do as it is," Papa said

shortly, pausing by the picket fence and unlatching the gate. "We've been over this before, Patience."

"Well then, why can't I look after the two of us?" I countered. "I'm nearly fourteen now, Papa, and surely if we were at home on Nantucket you wouldn't think twice about it."

"We're not on Nantucket, are we?" Papa was growing irritated. "We're on the island of Maui, and it's no place for my children to go gallivanting about unattended."

I blew out my breath in a vain attempt to unstick the tendrils of hair that clung to my forehead like seaweed on a wet rock. Although the trade winds that blew steadily through these latitudes kept the heat from attaining the level of misery we often endured at home on Nantucket in high summer, the breeze didn't do much to offset the humidity. Even at this early hour the air felt sticky and dense, and I could feel sweat trickling down between my shoulder blades. "We could stay aboard the *Morning Star* then."

My father was deaf to my pleas. "Surely you can survive a few more days," he said. "Off with you now. There's a merchantman bound for New Bedford who may have room in her hold for the *Morning Star*'s oil, and I must arrange the transshipment with her captain."

Oil, oil, everlasting whale oil! Was it all Papa could

think about? As a whaleman's daughter, I was certainly well aware that the whole purpose of our three year voyage was to take as many whales as possible. Whale oil fueled lamps the world around, after all, and valuable whalebone was crafted into everything from buggy whips to corset stays. After a year at sea, the *Morning Star*'s hold was swelling with both. While we rested up here in Lahaina before resuming our cruise, Papa could speed our profits—not to mention free up valuable storage space—were he to transship a portion of our catch home to market. Still, I chafed at his complete disregard for my misery.

Closing the gate firmly behind him, my father shooed me back to the stifling care of Reverend Wiggins with a dismissive wave of his hand.

I scuffed my way gloomily back toward the parsonage, where Papa, my little brother, Thaddeus, and I were lodging temporarily with the missionary and his family. It was a most unhappy arrangement—at least for my brother and me. Papa didn't seem to mind, but then, he didn't have to spend his days cooped up with the Reverend Titus Wiggins.

Like Papa, Reverend Wiggins had shipped out from New England for this faraway place, but unlike the *Morning Star*, which fished for whales, Reverend Wiggins fished for souls.

A great walrus of a man with close-cropped brown

hair and exceptionally large ears that gave his head an unfortunate resemblance to a chamber pot, he clearly disapproved of Thaddeus and me. For one thing, he deemed us far too undisciplined, and possibly heathen as well. For another, he was pained to discover that my mathematical abilities—honed by my Nantucket tutor, Maria Mitchell—were far in advance of his.

"Entirely unsuitable for a young female mind," he had sniffed, peering over my shoulder to watch as I sifted through tables of logarithms and wrestled with the equations for solving a navigational triangle Papa had set for me.

As for the parsonage—a simple wood-framed structure that we were astonished to learn had been sent round Cape Horn from Connecticut and assembled on the spot like a puzzle—well, it was far too crowded already with Wigginses.

"'As arrows are in the hand of a mighty man, so are children of the youth. Happy is the man that hath his quiver full of them,'" Reverend Wiggins had boomed when he introduced us to his family. "Psalms, chapter one hundred and twenty-seven, verses four and five."

A quiver? More like an armory, I had thought, casting a skeptical glance at the five young Wigginses staring back at me. With another arrow soon to be

added as well, by the looks of Mrs. Wiggins's waistline, which was nearly as expansive as her husband's.

"Pleased to meet you," I'd said dutifully, not feeling pleased at all.

Their oldest child was a girl named Charity, who
had mousy brown hair like her father's and eyes to
match. She looked to be about my age, but she wore
her Sunday best and a prim expression, and I didn't
hold out much hope for friendship. Next to her, in
stair-step fashion, stood four boys, all towheads with
pale blue eyes like their mother. The youngest were a
pair of freckle-faced twins about Thaddeus's age.

"Matthew, Mark, Luke, and John," Reverend
Wiggins had boomed again. "Our very own Four
Gospels."

He'd laughed heartily at this display of wit, and
Mrs. Wiggins, a rabbit-faced woman whose worshipful gaze rarely left her husband's broad countenance,
giggled obligingly, though she'd obviously heard this
well-rehearsed tidbit before. I rolled my eyes at Papa,
who gave me a severe look and an elbow to the ribs.

Later, Thaddeus and I were lectured within an
inch of our lives on the importance of behaving like
Goodspeeds for the duration of our stay.

"Reverend Wiggins was very generous to open his
home to us," Papa had said, "and I expect you children
to be suitably grateful. After what we've just been

through, a spell ashore, some fine home cooking, and a chance to stretch your legs will do you a world of good."

Papa was referring to the *Morning Star*'s recent brush with disaster in the form of one Ezekiel Bridgewater, our whaling ship's rapscallion of a former first mate. Along with his thuggish fellow conspirators, Binyon and Todd, Bridgewater was now securely under lock and key, charged with mutiny and attempted murder and awaiting transport to the American consul at Honolulu, where the three of them would be tried and sentenced.

In light of the heartache they had caused, I had no sympathy for their plight. The trio had plotted against my father, taking over our ship and marooning him, Thaddeus, and most of the rest of our crew on a barren island. Only Providence, a batch of laudanum-laced biscuits, and my own modest skills as a navigator had allowed me and a small band of brave companions to retake the *Morning Star* and rescue our shipmates.

No, I had no sympathy for the evildoers. Not a wisp. I hoped they would never see the light of day again but rather measure out the remainder of their lives in some dank hole of a prison—or worse.

And yes, I was just as glad as the rest of my shipmates to be safely ashore for a spell. But fine home cooking? Papa must have taken leave of his senses—or his taste buds, at the very least.

Not only did Mrs. Wiggins look like a rabbit, she cooked like one too. Her meals were astonishingly bland, and she apparently mistrusted the island's bounty, for not a single piece of fish or fresh fruit ever made it to the table. Instead, we were inflicted with an endless parade of colorless porridge, rice, and potato dishes, along with stringy chicken, salt beef, and a choice between thin slices of white bread that tasted like sawdust or ship's biscuit—"zoological biscuit," as my shipmates waggishly dubbed it, on account of the abundance of small creatures that lived within and had to be chased out before one could eat it.

And as for a chance to stretch our legs, although the boys managed to escape quite frequently, Charity and I were allowed out of the house only in the late afternoon when Mrs. Wiggins received callers—native women, other missionaries, and the small band of whaling wives who were also boarding ashore for the summer while their husbands cruised the rich whaling grounds of the far north—and then only as far as the front porch. "Our daily airing," Reverend Wiggins called it, as if the two of us were a pile of musty linens that needed freshening on a clothesline in the sun.

Beyond that brief taste of freedom, our days spun out in a stultifying round of prayers, chores, and lessons, along with the troublesome task of keeping Thaddeus and the Four Gospels out of Mrs. Wiggins's hair.

"Mrs. Wiggins is in a delicate situation," Reverend Wiggins had informed me pompously, as if anyone with two eyes in her head couldn't see that. "She needs her rest."

Providing that rest was well-nigh impossible, as the two older boys teased Thaddeus and the twins unmercifully, and it was all Charity and I could do to keep them from beating the lard out of each other— or worse. What with their wriggling and wrestling, the boys had on several occasions nearly toppled Mrs. Wiggins's prized possession, a glass-fronted whatnot cabinet filled with curios, including her treasured set of silver apostle spoons, a blue-patterned Spode teapot just like the one Mama had had back home, a Dresden china shepherdess, and a lovely piece of red fan coral.

I chafed at the confinement, for I had longed to explore my new surroundings from the moment I first laid eyes on them. From the deck of the *Morning Star*, Maui had appeared like something from a dream, bobbing up out of the sea like a lush green dumpling. The sun-parched grasses of her lowlands had beckoned as they rose sharply upward into stunning emerald peaks, as did the port of Lahaina, which basked in the sun like a sleeping cat. My ocean-weary eyes had eagerly traced the narrow beach that ran the length of it, its gleaming sands hemmed with lofty coconut palms, their fronded tops waving in the wind like the parasols of proper New England ladies out for a stroll on a breezy day.

Now that I was marooned here with the Wigginses, however, exploration seemed out of the question.

I sighed and cast a final glance over my shoulder at Papa, who was striding purposefully down the dusty road toward town. Thaddeus and the Wiggins boys were nowhere to be seen—skived off for a quick game of mumblety-peg before lessons with Reverend Wiggins, most likely—so I headed for the coral-stone cookhouse that adjoined the rear of the parsonage. The clatter of dishes within told me that Mrs. Wiggins, her prim, silent daughter, and Pali, the native woman who helped with housework, had already begun washing up from breakfast.

Rescue arrived scarcely a quarter of an hour later in the unlikely form of Charlie Fishback, farmboy-turned-able-seaman and one of my dearest shipmates. He knocked at the door just as I dried the last dish.

"Charlie!" I said, spying his honest, freckle-strewn face in surprise. Turning to Mrs. Wiggins, who looked a bit shocked at this familiarity, I added more formally, "May I introduce Mr. Fishback, the *Morning Star*'s new third mate."

Papa had kept the promise he'd made after his recent rescue and after careful consideration had decided that my shipmate's bravery and pluck in helping quell the mutiny had earned him a promotion to junior officer. A well-deserved one, in my opinion.

Charlie grinned and removed his cap, revealing a shock of copper-colored hair.

"Your presence is requested at the wharf right away, Miss Patience," he said. "Captain's orders. Missionary ship *Mercury* just dropped anchor. And you're to bring Master Thaddeus as well."

Missionary ship? There must be letters from home. My heart clutched with fear. Was it bad news, then? Was it Martha, our beloved housekeeper? I didn't think I could bear it if something had happened to her, not after losing Mama just last year. I ran to find Reverend Wiggins and inform him of my father's request, then grabbed Thaddeus and followed Charlie into town.

Now here we stood at the wharf, open-mouthed in astonishment as Papa's proper schoolmarm sister from Boston clambered onto the dock. Behind her in the small craft that had ferried them to shore stood a batch of freshly minted missionaries, all of them looking about in wonder.

"Why, it's Aunt Anne!" I cried in delight. "Why

didn't you tell us she was coming, Papa?"

"I just got word a few minutes ago when the captain came ashore," he said, shaking his head. "If this don't beat all."

I waved my arms over my head. "Aunt Anne!" I shouted.

She spotted us and produced a wan smile. Suddenly I was filled with fresh hope.

"You know what this means, don't you, Tad?" I whispered to my brother. "No more Wigginses."

Thaddeus's face split into a grin, revealing the space where his two front teeth used to reside. But his smile quickly faded. "She doesn't look very happy to see us," he replied, sounding worried. "Perhaps she won't stay."

My brother was right. Aunt Anne was looking downright grim.

"She's probably just seasick," I said. "It's a long voyage from Boston, after all."

Then someone else climbed out of the ferry boat, and our jaws dropped even farther.

It was Fanny Starbuck.

"Thunder and lightning!" said Papa. "What is she doing here?"

Fanny spotted us and waved a lace-mittened hand. "Yoo-hoo!" she trilled. "Ahoy there!"

Fanny Starbuck? Not-enough-brains-to-butter-a-biscuit Fanny Starbuck, our neighbor from Nantucket? Impossible! No wonder Aunt Anne looked so sour. I felt a rush of sympathy for her at the thought of being trapped in close quarters for months on end with that silly chatterbox. It was a wonder Aunt Anne had survived the voyage at all. Or that she had any hair left on her head. I would surely have pulled mine out in exasperation.

"What's she so gussied up for?" asked Thaddeus.

What indeed, I thought, my eyes narrowing suspiciously. Next to Aunt Anne and the flock of missionaries—all sensibly clad in sober black— Fanny stuck out like a parrot in a cage full of crows. Her pink-and-white-striped silk parasol matched the fabric of her fashionably cut dress, which seemed to have magnetic properties, for it had drawn a cluster of sailors who were falling all over themselves helping haul her things up onto the dock.

Just exactly what was Fanny doing here, half a world away from home?

There could be only one reason.

Fanny Starbuck was one of Nantucket's most eligible widows. My father was one of Nantucket's most eligible widowers. I hardly needed advanced mathematics to calculate the answer to that equation.

"Oh, no!" I groaned aloud.

Thaddeus looked up at me. "What is it?"

I shook my head. No use alarming him. But if my suspicions proved correct, dollars to doughnuts Fanny Starbuck was angling to become our new stepmama.

Two

Paying and receiving visits is an
important feature in female education.
—*Etiquette for Ladies, or The Principles of True Politeness*

"I didn't invite her—she just came," said Aunt Anne in a low voice. Behind her, Fanny flashed her dimples at the helpful sailors clustered around her. "She turned up most unexpectedly on the day of our departure."

"Hang it all, Anne, couldn't you have discouraged her?" Papa did not sound at all pleased by this turn of events.

"At least someone's glad to see me," Aunt Anne retorted, embracing Thaddeus and me warmly as we flung ourselves at her. "You are a sight for sore eyes, children. How you've grown! I would hardly have recognized you, Tad. And what, may I ask, has become of your front teeth?"

My brother offered another gap-toothed grin and plucked the teeth in question from his pocket, where he had squirreled them away since Papa pulled them out for him two days ago.

"Very impressive," said Aunt Anne, poking at them gingerly. She ruffled his dark hair fondly and turned to me.

"And Patience—why, just look at you! You're almost a grown woman, dear heart." She gave me another hug, then turned to Papa. "I'm sorry if my arrival is unexpected, Isaiah. I sent word from Boston before I left, but apparently my letters never reached you."

"Apparently not," said Papa shortly.

"As for Fanny, you have Martha to thank for her presence. It was all her idea."

Meddlesome Martha! So our housekeeper was still bent on finding Papa a wife, was she? I eyed Fanny. She was certainly pretty, there was no arguing that fact. With her blonde curls and china doll complexion, she was as lovely a rose as had ever bloomed on Nantucket—aside from Mama, of course. But Fanny possessed none of Mama's keen intellect or wit. She was a frivolous, foolish, feather-headed creature, and I couldn't think of a worse match for my father.

Besides, he was immune to her charms, I thought, giving him a sidelong glance. Wasn't he?

"Hang it all, Anne," said Papa again. "This is most vexing."

"Well, there's nothing to be done for it now," Aunt Anne snapped. "You'll just have to make the best of it. Besides, as I recall, you were the one who asked me to accompany you on this voyage originally."

Papa's dark eyebrows arranged themselves into their storm warning position. "That was nearly a year ago, and you gave me an entirely different answer at the time!" he roared in a tone generally reserved for reaching sailors in the topmost rigging during a raging gale.

Behind him, Fanny flinched. I smothered a smile. It would seem that Fanny was unacquainted with Papa's Cape Horn voice.

"Well, I changed my mind, and you'll just have to accustom yourself to the idea, Isaiah!" Aunt Anne roared back.

As the two of them squared off, bossy older sister and blustering younger brother, I was struck, as always, by how alike they were. Two peas in a pod—not only in obstinate temperament but also in appearance. Both were tall and dark haired, with black eyebrows and snapping blue eyes that could blaze sparks at the drop of a penny. I knew those eyes very well, for they stared back at me from my mirror every morning, though my own hair was lighter, the same chestnut brown as Mama's had been.

"A fine welcome this is!" continued Aunt Anne.

Their raised voices had drawn a crowd of curious onlookers, and Papa's face turned a peculiar shade of purple as he struggled to compose his features.

"Of course I'm pleased to see you," he managed finally from between clenched teeth. He gave his sister an awkward hug, and I watched closely as he turned to Fanny and lifted his hat. "Welcome to Lahaina, Mrs. Starbuck," he said stiffly.

Surely this formal greeting was a good sign, I thought. Papa did not appear overjoyed to see Fanny, and it seemed to me that Martha's scheme was not off to a promising start. This pleased me greatly, as I did not want Fanny for a stepmother. I did not want anyone for a mother but my own dear Mama, and that, of course, I could never have, for she had departed this world over a twelvemonth ago.

"Thank you, Captain Goodspeed. I am very glad to be here." Fanny's dimples had vanished, and she sounded a trifle uncertain. "I do hope our arrival hasn't inconvenienced you."

Papa pursed his lips. "It's just—unexpected, is all. But rest assured that I'll make all the necessary arrangements." Turning toward shore, he squinted in the direction of the customs house. "Sprigg!" he hollered.

Our steward was loitering in the shade of a tree along with Charlie Fishback and half the crew of the *Morning Star.* From their smirks I could tell they were all thoroughly enjoying the sight of their captain and his formidable sister going at it hammer and tongs.

Hearing my father's call, Sprigg scuttled forward, his gray pigtail flapping in the brisk morning breeze.

"Sir?" he rasped. Sprigg's voice, as disagreeable as his temperament, was like sandpaper on sharkskin.

"This is my sister, Miss Goodspeed, and her, ah, companion, Mrs. Starbuck," Papa announced with a wave of his hand toward Aunt Anne and Fanny. Sprigg shot an appreciative glance at Fanny, then bobbed his head at them both and muttered a greeting. "See to their belongings, would you, while I pay a call on Reverend Wiggins and sort out the accommodations. Patience, I'm leaving Anne and Mrs. Starbuck in your care for a bit. Perhaps you and Glum can find them some refreshment aboard. I'll be back directly."

With that my father strode off, leaving us to make our own way to the *Morning Star.*

We stood there awkwardly for a moment or two, and then Sprigg cleared his throat.

"What shall I do with that?" he said, pointing to a large object that squatted amongst the jumble of trunks at the edge of the wharf.

"What is it?" asked my brother.

I turned to look. "Why, it's a piano! Who on earth brought that?"

"It's not a piano—it's a melodeon," Fanny corrected me haughtily. "Hester Halifax says that music is a delightful companion in our hours of solitude."

Hours of solitude? On a crowded whaling ship? I looked at her, incredulous. Fanny Starbuck was a bigger fool than I had thought. "Hester who?" I asked.

Fanny slipped a hand into the pocket of her dress and drew out a small crimson volume. On the cover, stamped in gilt, were the words *Etiquette for Ladies*. "Halifax," said Fanny. "The distinguished author of this book."

Aunt Anne closed her eyes wearily. I wondered if she had heard a great deal about Hester Halifax during the past six months at sea.

"Whoever she is, and whatever that instrument is, we haven't room for it aboard the *Morning Star*," I said firmly.

Fanny's face fell. "But I can't leave it here!" she wailed.

After some discussion, we decided to leave the melodeon temporarily on the dock under Charlie Fishback's watchful eye. Papa would be back soon, and he could decide what to do with it. Charlie didn't seem to mind this request, particularly not after Fanny showered him with an abundance of dimpled smiles and thanks.

Blockhead, I thought sourly, watching my shipmate as he blushed and stammered and clutched at his cap in response. Not that I was all that surprised.

Fanny generally had that effect on men—all except Papa, thankfully.

"We'll have you aboard quicker than Jack Flash, Mrs. Starbuck," creaked Sprigg, baring his teeth at her in an alarming manner. I inspected the smile carefully, for I couldn't recall having seen it before, and decided I quite preferred the grouchy Sprigg to this new and improved variety.

"Glum, might we have tea in the deckhouse?" I asked once we were aboard. It was a lovely morning, and it seemed a shame to shut ourselves below in Papa's day cabin.

Glum's gaunt face creased in displeasure. "I suppose," he said gloomily. True to his name, our cook was perpetually mournful. "Though I haven't anything much to offer. Civilized folk would have given me a bit of warning."

The deckhouse was a small shed of sorts that Papa had given over to Thaddeus and me for the duration of the voyage. Here, when the weather was fine, we sat and did our schoolwork, watched the crew as they went about their business, or just dreamed away the hours. Aunt Anne shooed Ishmael, my shipboard cat, off the small sofa within to make room for herself and Fanny. Meanwhile Thaddeus and I fetched a pair of buckets, which we upended for stools, and I dragged a bench between us to serve as a tea table. I even managed to rustle up a cloth to cover it, though I had to angle it a bit to hide the stain along one edge. *Etiquette for Ladies*, indeed. I'd show Fanny Starbuck just how civilized we could be.

Glum shuffled back in bearing a tray in his skinny arms as my brother and I launched into a description of our recent adventures.

"Did Papa tell you what happened to us?" Thaddeus asked.

"No," said Aunt Anne, leaning forward eagerly. "Do tell."

"There was a mutiny," he began, and her eyes widened in alarm. "Off the coast of—"

"Emily Hussey had a baby girl just before I left Nantucket," announced Fanny brightly, taking a sip of tea. "Cunning little thing. I think they're going to name her Lydia, after her grandmother. Died of measles not long after the birth, poor dear. The grandmother, that is, not the babe. Emily is a cousin on my mother's side, and what with her recent loss I felt it my duty to try to lift her spirits, so I sewed the most darling little layette all in violet-sprigged muslin. The fabric was straight from London and scandalously expensive—it's outrageous what that Ephraim Cole charges in his shop on Main Street— but what else was I to do?"

She took another sip of tea and rattled on. I stared

at her in fascination. Did she never stop to take a breath? Aunt Anne had a pained expression on her face, and I could only imagine that this was a question she had asked herself many times during their passage from Boston. Poor Aunt Anne.

Fanny continued blithely, "And of course you must have received word about—"

"PAPA AND I WERE MAROONED!" bellowed Thaddeus suddenly, causing Fanny to start and nearly spill her tea.

"Well!" she said indignantly. "Has no one ever taught you that it's rude to interrupt?"

My brother opened his mouth to protest. I kicked him in the shin.

"Ouch!" he said, rubbing the wounded limb. "What'd you do that for?"

Fanny frowned at us. "Martha was quite right," she said, her voice pinched tight in disapproval. "A whaling ship is no place for children without a woman aboard. You've both quite forgotten your manners, that's plain enough."

I opened my mouth to retort, but Aunt Anne broke in.

"Here, Fanny," she said smoothly, arching a warning eyebrow at me and passing Fanny a plate of sliced cake. A rather ancient cake, I thought, peering at it with some concern. I wondered where Glum had dug it up and hoped fervently that the petrified black lumps in it were raisins. "You were saying, Thaddeus?"

"Bilgewater took over our ship with Bunion and Toad," my little brother said.

Aunt Anne and Fanny regarded him with bewilderment.

"What Tad means," I hastened to explain, "is that our former first mate, Mr. Bridgewater—"

"—only we called him Bilgewater because he was a stinker," inserted Thaddeus.

"—and two of the hands by the name of Binyon and Todd—"

"—only we called them Bunion and Toad 'cause we didn't like them—"

"—mutinied and seized the *Morning Star*," I finished.

Aunt Anne, whose head had been swiveling back and forth between my brother and me like the pendulum on the grandfather clock in our parlor back home on Nantucket, put her hand to her throat.

"Merciful heavens!" she whispered.

"They left Papa and me and most everybody else on a deserted island, but they took Patience with them because she makes good biscuits," Thaddeus continued.

"They were planning to steal the *Morning Star*'s oil," I added.

"But Patience was too clever for them," said Thaddeus, stuffing a bite of cake into his mouth. Aunt Anne leaned forward in her seat again, straining to decipher my brother's mumbling. "She and Glum put laudanum in the biscuits, and when Bilgewater went to sleep, she and Sprigg and Chips and Glum and Charlie Fishback fought Bunion and Toad."

Fanny turned her gaze to me. "You were in a fight?" she asked.

I shrugged modestly.

"And she saved us too," my brother boasted. "Patience is good at mathematics—everybody knows that—and afterward she sailed the ship back to rescue us. I'm not so good at numbers yet, but I will be too someday, and then Papa will teach me to navigate just like he's teaching Patience." He finished in a spray of crumbs.

Aunt Anne gazed at me in silence for a moment, her expression a mixture of amazement and pride. My pleasure at her silent praise was short lived, however.

"Fighting is hoydenish," Fanny declared. "Hester Halifax says mildness in manner is an essential grace in woman."

I reddened. Trust Fanny to know exactly the wrong thing to say.

"And do try not to scowl so," she added smugly. "'A beautiful smile is to the female countenance what the sunbeam is to the landscape.'" Fanny took a sip of tea. "I believe I was telling you about Emily Hussey's new baby," she said, and began to prattle on once again.

I shot Aunt Anne a desperate glance and tried to force my lips to curve upward in a polite smile. I would have liked nothing better than to thump Fanny's empty head with the teapot, but we were attracting quite a crowd. Mr. Chase, our rotund first mate, had suddenly found work to oversee right in front of the deckhouse door, and he had been joined by Mr. Macy and a goodly portion of the crew.

"Perhaps your friends would like some cake," said Fanny, dazzling them all with a sunbeam of her own.

As the men rushed forward to be introduced, Aunt Anne leaned over to me.

"We'll have to try to convince her to take a nap after luncheon," she whispered. "Otherwise I'll never hear the rest of your adventure."

I stifled a giggle.

"I almost forgot, I have some mail for you." Aunt Anne reached into the pocket of her dress and drew out a sheaf of letters.

And leaving her to chaperone Fanny and her flock of new admirers, I retired to the quiet of my cabin below.

July 28, 1836

Such welcome news from all of our dear ones back home! I couldn't wait until tonight to record the tidings here on the pages of my diary.

Not unexpectedly, Martha spent four pages listing Fanny's many perfections and virtues and lecturing me on such subjects as the importance of avoiding night air in the tropics.

Patches, my island cat, was well, she wrote in closing, though clearly still pined for my absence as she spent most of her time curled up on my bed.

Miss Mitchell, my mathematics tutor back on Nantucket, wrote of her school—a success so far—and of her work at the Athenaeum. She says she sent a number of books along for me in Aunt Anne's trunk, including my very own Bowditch's New American Practical Navigator—*the latest edition! An early birthday present, she says. She also particularly recommends a biography of Sophie Germain that she has included as well. Sophie is a Frenchwoman who discovered a talent for mathematics when she was my age. The two of us would have gotten along famously, she says.*

Best of all, though, is the news from Cousin Jeremiah. He is Mama's first cousin and the Morning Star's very much missed original first mate, who broke his leg in a storm off Cape Horn and had to be shipped home to Nantucket to mend. He's been given command of his own ship, it seems, the Minerva, and is planning to bring his wife Lucy with him this time out. They hope to rendezvous with us here in Lahaina next spring!

—P.

Three

The business of dancing is to display beauty.
—The Young Lady's Book, a Manual of
Elegant Recreations, Exercises, and Pursuits

July 30, 1836

If there is any shred of a silver lining to Fanny Starbuck's unexpected appearance in Lahaina, it's that with Aunt Anne here too, Thaddeus and I are finally out from under Reverend Wiggins's thumb, even if only for the few remaining days until the Morning Star sails.

Papa has arranged for Fanny to take over our temporary quarters with the Wiggins family until he sorts out proper accommodations aboard. Meanwhile, Tad and I are back in our stateroom along with Aunt Anne. Papa has given his bunk to her, and he has set up camp on the sofa in his day cabin.

Papa is highly displeased at the prospect of shipping out with both Aunt Anne and Fanny Starbuck aboard.

"A whaling ship is not like a merchantman," he grumbles. "We are not set up for passengers."

While I am all for leaving Fanny here on Maui, both Papa and Aunt Anne say that it would be cruel to abandon her amongst strangers. Fanny seems oblivious to the fuss she has caused, brightly chirping on about the innumerable benefits to Thaddeus and me—especially me—of having her aboard.

"Patience could use some polish," I overheard her tell Papa just this morning. "Her education as a lady must not be neglected. Hester Halifax tells us that proper attention to the laws of etiquette will enable a lady to advance through life with ease to herself and with pleasure to others."

As if an assistant navigator needs polish! Or any education, beyond what Papa and Miss Mitchell have outlined for me. Just for that remark, I make sure to give her ridiculous melodeon, which squats smugly in the corner of the main cabin where it has been wedged, a kick every time I squeeze past.

—P.

Although Fanny Starbuck was not staying with us aboard the *Morning Star*, she might as well have been, for she spent nearly every waking moment in our company.

I had finally gotten my wish to see more of

Lahaina, though the experience wasn't nearly as enjoyable with Fanny in tow. For one thing, while Aunt Anne and Thaddeus and I were eager to explore the surrounding countryside, wandering its narrow lanes lined with thatched huts and friendly islanders, Fanny only wanted to shop.

"Can't we go back into town now?" she complained as we exclaimed over a towering clump of sword ferns and broad-leafed *ti* plants as big as Thaddeus.

"You are free to go anytime you wish," said Aunt Anne shortly. It was hot enough to blister paint, and Fanny had been whining all morning. Even Aunt Anne's patience was wearing thin.

"But I can't go unchaperoned," Fanny protested.

"Well then, you'll just have to stay with us, won't you?" said Aunt Anne.

As we stood there, an elderly islander approached and gestured toward a water-puddled patch of ground beside his hut. I recognized it as a taro plot, for Pali and her husband, Upa, had an identical one behind the parsonage.

"It's taro," I told Aunt Anne. "The islanders dote on it."

The old man tugged on one of the large, heart-shaped leaves and pulled up what looked like a fat potato. Smiling proudly, he handed it, dirt-encrusted roots and all, to Aunt Anne.

"Thank you," she replied politely.

"*Aloha*," said the man, using the all-purpose native word for "love" and "how do you do" and "good-bye," as we started down the road.

"*Aloha*," we echoed, and walked on.

"Whatever are you going to do with that?" asked Fanny, casting a dubious glance at the plant in Aunt Anne's hand.

"Cook it and eat it, of course," said Aunt Anne. "You know what they say: 'When in Rome, do as the Romans do.'"

Fanny pulled *Etiquette for Ladies* from her reticule, a small drawstring bag that hung from her wrist. She frowned. "Did Hester Halifax write that?"

I rolled my eyes at Aunt Anne.

"Taro is good," said Thaddeus, taking her free hand and swinging it as we walked along the dusty road. "We had it boiled at the Wigginses'. It's purple, but it tastes like potato. Except when Upa makes it into poi, then it's nasty."

Upa was the Wigginses' gardener and handyman, and just last week my brother and I had watched him roast taro roots. He dug a shallow pit in the ground called an *imu*, a sort of underground oven lined with stones. A fire was built on the stones to heat them, the taro roots were wrapped in *ti* leaves and placed upon the stones, and then everything was covered with earth. When they were done baking, Upa mashed them into a paste with a pestle and let it sit for a few days until he deemed it just right. He and Pali—and indeed all the natives we had encountered—were exceedingly fond of poi, but I agreed with Thaddeus on this point.

"Tad's right—it tastes like bookbinders' paste."

"And when have you eaten bookbinders' paste?" asked Aunt Anne drily.

Fanny heaved a dramatic sigh and fished around in her reticule again. This time she produced a whale-bone fan with which she swatted at the humid air around her face.

"I am sorely in need of refreshment," she said. "Aren't you weary of walking yet? Perhaps the hotel in town serves lemonade."

Aunt Anne held up the taro. "You could nibble on this," she said, and Fanny shot her a dirty look.

Eventually, Fanny managed to steer us back into the bustling center of Lahaina. Although Aunt Anne warned her that the prices of goods were inflated ("Those merchants are fleecing and shaving you, Fanny Starbuck"), Fanny just laughed. She dearly loved to shop, and she cruised the island's merchants with the same eagerness she approached the stores on Broad and Main streets back home.

She'd already had to purchase another trunk just to hold the silks and shawls and exotic curios she had amassed, and while we preferred to walk, her profusion of parcels meant that she had to be ferried around in one of the small handcarts that took passengers up and down the town's streets.

Fanny was enchanted with this mode of transportation but declared herself quite scandalized at the scantily dressed native men who pulled the handcarts. Their garments were indeed slight, just a loincloth made from a simple twist of *kapa,* fabric fashioned from the inner bark of a paper mulberry tree.

"It's called a *malo,*" Aunt Anne informed us over lemonade on the veranda of the mercantile. "I read about it in William Ellis's *Narrative Tour of Hawaii.*"

"Oh, Anne, trust you to know that," said Fanny with a laugh. "You've always got your nose stuck in a book."

Two spots of color appeared high on Aunt Anne's cheeks. "Well, you know what Hester Halifax says: 'The accomplishments of the mind are at all times more attractive than those of the person. The one dazzles for a time, the other shines more steadily and lasts for life.'"

I snorted, and gazed at Aunt Anne in admiration. Talk about fighting fire with fire! Across the table, Fanny's brow puckered becomingly. She sensed that she had been insulted somehow but couldn't quite put her finger on it. After a minute she gave up trying to figure it out and burbled on.

As we listened to Fanny chatter on, I noticed that Aunt Anne wore a pained expression. I suspected she was chiding herself for allowing Fanny to provoke her. My clever aunt was normally very good about holding her tongue. I, on the other hand, was not and had been hard pressed these past few days to bridle mine.

Papa had taken me to task several times already for not being mannerly.

"Since you are the lady of the house—or the ship, in this case—it is your responsibility to make all of our guests feel at home," he told me. He put special emphasis on "all," and I knew exactly whom he meant. And then he lowered his eyebrows into their storm warning position and I knew he meant business.

And so for the past few days I had continued to sigh, and pour tea, and offer plates of cookies, and pour more tea, and listen to Fanny's twaddle until I feared my eyes would roll out of my head, onto the deck, and out through the scuppers into the sea from sheer boredom.

"I simply must teach you how to tat lace," Fanny announced once we were back aboard the *Morning*

Star. With a little help from Thaddeus, who had sat upon the lid, she had managed to squash her latest purchases into her trunk and stow it under the bunk in the first mate's cabin, where she had taken up residence.

For in the end it was Mr. Chase and Mr. Macy and Charlie who had sorted out Fanny's accommodations, and not Papa at all. Mr. Chase had graciously offered up his tiny cabin to her, while Mr. Macy and Charlie nearly fell all over themselves agreeing to rearrange their living arrangements accordingly. Anything to ensure Mrs. Starbuck's comfort! Now, Mr. Chase and Mr. Macy were sharing the cabin normally reserved for the second and third mates. Charlie, the great mooncalf, had nobly volunteered to move to a hammock in steerage with Sprigg and Glum and Chips, the *Morning Star*'s carpenter.

Fanny, who was perched on Papa's red velvet sofa in the day cabin, leaned over and held her copy of *Godey's Lady's Book* under my nose. Next to *Etiquette for Ladies,* this magazine was Fanny's favorite text, and she had brought two years' worth of back issues with her from Nantucket. "Here, look at this," she said, tapping the page.

I squinted at the lace pattern she was pointing to and shrugged. Of all the useless skills for an assistant navigator, I thought in disgust. Would Fanny be pestering Mr. Chase or Mr. Macy, or Cousin Jeremiah if he were here, to learn to make lace? And what would I do with it once I was done—make a doily for my sextant?

Fanny saw my expression and pursed her lips in disapproval. "'A scowl always begets wrinkles,'" she informed me. "Hester Halifax is most insistent on this point."

Sprigg, who had surely done plenty of scowling over the years to beget the number of wrinkles lining his elderly face, poked his head into the room just then. "Miss Goodspeed," he creaked, "Glum wants to know if you found the currants at the market that he was asking after."

"Oh, Sprigg, I do apologize," said Aunt Anne. "I quite forgot about them." She rooted in the basket at her feet and produced the currants. Sprigg thanked her, bared his ivories at Fanny, and withdrew.

He and Glum had been bustling about all day like proud housewives, preparing the evening meal. It was to be a special farewell dinner, for tomorrow we would embark on the next leg of our whaling cruise. The Wigginses had been invited to join us, but Reverend Wiggins had declined. He and his family were about to set sail on an adventure of their own, it seemed, as he had been asked to start a school for native girls in Wailuku.

The seminary at Lahainaluna for the island's young men had been a resounding success, and the missionary board had decided that the time was ripe to expand their efforts and that Reverend Wiggins was just the man to do it.

"Time and tide wait for no man, eh, Captain Goodspeed?" he had boomed yesterday as he bid us all farewell. "Especially when there are heathen souls to be saved."

Sprigg and Glum had polished the best silver and concocted elaborate dishes—or as elaborate as could be expected from Glum, who was more at ease preparing salt horse (the time-honored name for the pickled beef that whaling ships fed their crews) than anything one might find in a formal dining room. Still, the scents that wafted from the galley weren't unpleasant, and mine wasn't the only stomach growling.

"My belly thinks my throat's been cut," complained Thaddeus.

Fanny gasped. "Why, Thaddeus Goodspeed, wherever did you hear such a vulgar expression?"

At this reproach my little brother's bottom lip stuck out and a mutinous expression crept across his face. Thaddeus was not one to be crossed when he was hungry. I decided to intervene.

"He heard it from Papa," I said.

Fanny's shocked look was most gratifying. It suddenly occurred to me that if I wished to scuttle her marital schemes, it might be helpful if I pointed out some of Papa's less admirable traits and qualities.

"You should hear him when he's angry," I continued, ignoring the warning glance that Aunt Anne launched in my direction. "He knows the most interesting words. But I don't think Hester Halifax would approve of most of them."

Fanny thought this over. "Well, I suppose that's only to be expected without the civilizing influence of a woman aboard," she said.

This was hardly the direction in which I had hoped to lead her. I opened my mouth to highlight another of my father's failings, but Aunt Anne broke in hastily.

"Patience, don't you think it's time you were getting dressed?" she said, with another warning look.

I sulked off to our stateroom, annoyed at having this promising new tactic sabotaged. I dragged my trunk from beneath my bunk as noisily as I could and fished out my white embroidered dress, the one with the blue sash that I had worn for my birthday party last fall. Both were crumpled, but I hadn't time to heat the iron now. I slipped the dress over my head and started to pull it on, but it stuck just below my ribs. I wriggled and squirmed and said a few words of my own that would have raised Hester Halifax's eyebrows, but it was no use. The dress simply didn't fit.

I struggled my way out of it again crossly and threw it on the floor. I must have grown in the months since I'd worn it last. And my Sunday muslin was torn and I hadn't had time (or desire, if truth be told) to mend it. There was nothing to be done for it now; I'd just have to make do with my everyday gray calico. Without the pinafore it was fairly presentable— if you didn't look too closely, you couldn't see the gravy stain—and perhaps the blue sash could be salvaged and used to perk it up a bit.

The blue sash was indeed salvageable, though a bit of a wash and a swipe with a hot iron would have improved its appearance. After I was dressed, I took Miranda, my treasured old rag doll that Mama had made for me when I was Thaddeus's age, from her place of honor on my pillow.

"You have a secret, don't you, Miranda?" I said, and lifting her skirt, I unclasped the pearls that I had wound around her cotton waist for safekeeping. They had been Mama's pearls once, and now they were mine, a gift from Papa on my thirteenth birthday.

Placing them around my neck, I peered critically into the cracked mirror that hung over the washbasin in the corner. By angling it downward, I was able to see small portions of myself at a time.

My hair was presentable, the pearls looked splendid, and the blue sash did indeed help, but still, the overall impression was not particularly favorable. I shrugged. It was only us, after all, just the *Morning Star* and her crew, the very same shipmates I'd seen each and every day now for nearly a year.

When I stepped back into Papa's day cabin, however, Fanny pursed her lips.

"Hester Halifax says that to neglect fashion altogether, or to affect a carelessness of it, is reprehensible," she informed me.

Bristling at the implied criticism, I opened my mouth to reply, but once again Aunt Anne neatly headed me off. "Wash your brother up, will you, Patience? And Fanny, if you don't get dressed now, you'll be late for the party."

A short while later, we were all seated around the table in the main cabin when Fanny made her entrance. And quite an entrance it was, too. She swanned in on a cloud of lilac satin, her hair swept up in an elaborate pouf of curls that echoed the billowy sleeves of her gown. The color set off her rosy complexion and ample charms to perfection.

Perhaps too much of certain ample charms, I thought disapprovingly, glaring at the dramatic swoop of her neckline. And said as much under my breath.

"Mind your manners," whispered Aunt Anne sharply, but the corners of her mouth twitched as she squashed a smile.

If I thought that rather too much of Fanny was on display, no one else seemed to mind. Papa and the three mates gazed at her in admiration throughout the entire meal, and Sprigg poked his head frequently out of the small pantry to have a good gawk as well.

If Aunt Anne and I secretly thought Fanny Starbuck was a ninny, our shipmates most decidedly did not.

Mr. Macy and Mr. Chase, bachelors both, continued to vie for her attention, and Charlie and Chips and the rest of the crew all took pains to show themselves to their best advantage whenever she was in their vicinity. Even Sprigg and Glum had fallen under her spell, mooning about in her presence like a pair of lovestruck schoolboys, the old seadogs.

It was Papa whom Fanny most aimed to please, however, that was entirely clear, and I was convinced she was succeeding. He smiled back now when she simpered at him, and laughed at her silly jokes. He had even begun calling her Fanny instead of Mrs. Starbuck—a development I found most worrisome. I feared that unless something was done, Thaddeus and I would soon be landed with a stepmama.

As dessert was served—a tasty tart made with

fresh pineapple—Mr. Macy rose to his feet. He was not quite as skinny as he had been when he first shipped out with us last year, and he had grown a beard, but his Adam's apple still bobbed noticeably when he cleared his throat.

"I have composed a small poem suitable for the occasion," he said, holding up his glass—toward Fanny, of course. "More of a toast, really."

I hoisted my glass morosely upward with the others as he began to recite:

> *It ain't polite to boast,*
> *But I must propose a toast*
> *To the loveliest of ladies in the fleet.*
> *We are proud they are aboard*
> *And we do not mean to hoard*
> *Them, but to share them with the rest would not be meet.*
> *We will soon be bound away*
> *To return another day,*
> *Our voyage blessed by these three beauties sweet!*

Everyone laughed and applauded, and Mr. Macy took his seat again, looking pleased. Afterward, there was dancing up on deck. Owen Gardiner, our cooper, played a spate of lively tunes on his squeezebox, accompanied by the German sailor Schmidt on the flute and Domingo, a Portuguese crew member from

Fayal, on the fiddle. I felt a pang at the first strains from the latter, for it reminded me of Long Tom, the fiddle's original owner, a gentle Swede we had lost last winter off Cape Horn.

While the rest of the crew looked on and clapped or swung each other round the fo'c'sle deck, Papa, Mr. Macy, Mr. Chase, and Charlie took turns dancing with Fanny and Aunt Anne. Fanny was as graceful as a feather, of course, and much to my surprise, my starchy aunt proved an equally lively partner. I, on the other hand, was stuck with Thaddeus most of the evening, thanks to my awkward, lumbersome plodding. Even Charlie spun me around only once—out of duty, most likely, I thought crossly, as he thanked me hastily and sprang back into line for another turn with Fanny.

Chips, a free Black from Nantucket and one of my most trusted shipmates, was leaning back against the waist of the ship watching the proceedings. He caught my eye and winked. "Give it a year or two," he said. "Then the shoe will be on the other foot."

"I don't know what you're talking about," I said, lifting my nose into the air.

He just laughed.

The kaleidoscope sunset faded and the sky turned a dusky blue. The party wound to a close. As Aunt Anne, Fanny, Thaddeus, and I bid our shipmates good night and started below, the crew struck up a chorus of "Good Night, Ladies." My brother protested loudly all the way down the companionway that he didn't know why they were singing *that* song, as *he* certainly wasn't a lady.

Neither am I, I thought miserably, tearing off my blue sash and wadding it into my trunk. Neither am I.

Four

Perfumes should be used, but with judgment.
—*The Ladies' Pocket Book of Etiquette*

"What is that awful *smell*?" cried Fanny, looking accusingly at Sprigg.

I laughed. Our steward, who was standing on deck with his back to us, was notoriously soap-shy, but the ripe odor assaulting our nostrils was not emanating from him.

"That," I said with relish, for I had been anticipating this moment since leaving Lahaina a week ago, "is the whale."

My own reaction to the *Morning Star*'s first cutting in—the process by which the whales we hunted were butchered and rendered for their precious oil—had been exactly the same many months ago. Before leaving Nantucket, I had no notion of the horrid stench a dead whale could create in close quarters. Now, while I certainly didn't find it pleasant, I had grown somewhat accustomed to it.

Fanny, however, had not.

To her credit, she had remained remarkably calm while witnessing her first whale hunt a short time ago—though she had refused to clamber atop the deckhouse with Aunt Anne and Thaddeus and me for a better view, citing Hester Halifax, of course. She had panicked only once, while watching Papa change places in his whaleboat with Big John, his harpooneer, in order to deal the whale a deathblow. It was a somewhat precarious process, and Papa had foolishly shown off a little, capering and striking a gallant pose as he raised his lance over his head. Just then the whaleboat bumped up against the exhausted leviathan and Papa lost his footing, teetering for a moment at the bow with his arms windmilling. Fanny shrieked at this sight and threw her apron over her head. She was coaxed out again only after we assured her that all was well.

As Fanny clamped a perfume-drenched handkerchief over her nose, I glanced over at Aunt Anne. Her nose was wrinkled in displeasure too, but she was watching the proceedings with her usual keen interest.

"Just wait till the blanket piece is aboard," said Thaddeus. "The gurry is even stinkier."

Fanny looked aghast at this piece of news. "Well, I for one am going below," she announced. "This floating butcher shop is no place for a lady. I am sure Hester Halifax would agree with me. Don't you, Anne?"

"It seems to me that this 'floating butcher shop,' as you put it, is what has kept you in style back on Nantucket," my aunt replied tartly. "I should think someone who was married to a whaleman would be interested in the trade."

Fanny reddened slightly at this. "I'm feeling a touch of the collywobbles, that's all," she protested. "You must have a stronger constitution than I do, Anne."

"Strong as a horse and tough as old boots," agreed Aunt Anne.

Fanny shuddered delicately at my aunt's forthright expression, and I suppressed a smile.

"Aunt Anne's a Goodspeed, through and through!" said Thaddeus proudly.

"Right you are, Tad," I echoed.

Fanny made no comment, merely simpered and waved her handkerchief at Papa and Mr. Macy. The two of them were perched above the dead whale on the cutting stage, a narrow length of suspended board that gave them a place to stand while they proceeded with the job of butchering our quarry. They caught sight of Fanny and raised their blubber spades in response. With a final flutter of her scented hankie, she flounced off below.

August 8, 1836

By the time we left Maui last week, we were the only whaler remaining in port, the rest of the fleet having long since sailed for the rich whaling grounds in the Sea of Okhotsk, off the northern coast of Kamchatka. Papa fears that we have already missed a goodly portion of the summer whaling season in those waters and consequently is acting on a tip from the captain of a merchant-man recently arrived, who sighted whales a week out from Lahaina. We have been making our way south by southwest in search of them ever since.

Papa has let me chart the course this time— my first solo effort since rescuing him and Tad. He watched over my shoulder only a few times and warned me to look sharp with my sextant, for we are due to pass through the Dark Isles, whose waters are filled with a host of dangers.

If today's prize has earned me his praise, along with that of the rest of my shipmates, my efforts in the galley have not. My modest talent for baking has been wholly eclipsed by Fanny, who merely has to dimple at Glum to send him running for sugar and flour and whatever other ingredients she requires.

No one asks for my humble biscuits anymore, what with Fanny's fresh yeast rolls gracing the table, and my gingersnaps, always a favorite amongst the crew (especially Glum), have quite fallen out of favor. "Mrs. Starbuck's shortbread!" is now the cry from fo'c'sle to quarterdeck. Even I *have to admit it is perfection, so crisp and buttery it fairly melts in your mouth.*

Not that I would ever tell Fanny so. She is already a paragon of virtue in her own eyes, and her vanity needs no further inflating from me.

Aunt Anne says I musn't be petty, that Fanny is young and eager to please and means me no harm. Eager to please Papa, I suspect, but I keep this uncharitable observation to myself. Fanny obviously thinks that the path to Papa's heart is through his stomach, and more and more now I find myself quite itching to toss her and her culinary creations overboard.

—P.

P.S. Fanny's piecrusts are perfection too, of course.

That first whale was the beginning of a string of remarkable luck, for over the coming days we sighted one spout after another. Hardly a watch passed when the cry of "She blows!" was not heard from the lookout. Again and again the whaleboats lowered, and again and again their forays were successful. Papa was in the pleasantest of moods, thanks to the steady crop of whales for the taking, and the fires under the try-pots blazed practically day and night. Once again the *Morning Star's* hold swelled with oil.

"Blubber, blubber, toil and trouble," I remarked brightly at luncheon one day, "try-pot burn and try-pot bubble."

Aunt Anne had me studying Shakespeare's *Macbeth,* and I was quite pleased with this literary allusion. I looked around the table at my companions for approval, but every pair of eyes was glued to Fanny, as usual.

I heaved a sigh, counting them. Three pairs of blue eyes (Papa's, Mr. Chase's, and Mr. Macy's), one pair of brown (Charlie Fishback's), and one of gray (my little brother, the traitor). Only Aunt Anne's eyes were focused on me, and she winked as I pulled a face.

"I do believe we have you to thank for this run of greasy luck, Mrs. Starbuck," said Papa gallantly, raising his fork in salute. "Neptune must love a lemon pie as much as I do."

Whether or not Fanny's presence was responsible for our good luck, it was certainly at least partly responsible for the collective good cheer of our crew. Although we were much crowded for space now with both Fanny and Aunt Anne aboard, not a peep of complaint had been heard. There'd been no griping about "hen frigate" or "petticoat whaler," as many a sailor was wont to term ships that carried women, and Papa wasn't the only one showing off when

Fanny was in the vicinity. Never had I seen the decks scrubbed with such enthusiasm, the rigging climbed with such gusto, or the whaleboats lowered with such vigor as when Fanny was watching.

Fanny played right along, lavishing the crew with compliments on their strength and bravery and laughing at their skylarking. She was still squeamish at the sight of the quarry so often chained now to the side of the *Morning Star,* however, and found excuses to remain below during each cutting in.

When she wasn't poring over *Godey's Lady's Book* or whipping up another path to Papa's heart in the galley, Fanny spent much of her time fussing over her cramped quarters. As austere as a monk's cell while Mr. Chase was in residence, now nearly every inch of space in the tiny cabin was covered with doilies and lace and brightly patterned quilts. I found it revolting, but Papa and the mates did not. They declared themselves enchanted and took every opportunity to admire the view.

One afternoon I looked up from the charts I had spread out on the main cabin table to see Mr. Macy hanging a hand-carved sign on Fanny's door.

"'Home, Sweet Home,'" Fanny read aloud. "Why, Mr. Macy, did you make that for me?"

Our second mate blushed beneath his beard. "Thought you might like it," he said bashfully.

"Indeed I do," twittered Fanny gaily in response, quoting the ever-more-tiresome Hester Halifax once again. "'Domestic life is woman's sphere.'"

What did that make me? I wondered sourly, for heaven knew I had little interest in all things domestic. Except baking, of course, but that was no longer appreciated. No, I was infinitely happier with a sextant in my hand than a feather duster.

I frowned and bent my head again over the charts.

"Land! Land ho!"

The cry came floating down through the skylight from the top of the mizzenmast above. Navigation and domestic embellishments alike were forgotten in the general rush for the companionway. I scrambled up the stairs behind Fanny and Mr. Macy and crowded past Chips, who was standing a trick at the wheel. The rest of the crew had gathered on the foredeck, where we joined them.

"The Dark Isles," I breathed.

I stood on tiptoe, gazing hungrily at the purple cloud-crowned smudges in the distance. We had not seen land for many days, and the sight of it drew our eyes like a magnet.

"Will we be able to go ashore?" asked Fanny.

Papa frowned. "Possibly," he said. "But these are dangerous waters."

"Plenty man-eaters," added Big John, snapping

his teeth together for emphasis. "No friendly."

Fanny shivered, and Thaddeus and I moved closer to Papa. Even Aunt Anne looked a bit taken aback.

"We need fresh water, and there are places where we will be welcome," Papa continued. "But Big John is right, and we must proceed with caution." He turned to Fanny. "Still, you needn't fear. We'll find a spot for you to try out your land legs again."

And shouting to Chips to hold the wheel steady, we set a course for the heart of the cannibal islands.

Five

August 10, 1836

We have been cruising for two days now while Papa studies the charts and warily circles one island after another. Every time Fanny sees land, she pouts prettily and begs him to take us ashore, but Papa will not be rushed. We came close to anchoring in a promising-looking cove yesterday afternoon, but then a small flotilla of canoes appeared bearing natives. After inspecting them through his spyglass, Papa announced that he didn't like the cut of their jib and gave the order to sail on.

Cannibals are all the talk of the foredeck, of course, and during the dogwatch the hands spin hair-raising tales for one another, like children telling ghost stories on All Hallows' Eve. Aunt Anne and I have our work cut out for us keeping Thaddeus out of earshot, but sometimes he slips through our fingers. At dinner last night, he looked at the roast pork on the table and asked Papa if it was "long pig"—what cannibals sometimes call their two-legged victims. Sprigg, the old barnacle, scuttled off to the pantry guiltily upon hearing this, so I'm quite sure he was the one who let that particular cat out of the bag.

Fanny, meanwhile, has pronounced herself wary of Big John and Kanaka Jim.

"They look like savages," she said with a ladylike shudder. "I don't know why you keep them aboard, Captain Goodspeed."

"Stuff and nonsense," Aunt Anne replied stoutly. "The Sandwich Islanders have never practiced cannibalism."

"My sister is correct, Fanny. Our fine harpooneers are no more man-eaters than I am," said Papa calmly, mopping the gravy from his plate with one of her tasty rolls.

But Fanny did not look convinced.

Even dour Glum has gotten into the spirit of things, and this morning, as the two of us scrubbed pots in the galley, he launched into a rendition of "The Cannibal King" in his deep, mellow voice—a voice that never fails to surprise me, emerging as it does from such a storklike frame. It didn't take me long to pick up the refrain, and we sang together like two companionable

*ghouls until Fanny spoiled our fun by scolding me
with dire warnings from Hester Halifax about the
fate of females who indulge in vulgar, hoydenish
activities.*

*We have sighted no more whales, and Papa
has declared make-and-mend to keep us all occu-
pied. Thaddeus is on deck at the moment polishing the binnacle, and I am supposed to be
changing the linens on our bunks, which I will do
just as soon as I finish petting Ishmael.*

—P.

*P.S. The linens will have to wait! I must go now,
for Thaddeus just ran in. He says that Papa
thinks he has found a safe spot for us to land and
has promised us a picnic ashore.*

The canoes came upon us without warning.

As sudden and silent as death, they rounded the
headland and shot across the reef, half a hundred
paddles or more flashing in unison as they sliced
through the sun-spangled waves and drove the boats
toward shore.

Thaddeus saw them first.

"Patience," he whispered, plucking at my sleeve.

I pulled away in irritation. My little brother had
been fidgety all day, and with the remains of our

picnic to clear up I had no time to humor him.

"Leave go, Tad," I said crossly.

"But Patience, look!"

With a sigh I turned, shading my eyes with my hand, and gazed out across the cove in the direction he was pointing. My heart jolted at the sight of the approaching boats.

"Papa!" I called. The word emerged a hoarse croak.

My father didn't hear me. He and the others were seated a short way off, shaded by a makeshift awning rigged from a sail. Mr. Macy was reciting one of his poems, and there was a ripple of appreciative laughter from Aunt Anne and Fanny.

"Papa!" I called again, louder this time, and my father must have heard the terror in my voice for he sprang to his feet. One quick glance seaward and his face drained of color.

"Hostiles!" he bellowed. "To the trees!"

There was a mad scramble as we all made for the meager shelter of the palms that fringed the beach. A sharp whistle pierced the air, and I looked back over my shoulder to see Papa frantically signaling the *Morning Star,* which lay at anchor beyond the coral reef skirting the cove.

A gray head popped up over the taffrail in response. Sprigg's spectacles glittered in the glare of

the tropical sun. He turned away and shouted something, and instantly two more heads appeared, one as
bald as a seal and the other a blaze of red. Glum and
Charlie were aboard with him, the three of them having drawn lots to serve as shipkeepers while the rest
of us went ashore.

"To arms!" Papa cried, gesturing madly at the
canoes.

Our shipmates nodded and disappeared. But what
could the three of them do against so many?

And how could a day that had begun so pleasantly
have turned so ugly and dangerous so quickly?

"Work first, then leisure," Papa had told the crew
after the *Morning Star*'s whaleboats ferried us to land.

Not a word of complaint had been heard as the
hands busied themselves filling casks with fresh
water and loading them into our ship's hold. Meanwhile, Aunt Anne and Thaddeus and I had whiled
away the morning exploring a small stream that led to
a picturesque waterfall. We'd left Fanny behind in the
shade of a coconut palm with only Hester Halifax for
company, as she had foolishly insisted on wearing her
fancy robin's egg blue dress for the occasion and was
concerned about muddying the hem.

"Don't worry about me. I'll be fine," she'd said.

"Don't worry, we won't," I'd replied sweetly.

Fanny had looked up at me sharply, but my smile

must have been convincing, for she didn't reply, just fished *Etiquette for Ladies* from her reticule and flounced down onto a quilt on the sand.

She did join us afterward, though, when Chips offered to row us out for a closer look at the reef. The five of us had spent a most agreeable hour leaning over the edge of the whaleboat and gaping in wonder at the multitude of brightly colored fishes that flitted through the crystalline water below—tiny wedges of vibrant pink and orange and yellow that flashed amongst the coral formations like bees through an underwater garden.

Once the hold was full of fresh water again, the crew cooled off by splashing about in the waters of the shallow bay, and then it was time for lunch. We all feasted on sandwiches and lemonade that Glum and I had packed that morning (followed by Fanny's short-bread, naturally). Later, some of the crew napped on the beach while others clustered around Mr. Macy, who obligingly held forth with his poetry.

Yes, it had been an altogether pleasurable day indeed. But there was no pleasure to be found now. Now we were running for our lives.

The war canoes—a small armada of double-hulled craft topped with sails—surged onto the beach. A fierce battle cry burst from the throats of the paddlers, raising the hair on the back of my neck and winging my feet with fear.

In my haste I stumbled and fell, and as I scrambled to get back up, I turned and stared at the men tumbling forth onto the shore. Tattoos spiraled across their bodies, and their hair shot out in wild dark halos around their heads. Their teeth—which I could plainly see grinning at me in triumph—were filed to sharp points, giving them the appearance of human sharks. I had not a particle of doubt that these were the dreaded flesh-eaters of whom I'd heard so many horrible tales from the foremast hands, the ferocious cannibals of the Dark Isles, who gloried in feasting on man-meat.

"Tad!" I screamed, trying and failing to scoop my little brother up in my arms. Nearly seven now, he was no longer the slight little sprout he'd been when we left our home on Nantucket almost a year ago, and I had to settle for dragging him by the arm as best I could.

In a flash, the howling horde was upon us. I cried out as strong hands pried Thaddeus away from me.

"No!" shouted Papa. He shoved his companions forward toward the trees and turned back toward my brother and me. I could see fear in his eyes— fear for us.

Papa never stood a chance.

A pair of warriors were upon him in an instant,

and as I watched, one raised his wooden club and swung it viciously downward. Papa staggered, fell to his knees, and, with one last stricken look in our direction, keeled over wordlessly onto the sand.

A sob tore its way from my throat. "Papa!" I cried. I struggled mightily with my captor, scratching and flailing at him as I tried to free myself. But it was to no avail, and in a trice I was bound up like a wild pig and tossed in a heap with my brother.

In a matter of minutes, it was over. Stalwart Chips held out to the last, but unarmed as he was, even he proved no match for the fearsome natives.

Shrieking in triumph, they dragged us into a pile around Papa's still form, poking and prodding at us with their clubs. Thaddeus was ashen faced, his eyes squeezed tightly shut in terror, and I couldn't tell if Papa was alive or dead. The howls of the savages rose to a crescendo as they hoisted us into the air and flung us into their waiting canoes. I grunted as Thaddeus landed atop me, and although my hands were firmly fastened behind my back and I couldn't reach out to comfort him, I was able to twist around and nudge his head with my nose.

"Be brave, Tad," I whispered. My brother didn't reply, and I wondered if he'd heard me, but after a minute he nodded and squirmed closer. I gave the top of his head a reassuring kiss. "That's it. Remember, we're Goodspeeds, through and through."

Brave words, but they rang hollow to my own ears. Fear traced its cold, bony finger down my spine at the thought of the fate that surely awaited us. As the boats slipped across the reef spanning the mouth of the cove, the warriors took up an exultant chant, their voices marking time with each thrust of their paddles. The canoes surged forward. I raised myself up slightly and peered over the gunwhale toward our ship.

A shot rang out from the *Morning Star,* and I saw a blubber spade flash in the sun as Glum raised it over his head. There was no hope of assistance from our shipmates at the moment; they had their hands full trying to repel boarders, for a canoe had pulled up to the stern and a horde of natives were trying to swarm over the taffrail.

This is all *her* fault, I thought bitterly, slumping back down and looking over at the sodden bundle of crumpled blue muslin that lay weeping near my feet. None of this would have happened if Fanny hadn't put up such a fuss about coming ashore.

Now, thanks to Fanny Starbuck, we'd likely never set foot on the *Morning Star* again.

Six

It is well to know how to enter a room, but it is much
better to know when and how to leave it.
—*Ladies' Indispensable Assistant,*
Being a Companion for the Sister, Mother, and Wife

I raised myself up again slightly, watching as the
Morning Star fell farther and farther behind. I could
only imagine what Sprigg and Glum and Charlie
Fishback were thinking as they saw us all carried
away. If they even had time to think of us, that was,
for the battle was still waging for control of our ship.

The warrior nearest Thaddeus and me noticed
that I was sitting up and fetched me a sharp smack on
the side of my head with his paddle.

Wincing, I fell back. I glared at him, and he
grinned, displaying his sharpened teeth. *The better to
eat you with, my dear,* I thought improbably, recalling
a line from a tale by the Brothers Grimm. I almost
laughed. Grim, indeed. How would we ever get out of
this predicament? Escape seemed impossible, with all
of our weapons far out of reach aboard the *Morning
Star.* We could only hope that if they managed to
hang on to the ship, our steward and cook and third
mate would somehow find a way to mount a rescue.

Nerving myself for another blow, I groaned and flopped around dramatically until I was half-leaning against the side of the canoe. The paddler eyed me warily, but I kept my eyes tightly closed for a minute or two to allay his suspicions. Then, when his attention returned to his paddling, I tipped my head back slightly and risked another peep through my eyelashes.

I could see the island clearly, from the turban of clouds that rested on the highest peak to the verdant hillsides seamed with valleys and waterfalls. I watched for a while, assuming that the land would fall away as we veered out to sea, for surely the paddlers had come from some neighboring archipelago.

But the island remained in view, and after a time it became obvious that, far from heading away from land, we were simply hugging the shoreline and circling the island.

The warriors continued their rhythmic chant, their paddles thrusting into the water with each beat, urging the canoes forward. I continued to watch and listen, and a short while later the flotilla angled sharply inland. I strained to see where we were headed, careful not to draw undue attention to myself. Before us rose a massive cliff face, a sheer wall of rock unbroken by greenery or anything that could possibly pass as a beach or safe harbor. My heart squeezed tight with renewed fear. Did the savages mean to dash us all to pieces upon this stone barrier?

The canoes, which had been traveling in a pack, now changed formation and lined up in single file. The chanting ceased, and the paddlers' faces grew tense with concentration. Our canoe was in the lead, and through slitted eyes I watched as a wave lifted us up and up, higher and higher. We paused, motionless it seemed, at the very top, then with a shudder the canoe tilted sharply downward as we pitched over the crest and dashed forward toward what looked like certain death.

I couldn't help myself, I cried out in fear. Too intent on their task to notice, the paddlers stroked the water furiously, working to keep the canoe perpendicular to the cliff's face as the roaring surf hurtled us toward our doom.

And then, at the very last second, when it seemed that all was lost, we shot through an all but invisible slash in the immense rock wall. The warriors raised their paddles and voices in triumph as we slid into the narrow opening.

The water stilled a second or two later, and the roar of the crashing surf ceased. I looked around, dumbfounded to see that we had entered a lagoon.

No wonder the island had looked safely uninhabited

from the deck of the *Morning Star*! A thousand ships might pass this place, and not a one would suspect its existence. The lagoon was completely shielded from the outside world.

The hidden pool of water on which we floated lay cupped at the bottom of a circle of low peaks, like a puddle at the base of a shallow well. Three quarters of the way around, the water was skirted by a narrow beach, behind which the land rose sharply upward into a tangle of greenery. A number of grass huts peeked out from behind the palms, and I could see the faces of curious women and children as we approached shore.

My heart sank. There was no hope of rescue now. Our shipmates would never find us, and even if they did, this natural stronghold would prove a fortress too formidable to breach. We were doomed.

My spirits did not improve as the canoes drew up on the beach and we were dumped unceremoniously onto the sand. We sat hunched together in a pile, the thirty of us, wretched at the prospect of our fate. Papa was still motionless, a trickle of blood visible on his forehead. Fanny's face was as white as her petti- coats. Chips and Aunt Anne both glared defiantly as our captors moved in, their clubs raised.

This must be the end, I thought desperately. I threw my body over my brother as a shield. But no, we were only meant to endure a spate of renewed gloating, and we were poked and prodded and shrieked over once again as the villagers turned out to view us.

The crowd parted as a tall man came forward. Like the other warriors, he was naked except for a loincloth, his body also covered in tattooed spirals and whorls. A strand of teeth encircled his neck— teeth that on closer inspection I was horrified to see were human. I glanced over at my brother, hoping he wouldn't notice.

From his proud bearing it was clear that the man was the chief or ruler of the village. He clapped his hands and shouted something, and the women and children withdrew, laughing and casting curious glances back at us. Whatever was to come next must not be deemed an appropriate sight for innocent eyes, I thought, which didn't bode well.

At the chief's next command, we were separated into heaps—Papa and the men in one pile, Aunt Anne, Fanny, Thaddeus, and me in another. My father groaned as they dragged him across the sand, and my heart leaped with hope. Papa was alive!

The chief gave an order and a pair of warriors dragged the four of us down the beach away from our shipmates, then pushed us down onto the sand under a coconut palm. Aunt Anne's left leg buckled under her as they did so and she cried out in pain.

"What is it?" I asked.

"My ankle," she replied, wincing. "When we were captured, one of them hit me on the leg with his club."

"Is it broken?"

She shook her head. "No, but I can't put much weight on it."

The younger of the two warriors, a boy who couldn't have been much older than I, remained behind to guard us. When he was satisfied that our bonds were secure, he turned his back on us and gave his attention to his companions. Just a few hundred yards down the beach, they were busy digging a large pit and lining it with stones.

My heart sank. I recognized that pit—it was an *imu,* an underground oven, just like the one Upa had used back at the Wigginses' in Lahaina to roast taro for his poi. Soon the savages would start a fire to heat the stones, just as Thaddeus and I had watched Upa do. Tears pricked my eyelids.

"We haven't much time," I said.

"What do they mean to do with us?" whispered Aunt Anne.

I inclined my head wordlessly toward the fire pit, and she blanched. "Merciful heavens!"

"Perhaps not the four of us," I whispered back,

though this was cold comfort. "From the tales I heard on the foredeck, women and children are usually made slaves."

My aunt glanced over at Thaddeus and Fanny, a bleak expression on her face.

Above us the sun slipped over the low rim of hills, and although it was not yet dusk, an early gloom descended on the lagoon. Frantically I tried to think of something—anything—that we could do to save ourselves and our shipmates. My mathematical abilities were of no use to me now, unless to merely calculate the grim odds. We were outnumbered by three to one, by my estimation.

I glanced over at the sentry. His face was set in resentful lines; clearly he'd much rather be engaged in the glorious work of building the fire pit that in just a few hours would begin roasting man-flesh.

"I have an idea," I whispered.

Thaddeus and Fanny still slumped listlessly on the sand, exactly where our captors had dumped them, but Aunt Anne listened closely as I outlined my plan.

"Merciful heavens, I can't let you attempt that," she whispered back when I was done.

"What other choice do we have?" I argued. "We can't just sit here and do nothing."

"Well then, I should be the one to go," said Aunt Anne. "Or Fanny."

"You've hurt your ankle, Aunt Anne, and Fanny, well . . ." My voice trailed off as I looked at Fanny, who was still sniffling. I certainly couldn't count on her for help. "Fanny can't swim," I countered, unable to mask the contempt in my voice.

"I can swim," whispered Thaddeus stoutly, struggling to sit up. It was the first true sign of life he'd exhibited since we were taken captive, and I wanted to hug him. "Can I come?"

"May I," I said automatically. I regarded him, considering his request. If truth were told, an extra pair of hands might be useful, though my brother was overestimating his prowess in the water. He had only just mastered floating. "Very well, then."

I explained to Aunt Anne exactly what I needed her to do, then inched forward slightly and reached out one foot. Bracing myself for a blow, I prodded the young guard with my toe. He whipped around in a half-crouch, club raised.

My nerve nearly failed me then, but I took a deep breath and mustered my most winning smile. His eyebrows disappeared up into his bushy halo of hair.

"Water," I said, and pantomimed sipping as well as I could with my hands tied behind me, by making slurping noises with my lips.

The boy crept closer, club still raised, his face clouded with suspicion. He looked so astonished that

I had to fight a wild impulse to laugh. Not used to having your dinner talk back, are you, I thought, my mind suddenly filled with the mental image of how surprised I would be if a pork chop rose up off my plate to address me.

"Water," I repeated.

The boy stared at me for a moment longer, and then understanding dawned in his eyes. Slowly, he lowered his club.

"*Wai?*" he asked, mimicking tipping a cup to his lips.

He understood! "*Wai!*" I said, nodding enthusiastically.

He gave me a curt nod in return and started off toward a nearby hut. As soon as he was out of sight, I sat up and scooted closer to Aunt Anne. Back to back we sat, working at each other's bands. I tugged and twisted until my wrists felt raw and finally managed to pull one hand free. In a trice I had Aunt Anne untied, then set to work on Thaddeus. Fanny would have to wait; there wasn't time.

"Keep your hands behind you when he comes back, Tad," I reminded him. "Best not to let on we've gotten loose."

The shadows were growing longer now, and the warriors were chanting again, a horrid, guttural sound that lifted the hair on the back of my neck.

Our guard returned bearing a calabash of water. He held it to each of our mouths in turn, watching us warily. I was the last to drink, and as I took a final sip, I brought my hands up and grasped his wrists.

Startled, he tried to draw back. I held him firm.

"Now!" I cried softly, and Aunt Anne brought the coconut she had been hiding behind her back crashing down on his head.

A surprised look flashed across the boy's face, then he toppled forward onto the sand and lay still. Fanny, who had finally managed to sit up, paled.

"Merciful heavens!" Aunt Anne exclaimed. "Have I killed him?"

I shook my head. "No, but he won't be gallying anyone for a while."

Crouching in the shadows, I undressed swiftly, down to my pantaloons and chemise. I took off my petticoat and folded it up, tucking it into the waistband of my pantaloons. I would be needing it shortly.

After I untied her, Fanny stopped sniffling long enough to help me bundle the unconscious boy into my gray calico dress, and we laid him back on the ground, heaping up a pile of sand beside him. Over that, I laid my pinafore to serve for Thaddeus.

I stood back and inspected the ruse critically. It was a paltry one and would fool no one in the light of day, but I hoped it looked enough like two bodies to buy us the few hours of time we needed for my plan to work.

"I think that dress looks better on him than it does on me," I whispered.

Fanny stifled a panicked giggle.

"I'll give him another whack if he wakes up," said Aunt Anne. She hugged me tightly. "Be careful, dear heart, and Patience?"

"Yes?"

"If it's not safe to return, save yourselves."

I looked at her and smiled. "We'll be back," I said. "We're Goodspeeds, remember?"

"Through and through!" added Thaddeus, and the two of us melted into the shadows.

Seven

*There are many ways that a woman of sense
will find to employ her leisure hours.*
—*Etiquette for Ladies, or The Principles of True Politeness*

"Patience, I'm—"

My brother's words were suddenly muffled as I clamped a hand firmly over his mouth. I pulled him into the shadows and held him tightly against me, our hearts pounding in unison as a group of native women passed by a few feet away, chattering amongst themselves. We stood there, motionless, until they were out of earshot.

Pressing my lips to my brother's ear, I whispered, "Don't make a sound until we're out of danger."

He nodded vigorously, and taking him by the hand, I led him from tree to tree, down the beach and away from our shipmates and the amassed warriors. Finally, when I deemed us far enough away not to be spotted, I broke across a clearing at a run and dove into a thicket of ferns. Thaddeus was right on my heels.

"This isn't going to be easy," I told him. "Just stay close."

We started upward, toward the low rim of hills

that encircled the lagoon. The sun was fading, and the sky above flushed a soft rose streaked with gold. It was dim in the undergrowth, and we stumbled and fell repeatedly as we clawed our way toward the top. I paused now and again to tear strips from the petticoat I carried tucked into my pantaloons, tying them hastily around a branch or a vine as a marker for our return trip.

Thaddeus proved a stouthearted companion and didn't once whine or complain, even when he tripped over a rock and splayed headlong into a streambed.

"Clever boy, you just plotted our course out of here," I told him, giving him my hand and hauling him back to his feet.

We followed the stream upward, the rush of water growing louder and stronger the higher we climbed. It pitched to a thunderous roar as we neared the top, its dizzying splash of white still visible in the waning daylight as it arced downward over a lip of rock and disappeared into a cloud of mist below.

Cautiously, we skirted the waterfall's foaming mouth and heaved ourselves up the final few feet to the rim. We rested there for a moment, panting. Overhead, a few stars were already visible.

"We need to keep going," I said, hauling myself to my feet.

Thaddeus did the same and we made our way to

the cliff's edge. I looked down at the sea below, but there was no flash of white from sails near or far to break the dark expanse of water.

"Do you see them?" asked my brother.

I shook my head and tried to think what I would do if I were in my shipmates' shoes. Surely they would have tried to sail after us, as short-handed as they were. But could they have done so with only the three of them aboard?

And if they had, would they have passed the opening to the lagoon and sailed on? Or would they have given up and doubled back? I stood there a long moment, pondering.

"Let's find another lookout," I said finally, and we moved westward, back in the direction of our picnic beach.

As we clambered over the uneven ground, Thaddeus stubbed his toe on a rock and nearly fell. He hopped about on one foot, nursing the other, and the words that came out of his mouth would have curled Hester Halifax's hair.

"Why, Thaddeus Goodspeed!" I said, feigning shock. "I do believe you've been spending too much time in the company of Pardon Sprigg."

From another rocky outcropping a quarter of a mile or so away we again scanned the horizon.

"There's our beach," said my brother after a minute.

"Where?"

He placed his hands on either side of my head and angled it a few degrees farther west.

"Sharp eyes, Tad!" I said. I'd remember that deadly crescent of sand until my dying day. Which I sincerely hoped would not be anytime soon.

And then, directly below us, a small craft floated into view, her sail a ghostly white against the indigo sea.

"It's a whaleboat!" cried Thaddeus. "And look, there's the *Morning Star*!

He was right. Our shipmates must have indeed ventured after us and, finding no trace, doubled back to anchorage for the night.

Grabbing my brother's hand, I pulled him to the rim of the hill and plunged down the far side. We crashed and stumbled and tumbled our way headlong toward the picnic beach, emerging at the bottom a short while later, panting, bruised, and sore but very relieved to see our ship at anchor.

I cupped my hands over my mouth. "Sprigg! Glum! Charlie!" I shouted.

There was no reply.

"Hang it all, I was afraid of this," I said. "You stay here, Tad, and see if you can raise them. I'll be back quicker than Jack Flash."

"Don't leave me," he said, clutching my hand. There was a note of panic in his voice.

I looked at him. This day had clearly taken its toll on my little brother. But despite his protests to the contrary, Thaddeus was not a strong swimmer, and I was certain he'd never make it out past the reef.

I bit my lip, considering, then scrounged a piece of driftwood and together the two of us waded out into the shallow waters of the cove. When it was deep enough, I gave the piece of log to my brother. "Hold on tight, Tad. I'll be right beside you."

Obediently, he clung to the driftwood and we started for the *Morning Star*. The water was soothingly warm, but as I swam I couldn't help wondering what creatures lurked in its depths. Eels, perhaps, as slick as seaweed, that might twine about my legs. Or strange spiny creatures. Or sharks—please don't let there be sharks! I prayed, and swam a little faster. Beside me, Thaddeus kicked sturdily.

When we reached the anchor chain, I grabbed it and hallooed with all my might. After a minute I heard someone respond from the deck above. It was Charlie Fishback.

"Throw me a line!" I called.

His face glowed like a pale moon in the darkness above me. "Is that you, Miss Patience?" he asked, incredulous.

"Well it's not Hester Halifax," I snapped. "Hurry up and haul us in!"

They had us aboard in a trice, and as we flopped

onto the deck Sprigg threw blankets over us both.

"We were so worried about you," he wheezed.

Glum patted me on the back as I coughed and sputtered. After I caught my breath, I quickly outlined what had befallen us since the cannibals had snatched us away, then told my shipmates of my plan.

"There's no time to be lost," Charlie said when I was done, and he and Sprigg sprang off in search of the weapons we would need. As Glum readied the larboard whaleboat, I ran down to Papa's day cabin to round up the other necessary items.

"You stay here and mind the ship," I told Ishmael, who was perched next to Miranda on my bunk. He blinked at me and purred.

I grabbed an old leather satchel of Papa's and stuffed everything in, then took one of his shirts and, discarding the blanket, drew it over my head. Sprigg would surely have something to say about this, I thought, but there was no time for niceties now. I buckled Papa's belt around my waist, slung the satchel across my chest, and ran back up the companionway.

If Sprigg thought my attire outlandish—which he surely did, for he peered at me disapprovingly over his spectacles—he kept his comments to himself for once.

"Will this do, Miss Patience?" asked Charlie.

Together, we counted up the weapons—not quite enough for all of our captive shipmates but still nearly more than we could carry. I paused.

"What we really need is a cannon," I mused.

"Afraid we're fresh out of cannons," said Charlie.

He was right, of course, for the *Morning Star* didn't carry one. But even if she had, we'd never have managed to drag it back to the lagoon. No, a cannon wasn't what we needed.

"How about spare gunpowder, Charlie?" I asked as a wild idea occurred to me.

He held up a small gunnysack in response. I turned to Glum. "Do you have any empty bottles?"

Glum scratched his hairless head. "Might be able to rustle up an old vinegar flask or two."

"You do that," I said, and he loped off toward the galley.

"We're going to need a diversion," I continued as I explained my idea to the others.

"That's a capital plan," Charlie replied, when I was done.

"Could work," agreed Sprigg grudgingly.

A few minutes later, we climbed down into the whaleboat, and as we rowed for shore Glum handed Thaddeus and me some bread and cheese. We tore into it hungrily, for we hadn't eaten since our picnic many hours ago. As Papa and Thaddeus liked to say, my belly thought my throat had been cut.

After we drew up on the beach, Charlie and Glum distributed the weapons and in a moment we were bristling with steel. I had a pair of pistols stashed in my belt, along with a cutlass. Charlie had all of that plus a musket slung over his shoulder, and Glum wore a rucksack full of pistols and was also armed with a harpoon. Sprigg, whose wizened frame was bowed nearly double under the weight of a cutting spade, fairly glittered with knives, and even Thaddeus had a weapon, a small dirk that he clutched proudly in one hand.

"Ready?" I asked.

Charlie held up a lantern in reply and the others nodded. We plunged into the forest. Although the moon had risen, its light offered little assistance, for it was as dark as a pocket under the canopy of trees. By the lantern's feeble glow we slashed our way through the deep shadows, and I was grateful that I had thought to leave strips of my petticoat as markers, or we would never have found the path back.

"Just like Hansel and Gretel," said Thaddeus, whom I had commissioned as scout, as he pointed out another one a few yards ahead.

"Exactly," I replied.

"Friends of yours?" asked Sprigg.

Charlie caught my eye and we both grinned.

We pressed on, up and up and up, finally straggling out onto the ridge at the top. We flung ourselves down, panting. I lay back for a moment and stared up at the sky. Broad as a whale's back and as black as lava, it was salted with stars. I whispered a prayer for our safety and for the safety of our shipmates.

The rest was brief. Leading my friends around the thundering waterfall, we began our descent to the lagoon. We emerged a short while later at the far end of the beach. We looked a fright. Glum's bald head was covered with scratches, Charlie was nursing his elbow, and Sprigg's spectacles were not only askew but one of the lenses was cracked. Papa's shirt was in shreds around me, and Thaddeus was limping.

"'The raggle-taggle gypsies, oh,'" I said softly.

"Raggle-taggle pirates is more like it," said Glum, his eyes glinting fiercely in the lantern light.

We crouched in the shadows and quietly loaded the weapons. My hands shook slightly as I poured in the powder and shot.

Removing the vinegar bottles from the satchel, I passed one to Charlie, and together we filled them halfway up with gunpowder, wadding in the remaining strips of my torn petticoat on top and leaving a long piece emerging from the neck as a fuse.

Glum raised his eyebrows at this and nodded approvingly. I handed one to him and one to Sprigg, who peered through the good lens of his spectacles as he inspected it closely. I handed them each a flint.

"On our signal," I whispered, and they nodded.

With as little noise as possible the five of us made our way to where I had left Aunt Anne and Fanny. My heart was in my throat—had they been discovered?

"Aunt Anne!" I called softly.

"Merciful heavens, you're safe!" she called back.

Fanny, who had dried her tears and was clutching a coconut, kept one eye warily on the still-motionless young sentry as we approached.

"What's that rascal wearing your dress for, Miss Patience?" rasped Sprigg.

Glum poked him in the back with his harpoon. "Hush, you old fool," he said.

Aunt Anne arched a warning eyebrow at me and pointed wordlessly toward the throng of warriors. I gasped.

Mr. Macy had been plucked from the pile of crew members and tied to a tree, and the chief was making a speech of some sort as he prodded him in the belly with a club bristling with shark's teeth. One of the onlookers licked his lips greedily. We had to act now.

"Wait here, Tad," I told my brother.

He scampered obediently over to Fanny and Aunt Anne, who put her arm around him and drew him close. She looked up at me and gave a short nod.

Leaving the lantern behind, Sprigg, Glum, Charlie, and I crept cautiously down the beach toward the fire pit. We clung to the shelter of the trees, and I was glad of the darkness now, for if the warriors saw us, our plan would fail. Our only chance for success lay in surprise, and we needed to make our way to Papa and the rest of the crew undetected.

Halfway to our goal, I motioned to Glum and Sprigg, who peeled off into the shadows to await the signal from Charlie and me. We stole on, and tree by tree we drew closer, until I could see Mr. Macy's face clearly in the firelight. I longed to call out to him, to let him know that help was on the way, but prudence dictated silence.

Any moment now, I thought, any moment. Closer and closer we drew—just a few more yards! By the last cluster of palms we crouched low.

"Now, Miss Patience," said Charlie, and taking a deep breath, I let out a low whistle.

From the shadows behind us I heard the click of steel against flint, saw the small plume of flame that bloomed as the spark ignited the strip of petticoat. The flicker of fire reflected in Sprigg's spectacles as he stood up and threw the bottle. It arced through the air just as it should, closer, closer, and then—

"Oh, no," I whispered in dismay, as the makeshift

explosive fell short of its target and rolled toward the shore, where a curl of surf quenched both the fuse and my hopes.

Charlie gripped my shoulder. "There's another," he reminded me.

Again came the click of steel against flint, and again came the responding flare of light. Glum stood up this time, hefting the bottle in his hand. Lifting a skinny arm over his head, he lobbed it toward the spot we had chosen, well away from our shipmates and us.

I held my breath. The vinegar bottle landed upright in the sand, and Charlie and I threw ourselves down behind the tree. The crack of the explosion was satisfying loud, and we looked up to see every head around the fire pit swivel in astonishment at the unexpected sound. A split second later, a herd of cannibals charged past us to investigate.

And then everything went horribly wrong.

As we ran from the cover of the shadows, my three shipmates firing on the startled warriors, their chief quickly sized up the ambush and moved to where Mr. Macy stood tied to the tree. He bared his jagged grin at us, then raised a wooden dagger, bristling with razor-sharp shark's teeth, over his head.

"No!" I shouted, racing toward him as Sprigg and Charlie worked to slice through our crew's bonds.

But it was too late. With a single swift, savage blow, the cannibal chief thrust his dagger into our second mate's side. Mr. Macy cried out, then sagged forward, his head dropping to his chest.

I stood there a split second, stunned.

"Get down!" shouted my father, wrenching the cutlass from my hand. He shoved me onto my knees and swung the steel blade over my head. Behind me, one of our captors fell face-first into the sand, his club still raised to strike.

"Thunder and lightning, Patience, get back with Anne and Fanny!" my father bellowed, slashing about wildly at the cannibals, who had quickly doubled back after realizing they'd been tricked.

I ignored him and raised my pistol. My father grabbed it away from me. "Get to safety!" he ordered, spitting the words out in fury as he fired at the chief. The warrior's grin faded, and he clutched his chest in surprise and then pitched silently forward. "This is no place for you!"

"But—"

"Now!" Papa planted his foot on my backside and shoved me out of harm's way. Humiliated, I stumbled into the nearby underbrush and took cover from the melee. Useless, was I? No place for me, was there? My thoughts whirled about in my head, as black as the night sky overhead. Had I not proved my worth during the recent mutiny? Had I done something to deem myself untrustworthy, or was Papa's determination to set me aside simply due to the fact that I was a girl?

Never had I felt so helpless and angry as I watched the battle play out before me. Mr. Chase had joined Sprigg and Glum near the fire pit, the three of them firing with deadly purpose at the howling horde that rushed to overtake them. Owen Gardiner, our cooper, was behind them hacking about with a blubber spade, while Schmidt and Domingo and several of the other foremast hands chased off another group with their harpoons. Directly in front of me, Charlie Fishback and Chips stood back to back, Chips's dark face a harsh mask in the firelight as the two of them grappled with a pair of snarling, raging, would-be man-eaters.

The fighting waged fierce and hot as the entire crew of the *Morning Star* struggled for our freedom. The entire crew except for me, I thought bitterly. Well, and Aunt Anne and Fanny and Thaddeus, but they didn't count as crew in my opinion, whereas an assistant navigator was an altogether different proposition.

In the end the cannibals and their wooden clubs were no match for guns and steel, but the victory was hard-won and it came at a terrible cost. There were no huzzahs from our exhausted crew when it was all over, no huzzahs as they trussed up the remaining natives and doused the fire pit with seawater, and no huzzahs as Papa and Mr. Chase cut down John Macy and laid him gently in the sand. I was shocked to see how pale and weary my father looked—himself still bleeding from the blow to his head back at the picnic beach—as he bent over our second mate and inspected his wound.

"I can only hope my meager doctoring skills will be sufficient to save him from the grave," Papa said grimly. He turned to me. "It seems Martha was right, after all. A whaling ship is no place for women and children."

Eight

Obedience is much demanded in the female character.
—*The Young Lady's Book, a Manual of*
Elegant Recreations, Exercises, and Pursuits

August 12, 1836

Disaster!
We are on our way back to the island of Maui
under a cloud of sail, for Papa is determined that
Aunt Anne, Fanny, Thaddeus, and I shall be set
ashore as speedily as possible.
My pen is shaking as I write this, for this is a
turn of events I could never have foreseen.

—*P.*

My father announced his intentions at dinner the
following evening, after we were safely back aboard
the *Morning Star* and the cannibal island just a distant speck on the horizon.

"It's a sensible solution," he said as Sprigg served
up a fish chowder Glum had prepared in haste. "And
after much consideration in light of our recent brush
with death, clearly the only one. It is only by the
grace of God, after all, that John is still with us."

Papa inclined his head toward the tiny cabin that Mr. Macy shared with Mr. Chase, where our second mate lay recuperating in his bunk. The door was open, and we all turned to look at him. Mr. Macy smiled wanly at us and waved.

Papa's prognosis was for a full recovery, and I was much relieved to hear this, for not only was I fond of my shipmate, but I also felt dreadfully responsible for what had befallen him. Although the outcome had been successful, it was my plan for the ambush, after all, that had triggered the cannibal chief's attack and nearly cost Mr. Macy his life. Fortunately, my father's doctoring skills—coupled with attentive nursing from Fanny—had proved equal to rescuing him from the brink of death. Mr. Macy would need to rest for a couple of weeks, Papa said, but he was out of danger.

My father cleared his throat, and we all looked at him expectantly, except for Mr. Chase and Charlie, who couldn't seem to pry their gazes away from Fanny Starbuck.

"I have set a course for Wailuku," Papa continued. "You will recall that Reverend Wiggins is starting a boarding school there for native girls. He told me that his daughter, Charity, will be enrolled, of course, so I am sure he will not mind having you as a student as well, Patience. As in Lahaina, I will recompense Mrs. Wiggins for caring for Thaddeus along with her own boys. Anne, you and Fanny will help teach."

There was a long silence. I stared at my father, thunderstruck. Boarding school? Could I possibly have heard him correctly?

"But you'll miss my birthday," said Thaddeus in a small voice.

"We'll be back in time for Patience's, and we'll have a double celebration then," Papa promised, reaching over and patting him on the head. "And meanwhile I'll just have to leave a special present for you, won't I?"

My little brother brightened at this prospect, but I was not so easily mollified. My fourteenth birthday was on the first of November, nearly three months away. Three months ashore! At boarding school! Before I could utter a word of protest, however, Aunt Anne carefully put down her spoon.

"Do you mean to tell me you came to this decision without consulting me first, Isaiah?" she asked calmly, but I detected a note of steel in her voice.

Papa shifted uncomfortably in his seat. Sensing a skirmish, Sprigg poked his head out of the pantry.

"It's the only logical choice," my father protested. "I cannot in good conscience continue to put your lives at risk."

"But Papa, surely we're safe enough now that we're back aboard the *Morning Star*," I said.

He shook his head. "No, Patience, my mind is made up. The four of you are better off ashore while we cruise these waters."

"And if I were to refuse this 'sensible solution' of yours?" asked Aunt Anne tartly.

"Why the devil would you do that?" Papa blustered.

"How would you feel if I signed you on for a voyage without asking your permission first?"

"It's hardly the same thing."

"It certainly is," snapped Aunt Anne. She pushed back from the table, her face flushed. "If you'll all excuse me." She stalked off into the day cabin, leaving us in uncomfortable silence.

"Well," Fanny chirped after a moment, dipping her spoon into her bowl. "I don't know when I've tasted a more delicious chowder. I must persuade Mr. Glumly to share his recipe."

August 12, 1836

P.S. I am stunned at this news! I do not wish to be shipped off to boarding school any more than Aunt Anne does. But Papa is deaf to our protests. He is the head of this family, he says, and whether we like it or not, his decision is final.

Aunt Anne says what's done is done, and we'll just have to make the best of things, but I am inconsolable, and will do everything in my power to persuade Papa otherwise.

—P.

Nine

French a young lady is not only permitted to learn,
but is laid under the same necessity of
acquiring as a gentleman is of acquiring Latin.
—*Young Lady's Own Book, a Manual of Intellectual
Improvement and Moral Deportment*

On our last night aboard the *Morning Star* my father called me up on deck.

We were anchored in Wailuku, and all the arrangements had been made for our removal to Reverend Wiggins's school. Reverend Wiggins had responded promptly to Papa's letter of inquiry, pronouncing himself delighted with my father's plan ("providential," he had called it, and reading his response, I could envision his chamber-pot ears waggling with approval). The *Morning Star,* meanwhile, would continue on to the Sea of Okhotsk and join up with the rest of the whaling fleet.

"We've likely wasted the summer season, but perhaps if I crowd on enough sail we can catch the tail end of it," Papa had grumbled to the mates.

Perhaps if I crowded on enough sail, I could still convince him of the foolishness of leaving us ashore. I rounded the mizzenmast to where he was standing.

"You wanted to see me, Papa?" I said.

My father didn't answer me at first. The sky was a deep plum color, and the first stars were out. He was gazing off toward shore, a faraway look in his eye. I wondered what he was thinking about and fervently hoped it wasn't Fanny Starbuck.

"Papa," I ventured, "I do wish you'd change your mind."

He sighed and turned to face me. "Patience, we've been over this too many times already. It's pointless to discuss it further."

"But you promised we would always sail together as a family."

"That was before I nearly got you all killed."

"It wasn't your fault!" I protested. "No one could have foreseen what happened."

Papa shook his head. "Nevertheless, the fact remains that I put you in danger. You cannot imagine how I felt, returning to consciousness on that blasted beach to find myself trussed up like a turkey and with no sign of you or your brother—not to mention my sister or Fanny. I cannot allow that ever to happen again."

I felt a pang at his inclusion of Fanny Starbuck in our family circle. How easily she had wormed her way in, with her dimples and her shortbread and her blonde ringlets! Had she wormed her way into my father's heart as well?

Thinking of Fanny's dimples made me angry.

"I think the real reason you're leaving me here is because I'm a girl," I said bitterly, thinking back to the night of the battle with the cannibals. "If I were a boy, you wouldn't fear for me so."

"I'm leaving Tad, too, aren't I?" Papa countered.

"He's practically an infant still—he doesn't count." I was being unreasonable and I knew it, but I couldn't help myself.

"Don't you see you're being unreasonable?" my father continued, as if reading my thoughts. "You have much to learn, Patience."

"What have I to learn that I cannot be taught aboard the *Morning Star*?" I cried.

"Etiquette, for starters," he said. "It is clear to me from your behavior toward Fanny these past weeks that your manners need polishing."

I gaped at him. What was he talking about? I had been the picture of politeness since she had arrived in Lahaina. Well, most of the time.

"Papa, I wasn't the one who turned up here without an invitation," I said, trying to keep my voice level.

My father sighed. "Fanny Starbuck is very young, barely over twenty, and very far from home," he replied. "It was foolish of her to come, I agree, but here she is. She's likely lonely and scared and wishing

she'd never left Nantucket, and it would please me
very much if you would make more of an effort to
help her feel welcome."

And make it easier for her to waltz into the role of
my stepmother? He was asking the impossible.

"Miss Mitchell sent along some new mathematics
books for me with Aunt Anne," I said, trying a different
tack. "*Bridge's Conic Sections* and *Colburn's Algebra*. I'll
need your help if I'm to become a truly able navigator.
Surely it can't be good for my abilities to let them
rust ashore."

My father shook his head. "There's more to life
than mathematics, Patience, and other seas to navigate."

"What are you talking about?"

"You should be spending time in the company of
other girls, other women," he said. "Not roistering
about on a whaling ship."

This sounded suspiciously like Hester Halifax
speaking. "You've been discussing me with Fanny,
haven't you?" I accused.

My father ignored me. "There are certain refinements you should be acquiring at your age."

"What refinements?"

"French, for instance," he said. "Reverend Wiggins
feels it is a necessary part of a young lady's education.
He plans to teach it to both you and Charity."

I stared at him in disbelief. Not only had he been discussing me with Fanny Starbuck, but he'd also been discussing me with the odious Reverend Wiggins!

"French?" I burst out. "What need does an assistant navigator have for French? There are no whales in Paris!"

"It won't harm you to learn a foreign language," Papa replied, brushing off my objections.

"Do you speak French?"

"That's beside the point," he said stiffly. "And you'll learn how to dance—"

So he had noticed how graceless I was. Stung, I turned away.

"—and you'll also learn music, and deportment, and of course needlework."

My father had just described Fanny Starbuck.

"You mean to turn me into a simpering fool," I said in disgust.

"Thunder and lightning, Patience!" Papa roared. "Can I never please you? On Nantucket last fall all you could talk about was your desire to further your studies, and now that the opportunity has arisen . . ." His voice trailed off and he threw his hands up in exasperation.

Papa was correct that I had wanted to stay on Nantucket last fall and further my education, but to fling it in my face at this late date was simply cruel.

Nor was it at all fair to compare a fine mathematics tutor such as Maria Mitchell with the likes of Reverend Wiggins. My face flushed with anger.

"I'm not putting this very well, am I?" my father said in a gentler tone, stepping closer and giving my shoulder a reassuring squeeze. I pulled away, and he sighed again. "I'm not abandoning my best assistant navigator, and it's only for a few months. A spell ashore away from a ship full of rough sailors will do you good, my girl."

I whirled around. "But I love the *Morning Star* and all of our shipmates!"

"I know you do, and you'll sail with us again, and soon, I promise. I'll be back by your birthday. This is only a temporary arrangement, until I can—"

"What, until you can marry Fanny Starbuck?" I shouted, unable to contain myself any longer.

Papa stopped in his tracks. His face registered shock, then outrage. "That is none of your business," he shouted back.

"Why not? Why shouldn't I have a say in who is to be my stepmama?"

"Fanny's not— I'm not— But even if I were—" Papa spun on his heel and stalked angrily back toward the companionway. He paused at the head of the stairs. "I refuse to discuss this any further. You *will* attend the Wailuku Female Seminary, and you *will* mind your manners, and you *will* act as befitting a Goodspeed toward Fanny Starbuck!"

And with that he stomped off, leaving me to stare up at the star-paved sky and wish with all my heart that Mama were here to set things right again.

August 20, 1836

Our trunks are packed and all is quiet aboard the Morning Star, but sleep is impossible.

Why can't I ever learn to hold my tongue? Must I sail through life perpetually at loggerheads with my father? I do know he loves me, as I love him, and our tiffs have lessened in the months since we left Nantucket, for which I am thankful. But still, when we quarrel and the full weight of his disapproval settles on me as it does now, I feel it keenly.

Could he be right—do I have much to learn? I suppose I am in need of dance instruction; that has been well established. I am as graceless as a blubber gaff.

But that is hardly a failing in an assistant navigator. An assistant navigator has no need of such graces. An assistant navigator has no need for men to gaze at her the way they gaze at Fanny Starbuck.

Or does she?

—P.

The *Morning Star* sailed the following day, after hearty handshakes all around and wishes of greasy luck in the northern waters.

Although Papa promised once again that it was only a temporary parting, still, we were none of us in high spirits. Glum barely looked me in the eye as we said our good-byes, just patted my shoulder feebly and turned away. Even Sprigg wasn't his usual surly self and moped about looking quite downhearted. Charlie Fishback promised to write, and Chips clasped my hand in his and whispered, "We'll take good care of your father for you, Miss Patience, have no fear."

At this, tears welled up in my eyes, for Papa and I were still on the outs. Thanks to our quarrel last night, he hadn't spoken a word to me all morning. I longed to bridge the rift between us before he sailed, but so far the opportunity to do so hadn't presented itself.

Mr. Macy and Mr. Chase fluttered around Fanny, but this was quite pointless, as she only had eyes for my father. I watched closely as Papa bid her farewell. Did he hold her hand in his longer than was necessary? Was there a note of regret in his good-bye?

Thaddeus flung himself between them just then, clamoring for a hug. Papa obliged him, tossing him in the air and catching him again with a hearty laugh.

His smile faded as he looked over my brother's shoulder and caught sight of me.

"Papa," I began, starting toward him, but he cut me off.

"Mind your aunt," he said, and with a curt nod he packed us into the whaleboat that would carry us and our trunks to shore.

We stood on the wharf afterward, watching as the *Morning Star* weighed anchor. A short while later her sails fluttered, hesitated, then caught the breeze, and she set a course for the far north, leaving me with a heart full of wounded pride and regret.

Ten

The education of women should,
of course, be strictly feminine.
—*Young Lady's Own Book, a Manual of Intellectual
Improvement and Moral Deportment*

August 27, 1836

*Just as Eden had its serpent, so this island para-
dise has something to mar its beauty as well: Reverend Titus Wiggins.*

*If Fanny Starbuck is a thorn in my side, Rev-
erend Wiggins is my cross to bear. Why oh why
did Papa see fit to leave us in his care? We have
been at the Wailuku Female Seminary for
scarcely a week now, and already I am desperate
for the Morning Star's return. Sour as a crab-
apple and twice as smug, Reverend Wiggins is a
self-righteous killjoy. Aunt Anne thinks so too,
though of course she is far too polite to admit it.*

—P.

If Aunt Anne was polite, however, she was also
still a Goodspeed, prickly and proud, and she and
Reverend Wiggins nearly came to blows over the

school's curriculum. It seemed the good reverend took a dim view of educating women, at least beyond a purely elementary level.

"I have been charged with a harvest of young souls!" he boomed the first night after our arrival, as if he were addressing us from the pulpit instead of across the dinner table. Reverend Wiggins was much given to booming pronouncements. "It is my task to provide these young heathens with a passport to glory! To mold them into shining examples of propriety, industry, and virtue so that they may become suitable helpmeets for the scholars of the Mission Seminary at Lahainaluna!"

Apparently the scholars were not interested in educated helpmeets, I thought sullenly. At least not according to Reverend Wiggins. Being able to read well enough to decipher the Scriptures was sufficient, he said, and while he approved of basic arithmetic—a good helpmeet must be able to track her household's pennies, after all—he was vigorously opposed to the study of higher mathematics.

"Female brains are not designed for such strenuous mental work," he boomed again. "They will overheat."

"Mine should have long since exploded, then," I muttered, but he pretended not to hear.

Fixing me with a disdainful eye, he declared himself quite scandalized that Papa allowed me to assist him in navigating the *Morning Star*, despite the fact that my skills helped rescue our marooned crew.

"If you were my daughter, I would forbid it," he said pompously.

If I were your daughter, I longed to say, I would have marooned you myself. But for once I held my tongue.

Aunt Anne was not one to give in easily, and daily she could be heard telling Reverend Wiggins that his views were outdated, and that in the fifteen years he had been away from New England many things had changed.

"Female education—proper female education—is fast taking root," Aunt Anne told him. "Why, there's even talk of a college for women in Massachusetts. Miss Mary Lyon has purchased land for it in South Hadley. Mount Holyoke Female Seminary, it is to be called."

Reverend Wiggins looked at Aunt Anne as if she had two heads. "College for women?" he blustered. "Bluestocking nonsense. You must be mistaken, Miss Goodspeed."

But Aunt Anne said it was true. "And have you not heard of the Female Academy in Ipswich? It was started five years ago and is thriving, as is the female department of Duke's County Academy on Martha's Vineyard." She shot me a triumphant look. "Which, by the way, teaches navigation to girls."

"Ridiculous notion," said Reverend Wiggins, refusing to be budged.

So, while the scholars at Lahainaluna were studying proper mathematics—not the piddling sum figuring that Reverend Wiggins allowed here—as well as such lofty subjects as natural philosophy, astronomy, oratory, Latin, and Greek, we were stuck with the three R's, as Papa called them (reading, 'riting, and 'rithmetic), music, deportment, the housewifely arts, and, for Charity and me, French.

Aunt Anne's plea for physical exercise went down in defeat as well. Reverend Wiggins frowned on dancing, of course, and decreed our twice-weekly walks to church sufficient movement for our limbs.

"I am training respectable females, not hoydens," he said.

Fanny Starbuck was quite displeased to learn of this pronouncement.

"But Hester Halifax says that dancing is both useful and ornamental in strengthening the body and improving the carriage," she protested. "She says it cannot be dispensed with in the education of young ladies."

Even her dimpled appeals were of no use, however, as Reverend Wiggins declared himself altogether willing to dispense with dancing and refused to hear any more about it.

August 28, 1836

If Aunt Anne was unable to budge Reverend Wiggins from his determination to have us spend the bulk of our days learning to sew, knit, spin, weave, clean house, set a proper table, and so on—all the detestable chores I find most tedious in life and for which I have the least talent—she did win one concession: I am to be allowed to continue my mathematical studies.

I may do so only at night, however, and only in our quarters. (Reverend Wiggins clearly fears my corrupting influence, which is a shame, for from what I have seen of her nimble work with sums, Charity might easily be instructed in more advanced mathematics.)

And Aunt Anne herself must supervise, to ensure that I don't overheat or otherwise do myself or my brain an injury.

Just the thought of the Reverend Titus Wiggins and his pronouncements makes me feel overheated. I think I'll step outside for a little fresh air before bed.

—P.

P.S. Only 64 more days until my birthday, and the Morning Star's return.

P.P.S. Aunt Anne has learned that our entire school will be traveling to Lahaina in November for quarterly examinations. There are to be competitions in all the subjects, including mathematics. I'm sure Reverend Wiggins will forbid it, but oh, wouldn't it be fine to test my mettle against the scholars of Lahainaluna!

"How can you bear him?" I asked Aunt Anne, pulling my pinafore over my head. The shell had just blown, summoning us to breakfast. Where life aboard the *Morning Star* was governed by bells, at the Wailuku Female Seminary our day was regulated by blasts from a conch shell. We had been awoken by the first blast at dawn, when Reverend Wiggins led the students in prayer and Scripture reading, though we were not obliged to join them until six, when breakfast was served.

Aunt Anne and I were getting dressed in the grass hut to which she and Thaddeus and I had been assigned while the school's adobe dormitories were built. I quite fancied our snug, sweet-smelling quarters—the whisper of the wind at night through the thatch was immensely soothing—but Fanny rebelled at first sight of it.

In fact, the closer we had drawn to Wailuku that first day a week ago, the lower Fanny's spirits had drooped. While the trek from the bay was hardly a lark—two miles overland, most of it uphill, with all of our trunks, half a dozen *malo*-clad guides, and the blasted melodeon, to boot, left none of us leaping for joy—it certainly didn't warrant the moans and groans that Fanny had produced.

Wailuku was on the island's windward side, and a mizzling rain had set in during the last hour of our journey. This had proved entirely too taxing for Fanny, who in the end had needed to be carried. A seat was crafted for her from vines, which two of our guides suspended from a long pole slung across their shoulders. They thought this was great sport, but Fanny only complained all the more loudly—of seasickness, this time, thanks to the swaying of her perch.

The grass hut was the final straw.

"It looks like a beehive!" she had wailed. "And it has a dirt floor! I can't be expected to stay here!"

"Merciful heavens, Fanny, do stop that racket," Aunt Anne had replied. "It's not that bad. Look, there's a carpet for the floor made of woven rushes—it's quite quaint, really."

That's just how Mama would have viewed it, I thought, as an adventure, not a trial. But Fanny was not Mama, of course.

Reverend Wiggins hastened to point out that the

lodgings were only temporary, and that the dormitory—a long, low building behind the parsonage, thatched with *ti* leaves and separated into sleeping compartments—was nearly finished.

But Fanny, who had mistaken the building for a stable (and, indeed, even I had to admit a resemblance), found this prospect equally appalling and refused to be comforted. "I won't be stuffed into a stall, either," she had sniffled, after inspecting it.

Even the promise of a room of her own in the upper story of the stone schoolhouse, also under construction, couldn't stem the flood of tears. She had looked so pathetically downcast that Mrs. Wiggins finally took pity on her and invited her to share a room with Charity in the already overcrowded parsonage.

The conch shell blew again and Thaddeus, the rascal, never one to allow niceties to keep him from a meal, scampered off before I could wash his face or comb his hair. If Mrs. Wiggins was distracted enough with her own brood not to notice, Reverend Wiggins surely would, and I was equally sure he'd let me know that he had noticed. I sighed and put my question to Aunt Anne again.

"How can you bear him? Does he not drive you to distraction?"

"His heart is in the right place, Patience," my aunt

replied, parting her dark hair down the middle and swiftly twisting the two lengths into a knot at the back of her neck. "And while I agree with you that his personality often leaves something to be desired, it cannot be denied that his efforts to do good here are most sincere."

I was well aware of that. Reverend Wiggins made sure we were all well aware of it. His chamber-pot ears grew pink with righteous enthusiasm at the thought of heathen souls to be saved—thirty of them right here at this school—and hardly a day went by when he didn't boom at least once that "we are embarked on a noble enterprise!" or "Providence has entrusted us with a mighty endeavor!" or "those who sat in darkness will soon see a great light!"

If I heard any more of his pronouncements, I felt I would burst.

I heaved another sigh. Aunt Anne patted my shoulder. "Chin up, dear heart. It's only for a few months. You know what your father says, 'What can't be cured must be endured.'"

She pushed me outside into the early morning sunshine. We both breathed deeply of the air, a soft, fragrant blend of earth and growing things overlaid with the invigorating scent of the sea, wafted up from the distant bay by the everpresent trade winds.

"How often I have dreamed of a place like this!"

Aunt Anne said, flinging her arms wide as if to embrace the view. She smiled at me. "If something must be endured, this is surely the spot in which to do it, is it not?"

She had a point. Even I, who had vigorously pouted every step of the way here, had to admit this was true.

While no place on earth could rival dear Nantucket in my affections—my heart still yearned often for home, and likely always would—her cool, salt-laced air and drifting gray fogs, the same gray as her shingled houses and sober-clad Quaker residents, seemed very far away. In the past week I had quite fallen under the spell of this glorious spot.

At home roses clambered over the fences in summer, perfuming the breezes, but here flowers grew wild everywhere we looked, fragrant hibiscus in an array of colors as intoxicating as the vibrant *kapa* cloth in which the natives wrapped themselves.

Equally intoxicating was the view. Set on a plateau above the tiny village, the school commanded a sweeping outlook. A meadow of deepest emerald surrounded us like a velvet cloak flung down by a benevolent deity, while to our rear a forest of darker, deeper hues beckoned the eye up the 'Iao Valley. There, a tangle of wild ferns and trees—breadfruit and koa, kukui nut, mountain apple, and bamboo—

sloped steeply upward toward the mist-capped mountains beyond. In the distance, unseen, a spike of rock
thrust heavenward like a finger raised in warning—
the 'Iao Needle. Aunt Anne and I had seen it on the
sole afternoon we had been able to sneak away for a
walk by ourselves. Cloud-crowned and remote, it was
a sacred spot, Aunt Anne had told me, reading from
her guidebook. Beneath it somewhere lay the bones
of the island's long-dead warriors and chiefs.

All around us, birds hung in the trees like bright
scarves, their cries mingling with the perpetual whisper of the wind. From where we stood, I could just
make out the turquoise water of Wailuku, and if I
closed my eyes, I could almost hear the low thunder
of the surf, as steady and constant as a heartbeat.

It was nearly impossible to be downcast in the
face of such beauty—or such resolute cheerfulness as
Aunt Anne's—and I followed her to breakfast in
much better spirits.

Eleven

Conversation, reading, and various sorts of needlework
are all pleasing and useful occupations for a lady.
—*Etiquette for Ladies, or The Principles of True Politeness*

Aunt Anne and I were late.

The others were already standing behind the benches that lined the long twin tables in the lanai—an open-air structure covered with plaited coconut leaves that served as the school's temporary dining hall and schoolroom. Work on the coral stone structure that would eventually house both was still many months from completion. We took our places, and after reprimanding us sharply with his eyes, Reverend Wiggins bowed his head for grace.

"'Bless the Lord, O my soul, and forget not all his benefits,'" he intoned. "Psalms, chapter one hundred and three, verse two."

As he led us in prayer, I peeped through my eyelashes at the other table, where the native girls stood with Pali, the Wigginses' gentle-voiced housekeeper.

Although I was, of course, acquainted with Pali and her husband, Upa, Charity and I were kept strictly apart from the native girls—to keep us safe from heathen influences, Reverend Wiggins said.

Naturally, I had developed a burning curiosity about our companions at the school, who ranged in age from six to fourteen. I was particularly intrigued by the eldest student, a girl by the name of La'ila'i.

Tall and slender, she had a cascade of dark hair and eyes to match—eyes that were enticingly merry, except when Reverend Wiggins was in the vicinity. La'ila'i was the daughter of a local *alii*, or chief, and had been enrolled along with her little sister Hi'iaka to encourage other island parents to entrust their daughters to the missionary school.

In a rare burst of confidence, Charity had informed me that the girls had shown up for the first day of school all but naked, clad only in lengths of native *tapa* draped about their hips.

"My father nearly had a fit of the vapors," she had whispered, allowing a small giggle to escape before she clamped her lips back into their usual prim line. "Mother and Pali and I stayed up all night sewing proper garments for them."

The girls certainly looked proper enough now, I thought. They were dressed alike in long, full-yoked garments that resembled my own Mother Hubbard–style nightgown. The girls called them *holokus*, and like my everyday gray calico frock, they covered them from neck to ankle. But whereas all the native girls were barefoot, my feet were crammed into shoes. Shoes that had grown uncomfortably snug in recent weeks, I thought, wiggling my toes. In fact, all of my garments had grown uncomfortably snug in recent weeks. My body seemed to be changing shape.

Across from me, I saw Thaddeus gaze longingly at the platter on the table between us. It was piled high with muffins—courtesy of Fanny, who had won kitchen privileges from Pali and Mrs. Wiggins as quickly as she had won them from Glum—as well as chunks of pineapple and banana, or *halakahiki* and *maiʻa,* as the girls called them. After some initial resistance Aunt Anne had managed to convince Mrs. Wiggins not only that the local food was not poisonous, but also that it was more charitable to offer it to native girls unaccustomed to plain New England fare. It was certainly a welcome change from the porridge we'd been dealt each morning back in Lahaina, and although none but the native girls would touch it, Aunt Anne even made sure that their beloved poi was added to the menu, along with an abundance of fresh fish.

Charity's four brothers stood flanking Thaddeus, not a hair out of place and as freshly scrubbed as my brother was not. With their hands clasped piously under their chins, they looked like angels.

That was a far cry from the truth, however, as well I knew. Reverend Wiggins may have dubbed his boys the Four Gospels, but Holy Terrors was more like it. Fortunately Aunt Anne brooked no nonsense, and while the scuffles and pranks they had inflicted on Thaddeus and me in Lahaina hadn't entirely ceased, at least they had lessened here in Wailuku.

"Amen," said Reverend Wiggins finally, and as we took our seats, Thaddeus dove for the muffins.

"May I serve you some pineapple?" I asked Mrs. Wiggins, who was seated beside me.

"No thank you, dear," she whispered. "I'll just have tea."

She looked a little paler than usual, but perhaps that was because she was "expecting a small messenger from heaven," as Reverend Wiggins put it. I remembered that Mama had sometimes been unwell in the mornings before Thaddeus was born. On the other hand, Mrs. Wiggins's pallor could have been heightened by the fact that she was seated next to Fanny. As fashionably dressed as always—she was clad this morning in a dress the shade of a ripe peach—Fanny was as vibrant and full of color as Mrs. Wiggins was lacking in it.

Reverend Wiggins didn't quite know what to make of Fanny Starbuck. He disapproved of her fripperies ("'As a jewel of gold in a swine's snout, so is a fair woman which is without discretion'—Proverbs, chapter eleven, verse twenty-two," I'd overheard him gripe to Mrs. Wiggins), but he couldn't fault her piety. No one steepled her hands more prettily, nor bent her head in prayer more dutifully, than did Fanny Starbuck.

And she had certainly captured the affection of the students. Irresistibly drawn to her beauty, the native girls regarded her with a worshipful awe that Reverend Wiggins could only hope to direct into more worthy channels. If Fanny sat up straight, they sat up straight. If she said "please" and "thank you," they said "please" and "thank you." If she walked with mincing steps—so different from Aunt Anne's and my own brisk stride!—they walked with mincing steps.

Reverend Wiggins might be a self-righteous killjoy, but he was no fool. If he truly wished to teach the girls manners befitting proper helpmeets, he could do no better than to enlist the aid of Fanny Starbuck, and well he knew it. So he mostly kept mum about her appearance, only grumbling occasionally to himself or his wife. Fanny, naturally, was blithely unaware.

There was a loud peal of laughter from the far end of the other table, and I looked down to see La'ila'i attempting to butter a muffin. She was watching Fanny and trying to mimic her movements, but she had grasped the wrong end of the knife and was making a hash of it. Using proper eating utensils was just one of the many things the girls would learn, Reverend Wiggins told us, as they relinquished their heathen ways.

La‘ila‘i shrugged and licked the butter off her hand. Her sister Hi‘iaka laughed, and so did I. La‘ila‘i looked over and flashed me a broad smile.

"Eve, mind your manners," admonished Reverend Wiggins, with a frown that encompassed us both. He had given all the girls Christian names when they enrolled; Hi‘iaka was now "Hannah," and La‘ila‘i was "Eve." La‘ila‘i's biblical name had been an apt choice, as her own came from a native legend about the first mortal woman. La‘ila‘i was a heathen name, Reverend Wiggins had said, but I thought it much prettier than plain Eve.

La‘ila‘i's smile vanished. I suspected that she was as unhappy at the school as I was, but I had no way of finding out if this were true, because I never had the occasion to speak with her privately. Or publicly, for that matter, so separate were our activities. Even if I had managed it, it would probably have been of no use. She spoke as much English as I did Hawaiian, and I wasn't likely to learn Hawaiian anytime soon, at this rate. Although Reverend and Mrs. Wiggins were both fluent—indeed, all the girls' classes were conducted in Hawaiian—speaking the native tongue was strictly forbidden to all of us children.

"'Learn not the way of the heathen,'" Reverend Wiggins boomed frequently, as if we might forget. "Jeremiah, chapter ten, verse two."

After breakfast, Aunt Anne supervised the group of girls whose turn it was to clear away the dishes, while Fanny inspected their sleeping quarters. Morning sewing instruction would follow—from which Charity and I were mercifully spared by the necessity of learning French.

Settling in to Reverend Wiggins's study for our upcoming lesson, I glanced out the window toward the distant sea. Not a sail was visible on the broad expanse of blue. I wondered idly where the *Morning Star* was headed today and whether she had taken many whales. Was Charlie proving himself an able third mate? How was Glum faring in the galley without me? Did Papa miss us?

"*Mademoiselle Patience, attendez-vous?*"

"What?" I replied, startled from my reverie.

Reverend Wiggins glared.

"*Ah, oui, Monsieur Wiggins,*" I said meekly.

Charity flashed me a sympathetic look but returned her gaze quickly to the textbook in her lap. In the beginning I had hoped that the two of us might become friends, for aside from a handful of the native girls with whom I was forbidden contact, she was the only one my age here at school.

But Charity was so proper and dutiful that I was beginning to wonder if she was a real girl at all. Perhaps she had been brought up in the whatnot cabinet with the apostle spoons and the blue Spode teapot and the fan coral, I thought. A smile crept over my face as I imagined Reverend Wiggins placing her in there carefully each night beside the Dresden shepherdess and perhaps giving them both a brisk swat with Mrs. Wiggins's feather duster.

Reverend Wiggins looked at me sharply. *"Nous commençons avec chapitre trois."*

As we stumbled through our French lesson, I could hear Mrs. Wiggins in the parlor with the boys. They were taking turns reading aloud from *The Pilgrim's Progress*, and I suspected Thaddeus's eyes would be well glazed over by about now.

"Je suis, tu es, il est . . ." recited Charity, and my gaze wandered over to the window again.

Out in the lanai, the girls were grouped around Fanny, stitching industriously. From the looks of it, Aunt Anne had decided to weave a little mental arithmetic into their handiwork, for she was holding up a slate with 6 + 5 written on it. Fanny's forehead was puckered in concentration, and a snort of laughter escaped me when I saw that she was counting on her fingers.

"Mademoiselle, s'il vous plait!" said Reverend Wiggins in exasperation.

An hour of his plodding instruction left me fairly limp with despair, and I eagerly moved to the parlor for recitation and reading with Mrs. Wiggins. Charity and I were working our way through *The Young Lady's Book of Elegant Prose,* fairly sluggish going but a definite improvement over *The Pilgrim's Progress* and infinitely better than *Willis's Guide to Conversational French.*

Aunt Anne took the boys into the study for their turn at arithmetic, meanwhile, and as Fanny bustled about preparing for the housewifery lessons soon to follow, Reverend Wiggins took over in the lanai, where he was teaching the native girls to read and write Hawaiian.

Before the missionaries arrived in the Sandwich Islands in 1820, Aunt Anne had told me, Hawaiian was a spoken language only. If there was one single accomplishment in the missionaries' endeavors that impressed her most, she said, it was their zeal in setting down the language on paper. Thanks to their efforts, she said, many people in the islands were learning to read and write, as numerous instructive works, including the Bible, were translated into their native tongue.

A few hours later our academic instruction—except for my mathematical studies, which would commence after dark—was finished. The rest of the day would be devoted to what Reverend Wiggins called "our real work"—needlework of various sorts, music, deportment, and the like.

The boys were sent outside to stretch their legs, but alas, young ladies were not allowed such a luxury. I had to content myself with resting my elbows on the windowsill and allowing my eyes to roam for me. I glanced across the yard to the lanai. La'ila'i was staring unhappily into the distance as well. I wondered what she was thinking.

Fanny caught sight of me and called, "Patience! Come and assist me for a moment, would you?"

Dutifully I went outside and began distributing the knitting projects we had begun a few days ago. La'ila'i and I exchanged smiles as I handed her a pair of whalebone needles and a ball of wool. She gestured toward the empty seat next to her, and I hesitated. But Reverend Wiggins was watching from his study, so I took my usual place between Charity and Fanny on a bench on the opposite side of the lanai and tried to ignore the disappointment on La'ila'i's face.

With a sigh I stabbed my needles into the sorry excuse for a sweater I had undertaken. Needlework of any kind was a struggle for me; I just hadn't the skill, the interest, or the patience for it. Sadly my name was no indication of my nature.

Charity, naturally, was an adept knitter. She bent her head obediently over the task at hand, producing great swaths of flawlessly formed stitches. Along with Fanny Starbuck's own creation—a muffler in a shade of blue suspiciously like the color of Papa's eyes that she was surely planning to twine about his neck—it was held up as a paragon of perfection for the other girls, who also appeared to be catching on quickly. Everyone but me was well on her way to becoming a virtuous helpmeet.

I, on the other hand—well, no one was likely to ask for my help anytime soon. My pitiable efforts looked like something Sprigg would have done, had he gotten into the grog, mislaid his spectacles, and stumbled down into the *Morning Star*'s hold to knit in the dark.

"For heaven's sake, try not to fidget so," said Fanny irritably. "You're jostling the bench."

I gave her a surly look.

"And don't slump, either," she continued. "You'll ruin your posture."

Fanny, of course, was seated as daintily as the Dresden shepherdess in the whatnot, her back as straight as her knitting needles, which clacked together in industrious reproof with every stitch.

I laid my knitting down beside me and made a show of stretching my legs out, then clasped my hands in front of me and stretched my arms as well. My limbs were cramped and sore, and I desperately wanted to go for a walk, run across the yard, turn cartwheels, climb a tree (or, better yet, a mast)—anything but sit here on this bench. Fanny might be content to sail through life perched on a parlor sofa, reading her *Godey's* magazines and tatting lace, but I certainly was not.

I glanced up at the sky and idly twisted a strand of my hair. If I was back aboard the *Morning Star* right now—where I ought to be, and where I would be were it not for Fanny Starbuck—it would nearly be time to take the noon sight.

My other hand strayed to my pinafore pocket, where I had taken to keeping my sextant as a talisman of sorts and a reminder of the real life that awaited me at sea.

"Keep your hands away from your hair," Fanny instructed. "You know what Hester Halifax tells us, 'Never scratch your head, pick your teeth, clean your nails, or worse than all, pick your nose in company.'"

I grinned. Fanny had just described most of the *Morning Star's* raucous and unmannerly crew. I was suddenly overcome with longing for my absent shipmates. "Hester Halifax is an insufferable prig," I said defiantly.

Fanny put her knitting down. She frowned. "I'll

have you know that *Etiquette for Ladies* is read in the finest households."

Aunt Anne materialized behind us. "I'm sure it is, Fanny," she said. She picked up my misbegotten sweater and handed it back to me with a warning look. "There's no need for you two to argue."

"I wasn't arguing," I protested.

Fanny emitted a tiny but decidedly unladylike grunt. "'A lady can never be polite and well-bred on special occasions, who is contrary on ordinary ones.'"

I turned my back on her and stabbed my knitting needles together once again. Fanny had no right to lecture me on my behavior. She wasn't my elder sister or my governess, and she certainly wasn't my mother, much as she might fancy that role for herself. Aunt Anne should have seen that and stood up for me.

My black thoughts were interrupted by a shriek, and Thaddeus rushed in.

"Tad, what is it? What's wrong?" I asked in alarm.

My brother ran to me, clutching his face and crying loudly. He buried his head in my pinafore. Outside, the Four Gospels scattered.

"What is the meaning of this ruckus?" boomed Reverend Wiggins, thrusting his head out of his study window.

Aunt Anne took one look at my brother, picked up her skirts and strode outside. Grabbing the nearest

Gospel by the collar—it was Mark—she questioned him closely. The hapless boy wilted under her stern gaze, and in a minute, she was back.

"Thaddeus shoved a pebble up his nose," she said crisply, shooting a look at Reverend Wiggins, who had come outside to determine for himself the cause of the commotion. Like Papa, Aunt Anne was formidable when she was angry, and Reverend Wiggins hesitated on the threshold of the lanai. "Your boys put him up to it. They said it was *hoʻo kala kupua*, magic, and that it would make him invisible."

I wrapped my arms around my brother, who was still howling like a gale wind through a ship's rigging.

"Preposterous! My children do not speak Hawaiian," said Reverend Wiggins, drawing himself up to his full height. "This young rascal must have cooked up that story to excuse his own foolish behavior."

Didn't speak Hawaiian? That was laughable—the Wiggins brood were as fluent as their parents. And how could they not be, having lived on this island all of their lives? And with Pali and Upa in attendance at all hours of the day and night? Even Thaddeus and I had picked up a smattering already. What Reverend Wiggins should have said was that his children didn't speak Hawaiian in front of him.

Mrs. Wiggins stepped forward and laid a restraining hand on her husband's arm.

"Perhaps we shouldn't worry about where to assign blame just now," she said gently. "Thaddeus needs to be seen to. Dr. Phillips is here in Wailuku this week. I saw him at Brother Chapman's after the worship service yesterday."

Dr. Phillips was the medical missionary assigned to Maui. He spent time at each missionary station on the island and was currently in residence with the Chapmans in the village.

"I'll take him," I said.

"I shall accompany you as chaperone," volunteered Fanny.

I shot Aunt Anne a pleading look, but her eyebrows had settled into their storm warning position.

"I'd like a word with Reverend Wiggins, if you don't mind," she said. "Go ahead and take Fanny with you."

Thaddeus's pride was more wounded than his nose, it seemed, as he managed to laugh at the steady stream of silly riddles and nonsense rhymes Fanny produced to distract him on the short walk to the Chapmans'. I listened to her, my thoughts churning, for it seemed that Fanny had not only set her sights on my father, but she was also trying to steal my brother's affections as well. On the other hand, I thought scornfully, perhaps it was only natural that Thaddeus would find her amusing, given that her wit was on a par with his.

Reverend Chapman, a tall, slender, gray-haired gentleman, bounded out of his front door as I opened the gate to his front yard.

"Greetings!" he cried, beckoning us up the steps. "Mrs. Starbuck, Miss Goodspeed! 'How lovely upon the mountains are the feet of them that bring good tidings.'"

Like Reverend Wiggins, Reverend Chapman tended to speak in scriptural terms, but his selections were a great deal more cheerful.

"Not so good today, I'm afraid," I replied. "Is Dr. Phillips in? My brother has a pebble stuck up his nose."

Thaddeus looked down in embarrassment and scuffed his foot against the doorway.

Reverend Chapman squatted down beside my brother. "Is that so, Master Thaddeus?" he said. "Pesky things, those pebbles. Well, Dr. Phillips is due back directly, and meanwhile Mrs. Chapman is baking a banana cake, which I suspect might help speed the cure."

Thaddeus managed a smile at this, and Reverend Chapman shooed him off toward the kitchen as he ushered Fanny Starbuck and me into his parlor. "A houseguest just arrived whom I think you know."

"Mrs. Russell!" I said in delighted surprise.

A small, plump woman dressed in gray rose from

her seat, her round face wreathed with smiles. Mrs. Russell was a Quaker and the wife of Captain Russell, a fellow whaleman from Nantucket. We had befriended the two of them last fall during a gam at sea, and Mrs. Russell's cat Abigail was mother to my own dear Ishmael.

"Thee is a sight for sore eyes, Patience Goodspeed," she said, embracing me. "And Fanny Starbuck, as I live and breathe! What is thee doing here in the Sandwich Isles?"

While Fanny and Mrs. Russell settled in for a chat—or, more accurately, while Mrs. Russell settled in to listen to Fanny's nonstop prattle—Dr. Phillips arrived. Reverend Chapman retrieved Thaddeus (now covered in icing) from the kitchen and hoisted him onto the sofa.

"Aha!" said Dr. Phillips, peering up my brother's left nostril. "I see the rascal."

Like Glum, Dr. Phillips was as bald as an egg. He had lively gray eyes and bushy blond eyebrows, which he furrowed in concentration as he drew a pair of forceps from his black medical bag and neatly extracted the pebble from my brother's nose.

"How old are you, Master Thaddeus?" he asked.

"I'll be seven tomorrow," Thaddeus answered shyly, clambering down from the sofa.

"And a stouthearted lad you are too, from what I

hear. Helped outwit a passel of cannibals, unless I'm mistaken?"

My brother's face grew pink with pleasure at the praise.

"I'll wager you're far too grown up to be hood-winked into doing something like this again, correct?" Dr. Phillips continued in a more serious tone.

Thaddeus nodded sheepishly, and after lecturing him about the dangers of inserting foreign objects into noses, ears, and all other places on the body that they didn't belong, Dr. Phillips packed up his medical bag and declined Mrs. Chapman's invitation to luncheon.

"As dearly as I wish I could stay and visit with all you fine ladies, I must be off," he said. "There's a set of twins due to put in an appearance shortly in the village, and it's best I be there when they do."

And tossing us a wink, he took his leave.

Fanny and Thaddeus and I were happy to accept the luncheon invitation in his stead, however, and we spent a most agreeable afternoon visiting with the Chapmans and Mrs. Russell.

"I hear those ruffians who mutinied aboard thy father's ship were packed off to Honolulu last week," Mrs. Russell said, when she was finally able to get a word in edgewise. "They've been the talk of Lahaina."

"Hanging's too good for them," said Reverend

Chapman severely. He was lying on the carpet with Thaddeus, playing a game of marbles. "Imagine, leaving a young sprout like this"—he inclined his head toward my brother—"on an island to starve."

"Heaven knows we Quakers are not a bloodthirsty folk," said Mrs. Russell, "but I'm inclined to agree with thee in this case. I'm just thankful that clever Patience was aboard, or the tale might have had an altogether different ending."

Although Reverend and Mrs. Chapman had heard of our run-in with the cannibals, they had not heard of my part in subduing the mutineers and navigating the *Morning Star* back to the island where Papa and the others had been marooned, and they begged for details.

"Brave as well as clever," said Reverend Chapman admiringly when I was done.

For once, Fanny didn't say a word.

It was late afternoon before we left our friends, and then only after extracting a promise from them that they would join us at Thaddeus's birthday celebration the following afternoon.

Back in our grass hut that evening, I tucked my brother into bed and pulled the mosquito netting closed around him. The gauzy fabric swayed lightly in the currents of air that sifted in through the thatch. He reached out through the slit in it and caught my wrist.

"Aren't you going to read to me, Patience?"

"Aren't you tuckered out?" I replied in surprise. It had been a long day.

He shook his head. "Not too tired for *Robinson Crusoe.*"

Aunt Anne and I had been taking turns reading *Robinson Crusoe* aloud to Thaddeus each night in our hut. Although I had read it myself several times before—and, as we rounded Cape Horn last winter, had thrilled to the sight of the island of Juan Fernandez, where the author, Daniel Defoe, had lived as a castaway—my little brother hung on every word.

It was our secret, just the three of us. Reverend Wiggins did not approve of fiction, of course. "Vile drivel," he called it, and "flash rubbish"—not to mention "heathen," his favorite seal of disapproval.

"Very well, then," I said.

Aunt Anne looked over at us and smiled. She was seated at the upended trunk that served as our makeshift table, writing a letter. The warm glow from the whale oil lamp softened her features. Like Papa, Aunt Anne could look severe, especially when she was gallied in some way, and between Reverend Wiggins and Fanny Starbuck, she had been looking quite severe of late.

I loved being in our hut at night, just the three of us—Goodspeeds through and through! This was how

I had imagined it would be on the *Morning Star*, except with Papa there as well to keep us company. With any luck, perhaps this was how it would be yet.

I opened the book. "'I was now entered on the seven and twentieth year of my captivity in this place,'" I began, looking over at Thaddeus. But he was already asleep.

August 29, 1836

I was of a mind to abandon my journal now that I have been marooned here ashore. It has THE VOYAGE OF PATIENCE GOODSPEED *stamped on the cover, after all, and I am most regretfully no longer at sea.*

But Aunt Anne has encouraged me to continue. In many regards, life itself is a voyage, she says. We never know where its winds and currents will carry us, she says, or what adventures lie ahead, and surely it's worth keeping record of this journey as well.

On the walk back from the village today, Fanny volunteered to bake the cake for Tad's birthday party. I had been planning to do this, but as my brother quickly pronounced it a capital idea, what was I to say?

If Mama were here, she would have known

what to say. If she were here, she likely would have insisted I bake the cake. But Mama is not here, and Fanny is, and if I don't think of something soon to discourage her, I am likely to be tied to her apron strings for life.

—P.

Twelve

Nothing beyond a simple, natural flower ever
adds to the beauty of a lady's head-dress.
—*Ladies' Indispensable Assistant, Being a Companion for*
the Sister, Mother, and Wife

"Patience! Patience! Look what Papa sent me for my birthday!"

With an effort, I opened one eye. It was barely daylight, and in the dim interior of our hut I could just make out my brother's face. He thrust a small bundle toward me and I groaned, rolling away from him.

"Go away," I mumbled, pulling the quilt over my shoulder. "It's not time to get up yet."

Something warm and wet snuffled in my ear, then gave it a lick. I shrieked and sat bolt upright, clutching the quilt around me.

Beside me, Aunt Anne's eyes flew open. "What?" she cried in alarm. "What is it?"

"It's a dog!" my brother crowed.

"We can see that," I said.

He deposited the creature on my lap and I prodded it gingerly. It gave a short bark, then cocked its head at me and wagged its tail, releasing a cloud of dust. I sneezed.

"Merciful heavens, Thaddeus, take that creature outside," protested Aunt Anne.

"But it's my birthday present," my little brother whined.

Aunt Anne raised herself up on her elbow. Bleary-eyed with sleep, the two of us stared at the dog.

It was small, not much bigger than my cat Ishmael. Its coat had once been white, possibly, but was now as dingy as the *Morning Star*'s sails after a bout over the smoky blaze of the try-pots.

"Tad, he's filthy," I said.

The dog panted happily and leaped up to lick my nose. I pushed it away. Thaddeus patted its head, undeterred by either the furry visitor's grimy state or its eager pink tongue. "He was waiting for me outside our hut. Papa sent him to me."

"Are you sure?" I peered more closely at the animal, dubious.

Not only was it the scruffiest canine specimen I had ever seen, it was also most decidedly cross-eyed. Born in the middle of the week and looking both ways for Sunday, as Mama used to say. Surely our father wouldn't have chosen such an ill-favored creature as a gift.

"He's from Papa," Thaddeus repeated. "He's mine."

Aunt Anne and I exchanged a glance. We both

knew that Thaddeus's real birthday present from my father—a fishing pole—was at the bottom of one of Aunt Anne's trunks, bundled up with the other gifts in her winter coat.

Heaving a sigh, Aunt Anne sat up. "Hand me my wrapper, would you, Tad?"

Thaddeus obeyed, and pulling the wrapper around her, Aunt Anne got up and drew back the tapa cloth that served as the door to our hut. A shaft of sunlight streamed in. The dog hopped down off our bed and trotted over to Aunt Anne. He sat down in front of her and looked up expectantly, his tail swishing back and forth furiously. He looked even worse in the light of day.

Aunt Anne shook her head. "Reverend Wiggins will never approve."

The dog sat up on its hindquarters and waved its front paws in the air.

"Look how smart he is!" Thaddeus exulted. "He knows how to beg!"

"He certainly does," said Aunt Anne, battling a smile. Then she sighed again. "Your sister is right, however—he's filthy."

Thaddeus's face fell. "But he's my happy birthday dog."

I held my breath. My little brother was tenderhearted, and I knew how much he missed Papa.

Aunt Anne was silent for a long moment. "Well

then, we'll just have to give your present a bath, won't we?" she said briskly. "Go fetch us a pail of water, will you, Tad?"

Before he could obey, the conch shell blew, summoning us to breakfast. Aunt Anne made Thaddeus tie his new pet—Friday, my brother dubbed him, after Robinson Crusoe's trusty companion—to a stake in the ground outside our hut for the time being while she decided how to broach the subject with Reverend Wiggins.

As it turned out, Friday broached it himself. He managed to escape somehow and appeared in the lanai just as we finished grace, looking nearly as smug as Reverend Wiggins himself.

"Amen," said Reverend Wiggins.

"Arf," said Friday.

Eyes opened wide around the two long tables.

"What is that beast doing here?" Reverend Wiggins demanded.

"He's not a beast—he's my birthday present!" said Thaddeus.

"Nonsense," said Reverend Wiggins. He pushed back from the head of the table and approached the dog, flapping his napkin angrily. "Shoo!"

Friday ran to where my brother was sitting and jumped up into his lap. Thaddeus wrapped his arms around him protectively.

"He's mine!" he said again. "My papa sent him!"

"That ugly mutt? Ridiculous."

"He's not an ugly mutt—he's my birthday present and his name is Friday!" Thaddeus said heatedly.

Beside me Charity sucked in her breath sharply. Defying Reverend Wiggins was strictly forbidden. I could only imagine what she'd think of some of Papa's and my loud arguments—or Papa's and Aunt Anne's, for that matter. The Four Gospels elbowed each other busily in the ribs as their father moved closer to my brother and his dog.

"Friday, is it?" said Reverend Wiggins, shooting a suspicious glance at my aunt. "And where did you get that outlandish name?"

I gave my brother a little kick under the table, worried that he might spill our secret. No point in adding fuel to this fire. The less Reverend Wiggins knew about *Robinson Crusoe,* the better.

Thaddeus barely hesitated. "Because today is Friday and today is my birthday."

Not bad, I thought in admiration. I couldn't have come up with a better answer myself.

"Birthday or not, the dog goes," said Reverend Wiggins. "It's heathen."

Thaddeus could contain himself no longer. "He's my dog and he's not heathen!" he shouted, his face red with rage. "I'll bet Jesus had a dog!"

Stunned by this blasphemy, Reverend Wiggins was at a loss for words for once. He stared at my brother, then at Friday, who wagged his tail and barked again.

Aunt Anne pressed her lips together, and I stared down at my plate, choking back laughter. A delicate snort even escaped from Fanny, who quickly raised her hankie to her face and blew her nose.

I did a rapid mental review of the Ten Commandments. I didn't think there was one forbidding the telling of a very small falsehood, especially when the happiness of that someone's little brother was at stake. Just in case, I decided to be as truthful as possible.

"Thaddeus is right," I said. "The dog is a birthday present."

From whom, I had no idea. But it had shown up today of all days, which surely qualified it as a gift, didn't it?

Aunt Anne squeezed my hand under the table. "Friday arrived just this morning," she added, in an ingenious twist of the truth.

My heart soared. Aunt Anne was a Goodspeed, through and through!

"Well, really," huffed Reverend Wiggins. "I am most provoked. What was Captain Goodspeed thinking? We can't have a dog at this school!"

Ignoring the blast of disapproval that emanated from the head of the table, Friday leaped down from Thaddeus's lap, stood up on his hind legs, barked, then did a backflip. The Four Gospels cheered, and La'ila'i, Hi'iaka , and the rest of the students at the other table dissolved into giggles. By now even Charity and Mrs. Wiggins were trying hard not to smile.

"That's quite enough," said Reverend Wiggins, who was not amused. "Thaddeus, remove this hound from my sight. I shall decide its fate later."

The rest of the morning passed without incident, though our lessons were accompanied by occasional yips and whines from Friday, who clearly preferred Thaddeus's company to that of exile under a hala tree. Thaddeus must have felt the same way, for from my seat in Reverend Wiggins's study I watched him wriggle and fidget his way through an arithmetic lesson, then burst outside when Mrs. Wiggins finally released him for recess.

As my brother and the Wiggins boys ran in circles through the garden with Friday in hot pursuit, I stretched my own cramped legs out in front of me and wished once again that I was back aboard the *Morning Star.* At least there I could walk the quarterdeck or busy myself with some physical chore—even jump rope if I chose—when my body felt stiff from inactivity. But alas, the only exercise I had to look forward to here was rubbing two sticks together in the vain attempt to spark a sweater.

The day crawled by. Thaddeus's birthday party had been set for teatime, and although Reverend Wiggins disapproved of "idle festivities," as he called them, since Fanny told him we had invited Reverend and Mrs. Chapman, as well as Dr. Phillips and Mrs. Russell, he couldn't very well forbid it.

"It will give everyone a chance to see what you've accomplished here at the school," Mrs. Wiggins consoled him, and he brightened somewhat at this prospect.

As teatime drew near, the native girls vanished, then reappeared a short while later, their long dark hair gleaming with fragrant coconut oil and wreathed with bright blossoms.

"Eve, you and the others know those heathen adornments are forbidden—*kapu*," said Reverend Wiggins.

The girls, who had been talking excitedly amongst themselves, grew quiet. Laʻilaʻi's eyes blazed in sudden anger, then she lowered them and stared sullenly at her feet.

Kapu. Forbidden. There was that word again. Must everything be disapproved of? Native dress, including flower and feather adornments—*kapu.* Native music and the dance called the *hula*—*kapu.*

Native language—for Charity and me and the boys at least—*kapu*. I suspected that even the island's lush sunsets would be *kapu* if Reverend Wiggins had his way.

Although he expressed a keen interest in the native flora and fauna of our surroundings, and in fact was hard at work on a scholarly guide to Maui's natural history, Reverend Wiggins cast a blanket of disapproval over the native people and their customs, dismissing it all as "heathen."

Oh, I had heard whispers of the old ways here in the islands, of the old temples where the *kāhunas*, or native priests, had reigned, overseeing the worship of idols—and worse. Some of the wild tales on the fore-deck of the *Morning Star* had told of human sacrifice. But that was long ago, and the natives we had encountered since sojourning here were as gentle and peaceable as Nantucket's most devoted Quakers, their lives moving to rhythms of earth and sea that would be instantly recognizable to my own island's farmers and fishermen.

And what could possibly be the harm in wearing a wreath of flowers? How was that any different from the daisy chain crowns I had made as a little girl back on Nantucket, or from the gaily decorated bonnets that Fanny and, yes, even Reverend Wiggins's own wife and daughter wore to church each Sunday? Was

Providence truly so grim, and the path to salvation so joyless?

Before Reverend Wiggins could send the girls to remove their adornments, the guests began to arrive, distracting him.

"What a lovely spot!" cried Mrs. Russell, drinking in the view from the lanai. "Thee must show us the grounds and all thy plans for the school."

Reverend Wiggins's chamber-pot ears grew pink with the prospect of an appreciative audience.

"We are planting the true vine in a heathen nation," he boomed, towing Mrs. Russell and Dr. Phillips off toward the construction site.

When they returned, Mrs. Russell took a seat at one of the tables and picked up a piece of needle-work—not mine, thank goodness.

"Why, just look at this, I couldn't have done better myself," she said, inspecting it closely.

"'She looketh well to the ways of her household, and eateth not the bread of idleness,'" boomed Reverend Wiggins again. "Proverbs, chapter thirty-one, verse twenty-seven."

"And these lovely girls, are they not the pride of the island? Such lovely flowers in their hair, such freshness and innocence!"

Reverend Wiggins looked slightly abashed at this.

"I remember when Captain Russell and I first

visited Lahaina many years ago, the natives wore nary a stitch of clothing." Mrs. Russell glanced over at Aunt Anne and me, a mischievous expression on her round, cherubic face. "The crew didn't seem to mind the view, but oh, it came as quite a shock to me. And just look at these children now—God-fearing, modestly attired, and properly instructed in the housewifely arts. Thy happy influence here is most apparent, Mrs. Wiggins."

"'A virtuous woman is a crown to her husband,'" said Reverend Wiggins pompously. "Proverbs, chapter twelve, verse four."

"Oh, and thee too, of course, Reverend Wiggins," added Mrs. Russell hastily. "Thee must be very proud of thy accomplishments here."

Reverend Wiggins swelled visibly at the praise. "All that I ask is a life spent bringing the light of salvation to souls shrouded in pagan gloom," he intoned.

As we took our seats for refreshments, I saw a flash of white out of the corner of my eye. Friday had managed to escape again and was creeping toward Thaddeus on his belly. One crossed eye maintained a sharp lookout for Reverend Wiggins, who was engaged in deep conversation with Reverend Chapman, while the other was fixed on a plate of Fanny Starbuck's shortbread. He wriggled his way to my brother and settled himself at his feet, as far out of sight under the table as possible.

As Charity pounded out "For He's a Jolly Good Fellow" on the melodeon in the parlor—the windows raised so we could hear the tune—Fanny swept in bearing the birthday cake. It was perfect, of course, swathed in shaved coconut and decorated with the same bright hibiscus blossoms that the girls still wore in their hair. She set the platter down on the table in front of Thaddeus to a chorus of delighted *oohs* and *ahs*. I wondered if everyone would have been as delighted with the humble spice cake I had planned to bake.

"Like manna from heaven," pronounced Reverend Chapman, taking a bite from the slice that was offered him, and even Reverend Wiggins couldn't find fault, although he made a great show of prying the flowers off his piece with his fork.

"This is better than Christmas," said my brother, as I presented him with his pile of gifts. The Four Gospels clustered around him, jostling for position.

"Open this one first," said Matthew, handing him a parcel. "It's from us."

My brother unwrapped it to find a copy of *The Pilgrim's Progress*. He drooped at the sight of it, and I kicked him under the table. He glared at me, then turned to Mrs. Wiggins and offered a dutiful if unenthusiastic thanks.

"For moral improvement and instruction," said Reverend Wiggins smugly. "Every boy should have his own copy."

The rest of the gifts were much more satisfactory. Besides the fishing pole from Papa—"Look, Patience, Papa sent me another present!"—there was a tiny box from Chips with a lid that slid open, into which my brother promptly dispatched his treasured pair of front teeth. Sprigg and Glum had sent along a pocketknife, and there was a set of small whalebone ninepins from Charlie Fishback and a bag of toffees and a book of fairy tales from Aunt Anne and me. Pali and Upa gave him a basket of shells, and from Dr. Phillips there was a pebble painted bright blue ("Just a reminder," he said with a chuckle) and a jar of pennies.

"Those are from Mrs. Chapman and me as well," said Reverend Chapman. "Save them for your trip to the quarterly examinations. Mrs. Russell tells us there's a new penny candy counter at the Lahaina Mercantile."

Fanny had knitted him a pair of socks with tiny whales on them—"These are capital!" exclaimed Thaddeus, giving her a hug, which I thought was overdoing it a bit—and Mrs. Russell gave him some licorice. Finally, I handed him an envelope.

"It's a poem from Mr. Macy," Thaddeus announced. He passed it to me. "You read it."

I accepted it gingerly, as it was sticky with cake. "This is from the *Morning Star*'s second mate," I explained to the gathered guests. "He has a knack for rhymes." I began to read:

> *He shipped aboard when just a lad*
> *And what adventures he has had!*
> *Marooned upon a desert isle*
> *Till rescued by shipmates in grandest style,*
> *He then helped save us from the fate,*
> *Of being served on a cannibal's plate!*
> *Arriving in Maui without delay*
> *To celebrate this special day,*
> *The anniversary of his birth,*
> *Seven short years upon this earth.*
> *We wish him health and many more,*
> *Greasy luck and a long life ashore.*
> *Yes, he shipped aboard when just a lad,*
> *And what adventures he has had!*
> *Who is he? Why, he's our TAD!*

The poem was greeted by a round of applause and a hearty "Hear, hear!" from Dr. Phillips. My brother grinned his gap-toothed grin.

"That's a capital poem," he said.

"It certainly is," I agreed.

"It's simply splendid!" gushed Fanny, her eyes bright with excitement. "May I see it?"

She read it over, a small smile playing across her lips. The poem probably reminded her of Papa, I thought crossly, and snatched it away somewhat rudely when she handed it back.

Not that I could blame her. As I returned the slip of paper to its envelope, I had to swallow hard to dissolve the lump in my throat. How I too missed Papa and Mr. Macy and all of my shipmates!

Suddenly, Fanny let out a yelp and leaped to her feet.

"Ouch!" she cried, swatting at her ankle. "Something bit me!"

A split second later, Mrs. Wiggins flinched and cried out as well, and then I jumped up as something pricked my lower leg. Quicker than Jack Flash, as Sprigg would have said if he'd been there, the party was in an uproar. Adults and children alike were soon leaping about, smacking at their legs and ankles.

"*Auē!*" cried La'ila'i, hopping on one foot and nursing her bare toes on the other. "*He 'uku!*"

I looked over at Charity. "What did she say?" I whispered.

With a quick glance toward her father, who was

too busy shaking out the legs of his trousers to notice us, she leaned toward me. "Jumping insects," she whispered back. "Fleas."

Fleas? My heart sank. There was only one possible culprit: Friday.

It would take nothing short of a miracle for Reverend Wiggins to allow Thaddeus to keep him now.

Thirteen

For a love letter, good paper is indispensable.
—*Ladies' Indispensable Assistant, Being a*
Companion for the Sister, Mother, and Wife

"That beast must go," said Reverend Wiggins flatly, who was, predictably, furious when the insects were identified as fleas.

Thaddeus looked so downcast at this pronouncement that Dr. Phillips stepped in.

"Don't you think you're being a bit hasty, Brother Wiggins?" he said.

"Nonsense—this heathen hound has brought a pestilence upon us," retorted Reverend Wiggins. "He must be banished."

Dr. Phillips rubbed his chin, his gaze shifting from my brother to Friday, who had slunk onto his belly next to Thaddeus and was looking suitably hangdog.

"Come now, Titus, this is an affliction that a good scrubbing will cure," he said. "Young Thaddeus here is obviously taken with the creature. It would do the boy a world of good to have a pet, what with his father so far away and all."

"But we have limited resources here at the school," protested Reverend Wiggins. "And I am highly vexed that Captain Goodspeed didn't see fit to send along a donation to cover its care."

"I'm quite sure table scraps will suffice. Having a dog is good for a boy's health. For that of your boys as well. Keeps them fit."

"Their health, you say?" said Reverend Wiggins suspiciously.

"Absolutely," said Dr. Phillips.

Reverend Wiggins looked down at Friday with distaste. Friday stared back up at him, panting happily. One eye was headed due east, the other due west.

"Oh, very well, then," he said, not bothering to disguise his irritation.

Dr. Phillips smiled. "It's settled, then."

Reverend Wiggins nodded reluctantly. "Doctor's orders."

August 31, 1836

After our poor flea-bitten guests had taken their leave, Mrs. Wiggins set us all to work vanquishing the intruders. First we boiled water, great vats of it, with which we doused the lanai's wooden floor. After the boards were duly scrubbed, we sprinkled them thoroughly with salt, making sure that plenty of it fell between the cracks. We left it overnight, then swept it up this morning.

The remedy appears to be effective, for the "pestilence of fleas," as the much chagrined Reverend Wiggins calls it, seems to be over.

I only hope that Thaddeus and Friday manage to stay out of further trouble.

—*P.*

At exactly ten minutes before noon a couple of days later, as Fanny was supervising Laʻilaʻi and the other girls in setting the tables for luncheon, Aunt Anne left the parlor and headed for the girls' privy.

I waited for a minute or two, then did likewise, looking back over my shoulder several times to make sure we weren't being followed. But no one paid us any heed.

Our privy was situated on a small rise on the far side of the dormitories, shielded from public view by a thicket of hala trees. Aunt Anne was waiting for me, gazing out toward the distant Pacific.

"Did you bring it?" she asked.

I patted my pinafore pocket. "Right here."

Aunt Anne checked the small gold watch pinned to the bodice of her dress. "It's time," she said.

I reached into my pocket, brought out my sextant, and handed it to her.

"Mathematics has never been my strong suit, but I firmly believe it's never too late to teach an old dog new tricks," Aunt Anne had told me last night when she asked if I'd teach her to navigate. "Plus, it will be a surprise for Isaiah. Two assistant navigators for the price of one."

Papa would indeed be surprised, I thought. I, on the other hand, was not. Aunt Anne's curiosity knew no bounds. Fanny was right; her nose was always stuck in a book, but only because she wanted to know about everything she encountered. The name of every bird, of every plant, of every constellation in the sky—Aunt Anne drank in information like a sponge. She'd even managed to inspire the boys with her enthusiasm for learning by setting them to collecting insects in pasteboard boxes. Reverend Wiggins had taken to calling her—albeit grudgingly—a "most efficient female."

Aunt Anne grasped the brass sextant with both hands and brought the telescope eyepiece up toward her face. As she swung the instrument skyward, I grabbed her arm.

"Never toward the sun," I said firmly. "You could damage your eyesight most severely."

That was the first thing Papa had told me when I was learning, as I had made the very same mistake. "Like this," I explained, reaching over and tilting the sextant downward. "Toward the horizon."

I flipped a filter over the end of the eyepiece to

lessen the glare. When the sextant was pointed into the distance, the index mirror would position the sun properly in the horizon glass.

"Aha," said Aunt Anne with satisfaction. "There it is."

"Now, set the orange on the table," I continued, using sailor's slang for adjusting the angle of the sextant until the sun appeared to come to rest on the distant line of the horizon.

"I have it!" she cried in triumph a moment later.

I smiled, recalling my own delight the first time I had managed it. Aunt Anne was a quick study. She tightened the tangent screw to lock the sextant's index arm in place, and we jotted down the reading from the scale on the arc. That number, which indicated the sun's altitude above the horizon, would help us determine our latitude when we did our calculations later tonight, back in the privacy of our hut.

As I tucked the sextant back in my pocket, I heard a rustling in the bushes behind us.

"Who's there?" I called, praying it wasn't Reverend Wiggins. He had made his feelings about female navigators abundantly clear, and after the recent fiasco with Friday I saw no point in gallying him further.

The rustling stopped. There was no reply. Then a nose poked out of the underbrush. A small, furry nose.

"Friday!" I said in relief. "Good dog."

The bushes rustled again and we froze. When they parted this time, Charity emerged.

"I didn't mean to startle you," she said sheepishly. "I was on my way to the necessary and couldn't help noticing what you were doing." She pointed to my sextant. "What is that?"

"It's a sextant," Aunt Anne replied. "It's a navigational tool, used for fixing a ship's position at sea."

"Is that what you used to save your father and Thaddeus?" Charity looked at me, her brown eyes alight with interest.

I nodded.

"Do you think I might learn to use it?"

I hesitated.

"It's what your father might call *kapu,* you know," Aunt Anne said gently.

Charity kept her eyes fixed on the sextant. "I know."

Would wonders never cease? I thought. First Friday was allowed to stay, and now this. Someone must have left the door on the whatnot cabinet ajar, for lo and behold, it appeared that Charity Wiggins possessed a spark of spirit after all.

Aunt Anne passed her the sextant without another word. Charity turned it over in her hand, fingering its fine brass fittings.

"Patience, why don't you show your new student how it works," my aunt said.

Charity's pale face was flushed with excitement by the time our lesson for the day was finished, and she eagerly swore an oath of secrecy on the way back to the lanai.

"Do you think you could come to our hut tonight without anyone knowing?" I asked.

Charity's face settled into its familiar timid lines. "I don't know," she said doubtfully.

"It's just that I'm going to work with Aunt Anne on her mathematics and show her the formulas for fixing latitude. I could show you, too."

Charity gave me a sidelong glance. "I might be able to manage it."

"There you are!" cried Fanny, pouncing on us as we rounded the corner of the lanai and causing Charity to start in alarm. "We're just about ready to be seated." She handed me a platter of sweet potatoes. "Put this on the table, will you, Patience? Wait, let me fix your hair—it looks like a bird's nest."

I pulled away in irritation. Fanny could never resist finding fault with my appearance, and her constant attempts at mothering me were growing most annoying.

Fanny sighed. "Do try and be more agreeable, Patience. 'A bad-tempered woman is a burden to herself, and a pest to those connected with her,' says Hester Halifax."

"Hester Halifax is the only pest around here," I muttered to myself, starting for the table. "Besides you."

At luncheon, Reverend Wiggins announced that a messenger had just arrived from Lahaina with a packet of mail. Our first news from the *Morning Star*!

"There's quite a stack," he said, holding up the envelopes. "And even one for me as well. I do hope that Captain Goodspeed has included a donation for the hound's care."

Aunt Anne and I exchanged a guilty glance. That was hardly likely.

Reverend Wiggins doled out the letters—one for Aunt Anne from Papa, one each from Charlie Fishback and Glum for me, and a full half dozen for Fanny Starbuck. She rifled through them, blushed, and tucked them into her pocket.

"Who are they from?" I asked, in as careless a tone as I could manage.

"Oh, just a few of your shipmates," she replied in an equally careless tone.

After lunch, Reverend and Mrs. Wiggins retired to the parlor with the latest edition of *Ka Lama Hawaii*— The Torch of Hawaii—a Hawaiian newspaper produced on the printing press at Lahainaluna. Fanny retired to her room, pleading a headache. I knew she wanted to be alone with her letters, and I longed to follow and see if I could discover who they were from. But Aunt Anne and Thaddeus were eager to hear all the news from our shipmates.

I read my letter from Glum aloud first:

"Dear Miss Patience," he wrote. *"Do you remember where you put the cloves? I have a hankering for gingersnaps and cannot find the blasted things. We gammed with the* Emily Morgan *out of New Bedford last week, and Sprigg acquired a monkey from one of her foremast hands. He paid three dollars for it, which he thinks is a fine bargain, but Chips and I suspect the former owner got by far the better end of the trade. Jocko is its name, and a wicked thieving creature it is. Just yesterday it made off with Chips's best wool socks and fired them into the galley stove. I caught him red-handed and chased him out with a broom. It could use a good thumping with Sprigg's thimble, but that is not likely to happen, as Sprigg spoils it quite shamelessly.*

"Speaking of the galley, it is altogether too quiet in here without you. I hope you and your aunt are well, and please give my best to Fanny Starbuck. Oh, and tell Tad that Daisy the goat

*has gone into a decline in his absence. Yesterday
she ate the lace curtains in the deckhouse."*

The letter was signed "*Obadiah Glumly*" and dated
nearly two weeks ago, shortly after the *Morning Star*
had sailed from Wailuku. Old news, but still, better
than no news.

"Read me the bits about Daisy and the monkey
again," begged Thaddeus, but I shooed him off so I
could read my letter from Charlie in peace.

It was much briefer, just a few lines in smeared
pencil telling me that they had taken a whale four
days earlier. Kanaka Jim, the harpooneer in Charlie's
own boat, had struck it, and Papa was pleased with
them both. Then he added: "*I wish to learn to navigate.
Will you teach me? I plan to have a ship of my own someday and will need to know how.*"

He had signed it, "*Your friend, Charlie Fishback.*"

I nearly laughed. All this sudden interest in navigation! Somehow I had obtained three students in one day.
And Charlie, of all people! It was hard to believe this
was the same farm boy who had shipped aboard the
Morning Star just a year ago, as green as a shamrock and
all thumbs. The only sea he'd ever viewed before that
was a sea of Ohio wheat, and now he was talking about
wanting to be captain of his own whaling ship? Smiling,
I reread the letter, then tucked it back into its envelope.

"Your father sends his regards," said Aunt Anne, looking up from her letter.

Not his love? I felt a twinge of sadness. Papa must still be displeased with me. My father could be as stubborn as a mule—or as his equally stubborn daughter. Perhaps I would relent and write him an apology after all.

"What else does he say?" I asked, wondering if he had mentioned Fanny.

Aunt Anne passed me the letter. I scanned it briefly, but it was mostly just a recounting of the weather and their taking of the whale, along with an admonition to Thaddeus to behave himself. He didn't mention either of our birthdays, or Fanny, and had signed it, "*Your brother, Isaiah.*"

"Not a very satisfactory letter," I grumbled.

Aunt Anne shrugged. "Isaiah never was one with words."

Fanny reappeared for our afternoon music lesson, looking flushed and pleased. I was fairly frantic with curiosity about her letters by now but couldn't bring myself to ask again.

Who could have written to her? Mr. Macy and Mr. Chase, surely, and possibly Charlie as well—but were all the rest from Papa? Had he asked her to marry him already? I could hardly bear not knowing.

As Charity launched into "Blessed Be the Ties

That Bind" on the melodeon—she was really quite good, much better than Mrs. Chapman, in fact, who barely managed to keep up with the congregation at our Sunday worship services—I offered to prepare tea.

"You just rest there, Mrs. Wiggins," I said, as she started to heave herself up from the sofa.

Mrs. Wiggins blinked her pale, rabbity eyes at me in surprise. Aunt Anne, who was helping the boys sort dead beetles into piles, gave me a sidelong glance. It was unlike me to volunteer for any household chore. But neither of them said anything.

Pasting a false-hearted smile on my face, I left the parlor, popped the teakettle on the stove to heat, then crept as quietly as I could upstairs to the room Fanny shared with Charity. The door creaked as I opened it, and I froze. No one appeared, however, and the only further sound was that of voices raised in song. I let out my breath and went in.

The room was small and plain, with a whitewashed floor and a tall window shuttered tightly closed against the fierce afternoon sun. Like our own, the quilt-covered bedsteads were draped with mosquito netting. Between them stood a battered chest of drawers. Against the far wall, an upended trunk with a mirror propped atop served as a dressing table. Fanny had flung large doilies over both.

I crossed the room to the chest of drawers first and rifled through it quickly. No letters, just neat stacks of undergarments, stockings, hair ribbons, and the like.

I looked around, biting my lip. Where could the letters be? My gaze fell on Fanny's jewelry box on the dressing table. It contained only jewelry, however—a large cameo brooch, a string of pearls nearly identical to my own, a watch fob that must have belonged to Fanny's dead husband, and her wedding ring.

This was a ridiculous idea. Fanny probably still had the letters with her in her pocket. I started to leave, then looked back at her bed. What about under her pillow? No, surely she wouldn't be so obvious. But this was Fanny, I reminded myself.

I crossed the room again and lifted Fanny's pillow. Underneath lay a small book covered in bottle-green leather. Fanny's name was stamped on the cover in gold. Her diary! And sure enough, beneath it lay the stack of letters. I picked up the diary, and my heart sank. The top envelope bore Papa's handwriting.

I started to reach for his letter when I heard the sound of rapid footsteps heading down the hall. I dropped the pillow and whirled around. The diary was still in my hand. As the door opened, I quickly tucked it into my pinafore pocket.

It was Fanny. "There you are, Patience, we've

been looking for you," she said. "I thought you were going to make tea."

"The kettle's on," I replied. "And I was, ah, searching for a hairbrush. You said I looked a fright."

Fanny cocked her head and regarded me. "Yes, you do." She crossed to her dressing table and picked up the hairbrush, which was in plain sight. I blushed. "Here, sit down and let me do it."

Reluctantly, I perched on the edge of her bed. Had I put the pillow back properly? Did she suspect anything? Fanny drew the brush through my tangled hair gently, working in quick, deft strokes until it was smooth again.

"What have you been up to?" she scolded, and I nearly leaped out of my skin. "Look at this! Your ribbon is torn, and there are brambles in it." She held it up for me to see. "Honestly, I fear you are in danger of becoming a hoyden. 'Personal appearance is always a matter of importance with a lady,' Hester Halifax tells us."

I gritted my teeth. It wouldn't do to lose my temper now.

"Here, I have an extra you can have." Fanny pulled a sky blue ribbon from the top dresser drawer and proceeded to tie it in my hair.

My heart was thumping so hard I was sure she could see the rise and fall of my pinafore on my chest.

And the diary was practically burning a hole in my pocket. What if she decided to look for it now?

"There, that's much better," she said, giving the ribbon a final pat. I stood up and she looked me over critically. I looked back at her. Fanny seemed shorter than she had back in Lahaina.

She frowned. "Good heavens, Patience, you're growing like a weed! That dress is much too short. I can see your ankles." She plucked at the bodice. "And look at the seams here, you're fairly bursting out of this dress. I'll speak to your aunt right away. We must see about getting you something more suitable." She hesitated a moment, then added, "Is there anything you'd like to talk to me about?"

My heart fairly shot out of my body. She knew!

"With all the work to be done here at the school, I've scarcely had a chance to talk with you," Fanny continued. "Isaiah—your father—said I might wish to advise you on certain things. Womanly things."

I nearly collapsed on the floor in relief. She didn't know about the letters or the diary. She was talking about my monthlies.

"No," I mumbled, for Mama had told me of them long ago. "Nothing at the moment, thank you."

Fanny smiled at me, and for a moment I imagined her up here at night, exchanging confidences with Charity, and felt a stab of envy. I loved sharing the grass hut with Aunt Anne and Thaddeus and wouldn't trade it for the world, but still, it might be nice to be closer to girls my own age as well. But I quickly banished the thought. I had no more desire to have Fanny as an older sister than I did to have her as my stepmama.

Linking arms with me, Fanny drew me out of her room and down the hall. The diary was still in my pocket. There was no way for me to put it back now, but I must find a way to do so, and soon, before she missed it. For she certainly would.

I sat through tea mute with guilt. When it was over, I excused myself and rushed outside. I needed a quiet place to think.

I made my way to the privy. Here, at least, I could be assured of being left alone. Closing the door, I drew the diary out of my pocket. I turned it over in my hands. It was so very much like my own, except for the color. I thought of my diary, and all the secrets it contained—all my innermost thoughts and yearnings. I would surely die of shame if anyone ever read it—even Aunt Anne, with whom I had shared so many passages about our adventures.

No, I couldn't read it. I could never inflict that kind of humiliation on anyone, even Fanny.

"Oh, but you could," whispered a little voice in my head. "For surely she has confided her true feelings

about your father on those pages. Surely she has outlined her plans—their plans—for the future."

No, I told myself firmly. It would be wrong. I
could only imagine what Mama would say about such
a breach of trust. I started to slide the diary back into
my pocket.

"But don't you want to know the truth?" the little
voice whispered again. "Don't you want to know once
and for all if Fanny is to be your stepmother?"

I hesitated. My fingers caressed the soft leather.
Would it be such a bad thing to read just a sentence
or two? Surely that would be understandable—surely
no one could fault me for that.

But I musn't. I had promised Papa I would act befitting a Goodspeed, and I must keep that promise. Resolutely, I put Fanny's diary in my pocket. There was
only one course of action—I must put it back. I would
return to the house, smile at everyone, then simply
walk upstairs and tuck it back under the pillow. If
Fanny followed me again, I'd tell her—I'd tell her what?

As I tried to think of some logical explanation for
my presence in her bedroom a second time, my fingers slipped unconsciously back into my pocket.
Once again, they caressed the diary's smooth leather
cover, and once again the little voice whispered to
me. "Surely there's no harm in one quick peek," it
said. "Who would ever know?"

Almost as if mesmerized, I drew the diary out. I stared at it for a long moment, and then I opened it.

The most recent entry was dated today. Fanny must have written in it just after receiving her letters from the *Morning Star.*

"Unworthy as I am, I have been spared to enjoy the privileges and blessings of another Sabbath."

Pious piffle, I thought. Fanny had been paying too much attention to Reverend Wiggins. I read on.

"And such blessings they are! I am all joy, for today I received not one but three letters from him whom my heart holds most dear, my bonny blue-eyed sweetheart."

I slammed the pages shut. Anger flooded through me. Anger that my suspicions were correct about Fanny and that she had indeed won my father's heart. *Three* letters! When he hadn't even taken the time to write me a single one! I wanted nothing further to do with Fanny and her silly lovestruck gushings. I couldn't wait to be rid of the diary now.

I opened the privy door and rushed outside to go put it back—and nearly tripped over Fanny and Aunt Anne.

"Are you all right?" Fanny cried. "You ran off so quickly, we thought you might be sick and need our help."

Her gaze fell on the small green book in my hand. She frowned. "That looks like my—" she stopped, and her face drained of color. "Patience Goodspeed, what are you doing with my diary?"

I had never seen Fanny Starbuck angry before. Her face turned from white to a mottled red.

"It's not what you think!" I cried.

Aunt Anne's eyes blazed at me. "For shame," she said.

"I didn't mean, I was just going to—"

Aunt Anne held out her hand. Miserably, I turned over the diary. "Honestly," I pleaded. "I hadn't planned to take it—it was an accident. I wasn't . . ."

My words trailed off. What could I say?

With a sob, Fanny grabbed the diary from Aunt Anne, picked up her skirts, and fled.

"For shame," said Aunt Anne again, and turning her back on me, she followed Fanny to the house.

Word of my wickedness quickly spread. No one spoke to me at dinner, not even Thaddeus, who regarded me with round, serious eyes. Reverend Wiggins glowered from the head of the table, and Mrs. Wiggins and Charity both dispensed frequent sorrowful glances in my direction. Aunt Anne ignored me, and Fanny didn't show up at all. Laʻilaʻi and the other girls whispered amongst themselves, and I felt sure they had been told as well. At this rate all of Wailuku would soon know.

Eating was impossible. I stared down at my plate,

consumed with anguish. Why oh why had I ever touched Fanny's diary? Finally, I could bear it no longer. I pushed back from the table and ran to our hut, where I flung myself on the bed and cried hot, remorseful tears.

I didn't hear Aunt Anne come in, and I started when she sat down next to me. She was quiet for a few minutes as I struggled to get my tears under control.

"Patience, what you've done is reprehensible," she said finally.

"I know!" I wailed.

"What on earth possessed you? Surely Caroline taught you better than that!"

A fresh wave of remorse swept over me as I thought of what my mother would say if she knew what I had done, and all of a sudden the feelings I'd kept bottled up these past weeks came rushing out. I sat up.

"It was the letters!" I cried. "I was looking for her letters! I had to know—I knew it was wrong, but I couldn't help myself. Oh, Aunt Anne, I simply don't think I'll be able to bear it if Papa marries her!" My outburst ended in another wail, and I flung myself back down again.

"I see," said Aunt Anne slowly. "So that's what this was all about. Well, curiosity certainly killed the cat, didn't it?"

She rose to her feet and paced the small floor.

"Patience, I have no idea whether your father plans to marry Fanny Starbuck or not. Frankly, it's none of my affair, nor is it yours."

"But—"

She stopped and held up a warning hand. "*Nor is it yours,*" she repeated firmly. "I know you think Fanny is a foolish creature, and I'll grant you that there are days that I am in full agreement. I for one would be delighted never to hear from Hester Halifax again. However, over these past months since I first met her in Boston, I have come to see that while Fanny may not be in possession of a keen intellect, and may whine a bit at hardship and spend too much time thinking about frivolous things, she has a true gift, the gift of making people happy. She is doing wonders for the students at this school, and for Mrs. Wiggins, who sorely needs female companionship, given that she spends most of her time with that, that—"

"Walrus?" I sniffled.

"Exactly—that walrus of a husband of hers. In fact a kinder heart and sweeter disposition than Fanny Starbuck's I have rarely seen. If that is simply due to the fact that there are no bothersome thoughts rattling around in that pretty head to vex her, well, so be it."

Aunt Anne began pacing again. "I know that your father loved your mother deeply, and I also know that it's not practical to expect him to voyage through life without companionship."

"But he has Thaddeus and me!" I cried.

Aunt Anne gave me a wry smile. "You'll understand better someday, dear heart. Meanwhile, I don't know what your father is looking for in a wife, or even if he's looking for a wife. What I do know is that whatever decision he makes will not be made in haste, and will certainly take into consideration both you and your brother as well. You are very dear to him, you know."

My lip quivered at this, and fresh tears spilled down my cheeks. Aunt Anne fished a handkerchief out of her pocket. "Besides," she added, passing it to me, "he's a Goodspeed."

"Through and through," I finished morosely. I blew my nose and drew in a ragged breath.

"That's the spirit!" Aunt Anne pulled me to my feet. "And you're a Goodspeed too, so now it's time to act like one. To begin with, you owe Fanny an apology, so I suggest you wipe away your tears and march over there and deliver it. As sweet-tempered as she is, I suspect she'll find it in her heart to forgive you."

I nodded, but I wasn't so sure. And the real question remained, could I ever forgive myself?

Fourteen

The gratification that friendship affords, will
always be a sufficient inducement to cultivate it.
—*Etiquette for Ladies, or The Principles of True Politeness*

Fanny barely glanced up when I knocked, and she
endured, rather than accepted, my apology. Only the
thought of Aunt Anne's confidence in me as a Goodspeed enabled me to stumble through my awkward
request for forgiveness.

When I finished, Fanny was silent. Her eyes were
red rimmed.

"Hester Halifax says that forgiveness is the odor
which flowers yield when trampled upon," she
informed me stiffly. "And although I am feeling quite
trampled upon, I am endeavoring to be a dutiful
blossom—though I hardly feel so inclined at the
moment."

I stared at the floor, my face flaming.

"I must say, Patience, I never would have thought
you capable of such a low act," Fanny burst out,
decorum giving way to fury. "Before I left Nantucket,
Martha made a special point of assuring me that you
were a well-behaved young lady."

"Oh, Fanny, please don't tell Martha," I begged.

"Please. I am most sincerely sorry."

"Hmmph," Fanny sniffed, clearly unconvinced. Then she added grudgingly, "Most likely I won't. But if I don't, it's better than you deserve."

And with that she bade me good night.

I returned to our hut in a turmoil, once again wishing with all my heart that Mama were here to comfort and advise me. But she wasn't, and never would be, and I would just have to muddle through on my own.

September 3, 1836

I dreamed of Nantucket last night.

I was back in my bed at home with the quilt pulled up under my chin. It was an early spring morning, and Patches was curled up next to me, purring. Light flooded in through my open window, checkering the rag rug on the floor with gold. I could smell lilacs and, from the kitchen, bacon.

Martha was downstairs bustling about, and I heard Mama call to her and laugh, and then I heard her light step on the stairs. A moment later my door opened a crack and she poked her head in.

"Rise and shine, daughter mine," she said, as she did every morning. She smiled at me, that

sweet smile that had etched itself forever on my heart.

Papa came in my room behind her just then, and he put his arm around Mama's waist and laughed, his blue eyes alight with love for both of us.

Then I heard the conch shell announcing that another day had begun at the Wailuku Female Seminary, and I awoke.

The image of my parents' smiling faces lingered in my mind's eye for a long moment. They faded as I recalled yesterday's humiliation, and for the very first time since her passing I was glad that Mama was no longer here, for now she would never learn of the wretched thing that I had done.

Whether or not Papa will remains to be seen. And as I think of my fading dream and of that look in my father's eyes I can't help but wonder if I will ever see it again or whether his heart now belongs to Fanny. Am I going to lose him, too, the way I lost Mama?

—P.

A few evenings later, Charity and Aunt Anne and I were gathered around the makeshift table in our hut. Charity was looking pleased with herself for managing to sneak away (she'd waited until Fanny was asleep, then crept out), and while Fanny was still treating me coolly, she had made no further mention of my transgression and I was in somewhat better spirits.

Thaddeus was asleep on his pallet, one arm flung around Friday, who was snoring loudly.

"Almost as loud as Fanny," whispered Charity.

The two of us giggled. Aunt Anne subdued us with a glance over her reading spectacles, and we quieted down and bent our heads over our mathematics texts once again.

As I suspected, Charity indeed had a head for figures. I had pulled one of my old mathematics books from the bottom of my trunk and was introducing her to some basic geometry concepts. Aunt Anne, meanwhile, was frowning over *Bowditch's,* attempting to fix our latitude. Her first effort had put us so far below the equator as to be nearly in Antarctica, and I had set her to work trying again.

There was a soft scratching on the *kapa* cloth that hung across the doorway to our hut, and Charity jumped. My own heart nearly stopped—what if it were Reverend Wiggins? But Aunt Anne calmly gathered our books and papers together and shoved them under the quilt on our bed, then reached down and plucked *The Pilgrim's Progress* from a pile of books at her feet and placed it on the table in front of us.

Charity gasped. I grinned. Trust Aunt Anne to have a battle plan ready.

Aunt Anne winked at us. "Come in!" she called.

The cloth was drawn aside, and La'ila'i walked in. We all stared at her in surprise.

"*Aloha,*" she said softly.

"*Aloha,*" Aunt Anne and Charity and I replied.

"Is anything wrong, La'ila'i?" asked Aunt Anne in concern.

La'ila'i looked at Charity, who translated the question into Hawaiian. La'ila'i returned her gaze to Aunt Anne and shook her head, her hair rustling gently around her shoulders like a dark cloud. She glanced around the room, smiling at the sight of my sleeping brother and his dog. Then she pointed to herself and to me and Charity.

"*He Makamaka,*" she said.

"That means friend," said Charity.

"You want to be friends with us?" I asked.

Charity repeated the question in Hawaiian. A broad smile appeared on La'ila'i's face, and she nodded. Charity and I looked at Aunt Anne. Studying mathematics in secret was one thing, but this was severely *kapu.*

"*He Makamaka,*" repeated Aunt Anne thoughtfully, regarding the three of us.

La'ila'i nodded. I held my breath.

"We can't let Reverend Wiggins know," Aunt Anne warned, with an apologetic glance at Charity.

Charity's cheeks were flushed, her eyes bright with excitement. There was no doubt about it, I thought, the whatnot cabinet door had been flung wide open.

At the mention of Reverend Wiggins's name, La'ila'i's smile faded. "Reverend Wikkins *pilikia*," she said.

"*Pilikia* means trouble," said Charity, her smile fading too.

Reverend Wiggins would most definitely create plenty of *pilikia* if he found out, I thought.

"Hmmmm," said Aunt Anne.

La'ila'i rattled off another question in Hawaiian, and we looked over at Charity.

"She wants to learn English," she said.

"English," repeated La'ila'i, nodding eagerly. She said something else in her native tongue.

"If we teach her English, she'll teach you both Hawaiian," Charity said.

The prospect of new knowledge was too tempting for Aunt Anne. "This is against my better judgment," she said, "but let's get started."

And reaching out her hand to our new *makamaka*, she invited her to join us at the table.

Fifteen

Music has the double advantage of being a pleasing accomplishment, and an unlimited source of amusement.
—*Etiquette for Ladies, or The Principles of True Politeness*

September 23, 1836

Suddenly I find myself with three students—four, counting Charlie Fishback!

I never pictured myself in the role of teacher, but I find I'm quite enjoying it. And although the language barrier between Aunt Anne and myself and La'ila'i seemed insurmountable at first, with Charity there to help, we're making speedy progress. Laughter, of course, needs no translation.

Despite Reverend Wiggins's admonition to "learn not the way of the heathen," I have learned more Hawaiian in these past weeks than I have in a whole month of French. I know dozens of words now—including koholā, *which is the word for whale, and* ōkoholā, *which means harpoon, and* haole, *which is their word for off-islanders like us. If I keep this up, by the time the* Morning Star *returns I'll be able to speak to my Kanaka ship-mates in their own tongue!*

I am determined that for every word or phrase
I learn in French (graisse de baleine means
whale blubber. Now won't that be useful if I ever
visit Paris?), I will learn ten in Hawaiian. I only
hope Reverend Wiggins doesn't discover the clan
of "rebel female scholars," as Aunt Anne calls us,
living under his roof.

—*P.*

The following Sunday, Charity and Thaddeus and the Four Gospels and I were gathered in the parlor as usual for an afternoon of quiet reading and "contemplating higher things," as Reverend Wiggins put it. Rain had blown down from the mountains after church, a misty, sun-pierced shower that held the promise of rainbows, and I was at the window looking for them.

Mrs. Wiggins had retired upstairs for a nap, the boys were drooping over their copies of *The Pilgrim's Progress,* and Reverend Wiggins was outside under the lanai with Laʻilaʻi and Hiʻiaka and the other students, helping them memorize passages from Psalms for the upcoming quarterly examinations. There was to be a recitation prize, and Reverend Wiggins had his eye on it.

"Not out of vanity," he'd hastened to assure us all, "but rather to show that the light of salvation is indeed shining here in Wailuku."

He had collared Aunt Anne to assist him, and I could tell from the look on her face that she was wishing she were somewhere else.

Fanny was supposed to be setting an example for us children and was seated primly on the horsehair sofa with a Bible on her lap. She was giving it such close scrutiny that I grew suspicious, however. Craning my neck, I saw a copy of *Godey's Lady's Book* propped inside. I smiled. Fanny was examining dress patterns.

Not that I was in a position to point a finger at her. My own Bible held a copy of *Colburn's Algebra*, and Charity's concealed the biography of Sophie Germain that Miss Mitchell had sent. I had smuggled it into the parlor and given it to her after luncheon.

"It's capital!" I told her, which was true. Sophie's tale was a splendid one, and from the speed with which Charity's eyes were flicking back and forth across the pages, I could tell she thought so too.

I gazed out the window again, searching the clouds. Sophie Germain was thirteen, exactly my age, when the French Revolution began. The Bastille prison was overthrown and all of Paris was in an uproar, with riots in the streets and roaming mobs on the hunt for aristocrats. Frightened by the havoc, Sophie's parents kept her locked up safely in the house.

She spent her days in her father's library, where she discovered mathematics and read every book on the subject he owned. She persevered in her studies in spite of her parents' disapproval, for like Reverend Wiggins, they feared that academic study would do their daughter's delicate brain harm. Sophie's parents took away her candles, the heat in her bedroom, and even her clothes at night to keep her from her books.

One morning, they found her asleep at her desk, wrapped in a quilt, the ink in her ink well frozen solid. Her slate was covered with calculations. I wondered what Papa and Mama would have done had they been in Sophie's parents' shoes. Would they, too, have realized that their efforts to prevent their daughter from learning were in vain? Would they, too, have relented? I did not know the answer to this, but Sophie spent the rest of the Reign of Terror teaching herself calculus.

Calculus! Miss Mitchell had told me that if I kept up my studies, someday I might be ready for this difficult subject. That day seemed quite far away at this point, however. And to think of learning it by oneself!

French universities didn't accept female students, so Sophie took a man's name—Monsieur Le Blanc—and enrolled in correspondence courses. Her secret was eventually discovered by one of her professors, who was so impressed with her abilities that he championed her cause.

I stared at the rain clouds—no sign of a rainbow yet—and wondered if I'd ever become a famous mathematician or navigator or win a prize like Sophie did. The mathematics prize at the quarterly examinations in Lahaina was hardly the Grand Prix from the French Academy of Sciences, but still, it was something.

"Patience, keep an eye on the boys would you?" said Fanny, yawning. She stood up and stretched. "I'm going to see if Pali has started tea."

The minute she left the room, Matthew and Mark jumped up out of their chairs and started to wrestle.

"Boys, stop that this minute!" I whispered as loudly and severely as I could. "Get back in your seats!"

They ignored me, as did Luke and John and Thaddeus, who had withdrawn into a corner for a whispered consultation. My brother looked over at me.

"Want to see what we've taught Friday to do?" he asked.

"In a minute," I said, distracted. I had Matthew by the ear and Mark by the collar and was struggling to separate them.

Behind me, Charity squeaked in surprise and I turned around to see Friday leap up onto the melodeon bench. The two older boys paused their wrestling match to see what would happen next.

Thaddeus snapped his fingers, and Friday stood up on his hind legs and placed his paws on the keys.

"Play a song, Friday," my brother coaxed. He and the twins could hardly contain their glee.

Friday obligingly batted his paws on the keys, producing a cacophony of sour chords. The boys snickered.

Friday wagged his tail, his pink tongue lolling out of the side of his mouth. Charity looked at me and smiled. I smiled back.

"Sing, Friday!" Thaddeus commanded.

The dog lifted his muzzle into the air and howled obediently. The boys' snickers turned to laughter. Encouraged, Friday howled again. Soon, all six of us were laughing. The louder we laughed, the louder Friday howled and the louder he banged on the melodeon keys.

"Maybe he could play at church next Sunday," I gasped.

"He certainly sings better than Mrs. Chapman," said Charity, her eyes widening in shock at her own boldness. Then she laughed and that set me off again, for it was true—as kindhearted as she was, Reverend Chapman's wife was tone-deaf. Soon we were both rolling on the floor, clutching our aching ribs.

"What is going on in here?"

Reverend Wiggins stood in the doorway, his hands on his ample hips. He glowered at us. Friday leaped nimbly off the melodeon bench and sat down beside Thaddeus, both of them the picture of innocence. Charity and I scrambled to our feet and Charity hastily closed her Bible, concealing all evidence of Sophie Germain.

"Don't you children know what day it is?" Reverend Wiggins boomed. "'Remember the Sabbath day, to keep it holy.' Exodus, chapter twenty, verse eight." He skewered me with a look, then swiveled his head toward Thaddeus. "You Goodspeeds are behind this—I know it. And my own daughter, encouraging such nonsense. You will go to your room at once, Charity, and remain there for the rest of the afternoon."

"We were just having a bit of fun," I protested. "We didn't mean any harm."

"The Sabbath is hardly a day for fun," objected Reverend Wiggins.

Fanny reappeared, looking concerned. Aunt Anne was right on her heels.

"Is someone hurt?" Fanny asked anxiously. "I thought I heard cries of pain."

Matthew snorted. Reverend Wiggins quelled him with a single glance and pointed dramatically at Friday. "The dog was playing the melodeon."

The room fell silent.

Aunt Anne looked at Reverend Wiggins for a long moment. She arched a dark eyebrow. "You don't say."

Thaddeus and the Four Gospels examined their toes. I could see their shoulders shaking with suppressed laughter. I had to bite the inside of my cheek to keep from smiling.

Reverend Wiggins reddened. "Well, not exactly playing it," he said. "It was a trick. Cooked up by this niece and nephew of yours. They put my children up to it. And on the Sabbath!"

The corners of Aunt Anne's mouth tugged upward as she fought back a smile. She turned to face us so that Reverend Wiggins couldn't see the twinkle in her eye.

"Well now, children, Reverend Wiggins is right. The Sabbath is not a day for idle amusement," she said briskly. "Patience, Thaddeus, if you'll come with me perhaps I can find you something more productive to do with the rest of your afternoon."

With a dignified nod to Reverend Wiggins, she placed her hands on our shoulders and swept us from the room. Friday brought up the rear, wagging his tail.

Sixteen

Ladies should particularly avoid being out after dusk;
necessity alone, and that the most urgent, can
afford an excuse for such impropriety.
—*Etiquette for Ladies, or The Principles of True Politeness*

October 12, 1836

It is exactly a year since we set sail from Nantucket.

I read back over my diary to mark the occasion and am amazed at all that has transpired. I sorely miss my shipmates, and although my days here at the Wailuku Female Seminary have become almost bearable, thanks to my new friends, I am still eager to be back aboard the Morning Star.

Papa said he'd return by my birthday, which is in less than three weeks. Meanwhile, we have received several more batches of letters—mostly for Fanny Starbuck.

I finally relented and wrote a letter of apology to Papa for my behavior the night before he left. I told him I am endeavoring to fulfill his expectations of me and act befitting a Goodspeed. I told

him about the mathematics prize too. I signed it
"Aloha." I'm not sure if Papa knows any
Hawaiian, but he can get Big John to translate
for him if he doesn't.

—P.

The weeks passed, and as October sailed on
toward November, our days fell into a predictable
pattern.

By day we followed the rhythms set by Reverend
Wiggins for the school, with needlework and academic studies in the morning, followed by household
arts (we were braiding bonnets now from sugarcane
fiber), music, and deportment in the afternoon.

By night the rebel female scholars continued to
meet in secret—in our room in the new adobe dormitory now, for the building had finally been finished—
and we were forging ahead in mathematics,
navigation, and the finer points of English and
Hawaiian.

Hester Halifax was frequently invoked at the dining table ("A young lady cannot eat too quietly"), in
the parlor ("Mumbling to yourself while reading is a
very inelegant habit"), on the long walks to church
("Avoid all appearances of bustle; a lady is never in a
hurry"), and in the lanai ("Preserve a becoming
silence, until your opinion is asked"). Fanny read her

pearls of wisdom aloud to Charity and me as we learned to set a proper tea table, marched back and forth with books atop our heads to perfect our graceful carriage, and practiced our curtsies.

"Do try not to stick out in back like that," reprimanded Fanny, whacking me on my behind with *Etiquette for Ladies* as I lowered myself awkwardly toward the floor. "This is supposed to be a curtsy fit for the royal court, not a grog shop in Honolulu."

Why Fanny thought I needed to learn a curtsy fit for royalty was a mystery, as it was highly unlikely I would ever encounter any, but I held my tongue, and waited as patiently as I could for nightfall.

The quarterly examinations were only a few weeks away now, and there was a rising air of excitement at the school. La'ila'i and her sister and the other native girls were memorizing Bible verses with a vengeance, and even Thaddeus and the Four Gospels had gotten into the spirit of things and could be found poring over maps in hopes they'd shine in geography.

Reverend Wiggins had arranged for Charity and me to sit for the French examination, which was laughable, but I didn't say a word, just nodded obediently and said, *"bien sûr."* I planned to shine in an entirely different subject area, meanwhile, and had persuaded Aunt Anne to write to the board of examiners in secret and enter me in the mathematics competition (under "P. Goodspeed," just in case anyone else subscribed to Reverend Wiggins's misguided notions about female brains). We entered Charity as well ("C. Wiggins, Esq."—the latter a nice touch, I thought), for she was flying through my geometry text at a cracking rate.

If there was anything to cloud this blaze of industry, it was the fact that we had not heard from the *Morning Star* in several weeks. A number of the whaling ships had returned to Lahaina from their summer cruises already, and each few days brought news of this one or that one spotted in the harbor, but never was it the *Morning Star.*

Even the *Rambler* had returned, and Captain Russell visited us when he stopped briefly with the Chapmans in Wailuku.

"Thee musn't be concerned, Patience," he told me, just before he whisked Mrs. Russell back to Lahaina. "Thy father is a fine sailor, and remember, the *Morning Star* got off to a late start. Thy father is likely just making up for lost time."

He was probably right, but I still couldn't squelch the niggling worry. Every night before sleep, my thoughts flew as swift as swallows to Papa and my friends aboard the *Morning Star.* And every morning when I awoke, I said a prayer for their safety.

A week before my fourteenth birthday there was a

full moon. Aunt Anne had set her heart on learning to take a lunar—a complicated method of determining a ship's position by the moon instead of the sun—and we decided this would be the perfect opportunity.

Thaddeus took forever to fall asleep, but finally, after two entire chapters of *Robinson Crusoe*, he closed his eyes and drifted off.

"Keep an eye on him, Friday," I instructed the dog. "Both eyes, in fact."

Friday wagged his tail, and Aunt Anne and I set off. Charity and La'ila'i, who was curious to see what we were up to, were waiting for us on the hillock beyond the privy. La'ila'i understood the concept of navigation—long ago, she had told us, her Polynesian ancestors had sailed thousands of miles from Tahiti to the Sandwich Isles with nothing but the stars to guide them—but was eager to see how we accomplished this using a modern sextant.

Aunt Anne and Charity and I each took several readings, and we showed La'ila'i how to take one as well. The four of us compared our numbers—all within a couple of degrees of each other, which was promising—and after I slipped the sextant back into my pocket, we sat down in the meadow for a moment to drink in the view.

Stars as white as whalebone glittered against the dark curtain of sky, while the moon strained at the

tether of silver light that anchored it to the distant
sea. From somewhere far up the ʻIao Valley behind
us, we could hear the sound of drums. Laʻilaʻi closed
her eyes and began to hum. The melody was sad and
haunting.

"What is that song?" I asked.

Laʻilaʻi opened her eyes. "Tonight my people
remember *Kepaniwai*," she said.

"The damming of the waters?" said Charity. "I
heard Reverend Chapman and father speak of that
once."

Laʻilaʻi had told Aunt Anne and Charity and me
many tales over the past weeks, of kings and queens
in feather cloaks, of Pele the fire goddess and the
dead volcano at the other end of the island called
Haleakalā—the house of the sun—and of the trick-
ster Maui, who had fished up the Sandwich Isles at
the beginning of time. But *Kepaniwai*? I didn't know
this story.

"Forty years ago and more it happened," Laʻilaʻi
began, rising to her feet. We watched, entranced, as
her hips began to sway to the rhythm of the distant
drums, and her hands scribed graceful arcs in the
moonlight.

"Kamehameha, the man who would be king of all
the islands, he brought his warriors here," she said.
"They had a long gun, a cannon, from a *haole* ship.

Up from the sea they came, thousands of them, up through the valley where we now stand."

The story unfolded before us as she danced, interpreting the words with her hands. We saw the warriors swarming up the 'Iao Valley in pursuit of La'ila'i's ancestors, who retreated up the steeply sided canyon.

"They were trapped beneath the *kūkaemoku*," she said, thrusting her finger sharply upward, and we saw the 'Iao Needle itself, that spike of rock rising like a gravestone from the hills behind Wailuku. The drums beat more urgently now, and in their rhythm we heard the relentless boom of Kamehameha's cannon.

La'ila'i's bare feet beat a tattoo on the meadow beneath us, and we felt the fear of her trapped ancestors. She flung her hands to one side, and we saw the women and children clustered on the cliffs above. She flung them to the other, and we saw the doomed men in the valley below. The drums grew louder now, and although they were far away I wanted to cover my ears, for in their rapid beating I heard the beating of frantic hearts, of women and children forced to watch while husbands and fathers and brothers were slaughtered in the valley beneath them.

La'ila'i fell to her knees, reaching her hands out toward us in a gesture of yearning. The drums' frantic pace lessened, and her dance grew quiet and plaintive.

With a final downward sweep of her arms, we saw the bodies of the fallen warriors clogging the stream, a stream that now ran red to the sea. *Kepaniwai*. The damming of the waters.

I shivered. I had never seen anything so terrible or so beautiful.

"Miss Goodspeed!"

The two words rang out behind us, and we leaped to our feet. Laʻilaʻi's hands dropped to her sides. Reverend Wiggins stood behind us, and even in the moonlight I could see that his face was purple with rage.

"I am shocked!" he began, spitting the words out angrily. "Mrs. Starbuck was woken by the drums and found Charity missing. I venture out into the night to ensure her safety, and what do I find?" He leveled a rigid finger at my aunt. "I find that I have nursed a viper in my bosom! Have I not made it abundantly clear that this vile dance, this *hula*, is forbidden? *Kapu*! And you, Miss Goodspeed, leading these young girls astray. I am more than shocked—I am speechless!"

He was nothing of the sort, but I decided this was perhaps not the best time to point that out.

"The *hula*!" repeated Reverend Wiggins in disgust.

I looked at Laʻilaʻi. She was quiet, her eyes fixed firmly on the ground. So this was the *hula*? I thought.

I couldn't understand why Reverend Wiggins was so incensed. From all his fuss about *kapu* I had expected something . . . something . . . well, I wasn't sure what I had expected. But certainly not this heartbreakingly graceful display.

"It's just a dance," said Aunt Anne tartly, regaining her composure. "Neither more nor less than that."

"A wicked, corrupt dance."

"Only because you deem it so," she retorted.

Reverend Wiggins held up his hand. "Silence!" he thundered. "I will not countenance your disrespect. Eve, you will return to your quarters. Miss Goodspeed, you and Patience will return to yours. Charity, you will come with me, where I shall deliver you to your mother. I will retire to my study, where I shall remain in seclusion until I decide how best to deal with you all. I am most seriously displeased."

And with that he turned and left, dragging an ashen-faced Charity behind him.

La'ila'i padded away into the shadows before I could speak to her, and Aunt Anne put her arm around my shoulder.

"Come, Patience," she said. "Things will look brighter in the morning."

Seventeen

All amusements that require outdoor
exercise are particularly to be recommended
as being conducive to health and vigor.
—*Etiquette for Ladies, or The Principles of True Politeness*

But things did not look brighter in the morning.

"What do you mean, ill?" I demanded. "How can she be ill? She was fine last night."

La'ila'i had not shown up for breakfast, and Aunt Anne had been sent to fetch her. Now here she was back again, bearing bad news.

"Reverend Wiggins, I suggest you send for Dr. Phillips at once," Aunt Anne said. "La'ila'i is not herself at all. I fear she has a fever."

Reverend Wiggins turned to the nearest Gospel. "Matthew, you heard Miss Goodspeed, go and fetch Dr. Phillips. Tell him that *Eve*"—he shot a pointed glance at Aunt Anne—"is ill."

Our morning lessons were subdued. Aunt Anne and Fanny and Pali took turns going to the dormitory to check on La'ila'i. Mrs. Wiggins, whom Reverend Wiggins had strictly forbidden to accompany them, in case the fever proved contagious and harmed their "small messenger from heaven," looked stricken. So did Hiʻiaka and the other girls, who whispered amongst themselves every time Reverend Wiggins turned his back.

Despite the distraction, Reverend Wiggins had not forgotten about the *hula* incident, and every time his gaze fell on either Charity or me, he shook his head and repeated, "I am most seriously displeased." But every time he began to lecture us about our transgression, either Mrs. Wiggins or Fanny or Aunt Anne appeared to interrupt with a question or an update on Laʻilaʻi.

By teatime there was more bad news. Three more of the girls had fallen ill, all of them victims of the same mysterious malady Dr. Phillips called a "bilious fever."

Two days passed this way, with no improvement in anyone's condition. Word of the school's predicament spread quickly, and several of the girls' mothers and aunts arrived from Wailuku and Lahaina to volunteer their services. Even Friday sensed that something was not right, and slunk around anxiously all day, whining and rarely letting Thaddeus out of his sight.

My birthday came and went without notice, so wrapped up were we in the calamity that had befallen us. I would have forgotten it myself, except that I happened to glance in my diary and see the date. By now, fully half of the girls were confined to their beds, including Hi'iaka. Lessons were suspended, and Aunt Anne and Fanny and Pali were running themselves ragged trying to care for all of them. Wanting to shoulder our fair share of the burden, Mrs. Wiggins and Charity and I toiled in the coral stone cookhouse, washing sheets and other laundry and keeping a steady supply of food available for the dormitory sickroom.

On the morning of the fourth day, I rounded the corner of the dormitory with a tray of water glasses just as Dr. Phillips and Reverend Wiggins emerged from one of the rooms. They didn't see me, as they were deep in conversation. They both looked very grave. I hesitated, not meaning to eavesdrop, but I couldn't help hearing Dr. Phillips's report.

"I fear for their recovery," he said wearily. He removed his spectacles and pinched the bridge of his nose, shaking his head. "Particularly La'ila'i. The ipecac doesn't seem to be making any difference at all. Unless there's a change soon, I fear she may not survive the day."

The news struck me like a physical blow. I nearly dropped the tray of water glasses that I was carrying as I stumbled back around the corner of the hut. I leaned against it, trying to steady my breathing. La'ila'i near death? Surely Dr. Phillips must be mistaken!

I didn't care what they said about contagion, I must see my friend for myself. I waited until Dr. Phillips and Reverend Wiggins left for the parsonage, then set the tray down by the first door—La'ila'i's door—and crept back around the corner out of sight. A minute later, I heard a rattle—that would be Aunt Anne retrieving the water glasses. There was a low murmur of voices inside, and again I waited. My patience was rewarded; shortly, she reappeared with Fanny, and the two of them headed back toward the lanai as well.

As soon as they were out of sight, I dashed around the corner and lifted the *kapa* cloth. It was stuffy inside, and a flickering whale oil lamp on a table in the center of the room provided the only light in the dim interior. Careful to avoid tripping over the other two beds in the small space, I made my way to my friend.

Sitting down beside her, I took her hand. It was fiery hot. Mama's hand had felt just so, right before she died. I stroked it gently, and tears flooded my eyes.

"La'ila'i," I said quietly.

There was no response. I tried again. *"Aloha, La'ila'i, makamaka."*

Her eyelids fluttered open. She saw me and smiled weakly. *"Aloha,* Patience," she whispered.

I held a glass of water to her lips and she took a feeble sip. "La'ila'i, you must get well, you have to get well," I said. I squeezed her hand and ventured a small joke. "You have to teach me the *hula*."

She closed her eyes again and lay back. A weak smile hovered on her lips. "*Hula kapu. Pilikia.* Reverend Wikkins *huhū*."

Forbidden. Trouble. Reverend Wiggins in a huff. I squeezed her hand again.

"I don't care," I said. "Reverend Wiggins is a—" I searched wildly for the right word. How did one say "smug, self-righteous walrus" in Hawaiian? "—he's a *pua'a*."

A pig. That covered it.

La'ila'i's laugh quickly turned to a cough. "*I wai*," she whispered. Give me water.

I held the water glass to her lips. After she drank, she lay back on her pillow and closed her eyes again, and from the sound of her ragged breathing I knew she had fallen asleep.

I held her hand in mine for a few minutes more, then left, pulling the *kapa* closed behind me.

Back in the parlor, Dr. Phillips was questioning Reverend Wiggins closely.

"Needlework, you say? Music? Deportment?" He regarded his colleague thoughtfully. "But they do get out of doors each day as well, do they not? Growing girls need plenty of fresh air and exercise, just like growing boys."

Reverend Wiggins glanced guiltily at Aunt Anne, who cocked an eyebrow at him as if to say "I told you so." He cleared his throat.

"Well, ah, no, Brother Phillips," he replied. "I felt the girls got plenty of exercise walking back and forth to church. After all, 'A young lady's sedentary way of life disposes her best to such domestic, quiet amusements as reading,' Hester Halifax tells us."

"Hester who?" Dr. Phillips looked at Reverend Wiggins as if he were unhinged.

"Halifax," Fanny replied, stepping forward. Her pretty face was clouded with a frown. "And I must say, Reverend Wiggins, it is hardly fair to characterize such an esteemed authoress's opinion on a subject by a single quote. She has a great deal more to say about the importance of physical activity in a young woman's education." Fanny pulled *Etiquette for Ladies* from her apron pocket and riffled through the pages. "This, for instance: 'Recreation and amusement is as necessary to recruit the wasted energies of the mind, as sleep to restore bodily strength.'"

This was a side of Fanny I had never seen before. She was standing toe to toe with Reverend Wiggins, her face flushed with conviction. Clearly she cared deeply for the students in her care—including my dear friend La'ila'i—and I felt slightly ashamed of all the uncharitable thoughts I had harbored toward her.

Dr. Phillips nodded in agreement. "Sensible woman, this Hester, Hester—"

"Halifax," said Fanny again.

"Just so," said Dr. Phillips. "Brother Wiggins, these young island girls are not used to a life of confinement. You must have observed that in your years here in the islands. Swimming, surf playing, horseback riding, plenty of long walks, and dancing are what they are accustomed to."

"Dancing!" exploded Reverend Wiggins. "Surely you're not expecting me to countenance the *hula* and other heathen customs—"

Fanny waved *Etiquette for Ladies* under his nose. "Hester Halifax is hardly speaking of the *hula* when she tells us, 'Dancing is not only necessary as an accomplishment, but also very beneficial as an exercise,'" she said triumphantly.

Dr. Phillips took off his spectacles and polished them vigorously. "Brother Wiggins, I'm not saying that these customs are not heathen, simply that this is what the girls are accustomed to. To pluck them from their families is shock enough, but to suddenly deprive them of all familiar activity as well is simply not natural and may have contributed to this illness."

Reverend Wiggins grew pale.

"It's not that you are responsible for this epidemic—

it's simply that we must all do everything possible to prevent it from happening again," continued Dr. Phillips.

"But the missionary board has entrusted me with their schooling, not with—"

"If it comforts you to present physical activity under the guise of education, so be it. Natural history would serve well as an excuse to take them out of doors. But the girls simply must spend part of each day in the sunshine and fresh air. Sea bathing as well from time to time." He gestured at Charity and me. "And it wouldn't do these two any harm to be allowed to join in the activity."

Reverend Wiggins bristled at this suggestion. "No daughter of mine—"

"These girls are *all* your daughters while they're in your care," said Dr. Phillips sharply. "You cannot expect them to sit still the whole day long. It's simply not natural. They are human beings, not hothouse flowers."

Reverend Wiggins wilted under the doctor's fierce scolding. "If you insist, Brother Phillips."

"I do."

"In that case I bow to your wishes," said Reverend Wiggins grudgingly. "When the girls are well again—"

"*If* they are well again, Providence willing," Dr. Phillips interjected.

"—I shall take them on nature walks. As for sea

bathing, well, as I do not swim myself I cannot supervise, so perhaps we can dispense with that activity," he concluded, grasping at the remaining shreds of his authority.

"Perhaps you should learn," said Dr. Phillips. He looked pointedly at Reverend Wiggins's waistline, or where his waistline would have been had he possessed one. "Healthful activity is beneficial at any age, and you know what the ancients said: '*Quod delectat juventutem jucundum est viro*'—that which delights the youth is pleasing to the man."

Reverend Wiggins waggled his chamber-pot ears in displeasure at this thought.

"I can swim," said Aunt Anne.

Both men turned to look at her in amazement.

"So can I," I said.

Their heads swiveled back toward me.

"Why does that not surprise me," muttered Reverend Wiggins under his breath.

"Splendid," said Dr. Phillips, who was beginning to sound quite jovial. It occurred to me that he might actually be enjoying tweaking Reverend Wiggins. "Miss Goodspeed and young Patience here can supervise the sea bathing."

Reverend Wiggins looked as though he'd swallowed a blowfish. He opened his mouth to speak, then snapped it shut again and drew a deep breath. "Very well," he said finally.

"And Mrs. Starbuck can supervise the dancing," added Dr. Phillips.

Fanny inclined her head in gracious acceptance. Reverend Wiggins puffed out his cheeks again in annoyance, but in the end he gave in and even agreed to relax his insistence that Charity and I be kept apart from the other students.

"Your daughter and Patience here will be fine examples to the girls of respectable young womanhood," Dr. Phillips pointed out.

And so it was settled. Our routine at the Wailuku Female Seminary would be undergoing some changes when Laʻilaʻi and the other girls recovered—if they recovered, that was.

November 3, 1836

I met Laʻilaʻi and Hiʻiaka's parents today.

They came to visit after the special church service that Reverend Chapman arranged, a service of gratitude that the lives of our school's students have been spared.

Everyone is on the mend. Hiʻiaka is already up and about, and all the others need is a few more days of rest and quiet and they'll be as good as new, says Dr. Phillips.

When Hiʻiaka introduced me to her parents,

I decided that was as good a time as any to practice my curtsy. While her parents aren't exactly
royalty, just a chief and chiefess, they're the next
best thing.

La'ila'i's mother laughed in delight as I
dipped my knee and bobbed my head. She took
my face in both of her hands and pressed her nose
to mine, then gathered me into her arms. She was
immense, a veritable Amazon, like so many of the
noblewomen of her race, and I all but disappeared into her folds of flesh.

On her head she wore a wreath of yellow
feathers—plucked from the o'o bird by special
bird catchers during moulting season, Hi'iaka
told me—and around her neck she wore a lei
made from matching feathers.

Her husband was equally tall but slimmer. He
wore a cape of bright red and yellow feathers
draped over his shoulders, and looked very regal.
His legs and chest were covered in interesting patterns of geometrical tattoos, and he reminded me
a bit of Papa. Not the tattoos, of course, but I
could tell he is proud, and I'd wager just as
prickly.

La'ila'i's parents presided over the feast that
was prepared to celebrate the girls' recovery.
Upa dug a great pit out behind the coral stone

cookhouse, an underground oven just like the one he uses to roast taro for poi, only bigger. Thaddeus's eyes grew round when he saw it, and I must admit it gave me pause as well, for it was nearly identical to the one the cannibals made.

First it was lined with stones, upon which a fire was built. When the stones were heated, a pig wrapped in ti leaves was placed on them. More ti leaves and grass were piled atop the pig, and then the whole was covered with earth while the pork roasted. The smell was heavenly! Reverend Wiggins protested a bit at first at the "heathen cooking arrangement," as he called it, but I noticed he ate more than anyone else in the end.

La'ila'i's parents spent the day hovering around their daughters most protectively, and I found myself missing my own father very much.

There is still no word from the Morning Star. Papa promised he'd be back in time for my birthday, but that has come and gone. I'm fourteen now. Mama was just sixteen when she married Papa—imagine that!

Aunt Anne and Fanny gave me belated gifts—a beautiful gold watch to pin on my dress from Aunt Anne, just like her own. It was her mother's—my grandmother's—and she said she would have wanted me to have it.

Fanny gave me a handkerchief on which she'd embroidered my initials, along with a paper of hairpins. She offered to teach me how to put my hair up now that I am officially a young lady. I started to tell her that assistant navigators have no need of fancy hair arrangements, but then I thought of how she had stood up to Reverend Wiggins for La'ila'i and my other friends and how selflessly she had cared for them when they were ill, and I relented. Even Papa couldn't have faulted me for not acting befitting a Goodspeed, and Fanny looked pleased.

—P.

P.S. Fanny Starbuck may be a bit less of a ninny-hammer than I thought, but that still doesn't mean I want her for a stepmama.

Eighteen

Never commit a boisterous action. What could be
more disreputable than the character of a hoyden?
—*The Ladies' Pocket Book of Etiquette*

By the second week of November, Wailuku Female
Seminary had fully recovered from its bout with the
mysterious fever.

Thanks to Dr. Phillips's prodding, Reverend Wiggins had indeed altered our curriculum, and each day
now included time for gardening (we were each given
a small flower patch to tend), dancing lessons, and
nature walks or outdoor sport. The meadow rang
with our laughter now as well as that of the boys, and
we played catch and blindman's bluff and hide-and-
seek after breakfast, and after luncheon, and sometimes after supper as well.

"I have an announcement to make," said Reverend Wiggins one morning. "We will be making our
first school outing to the seaside on Friday."

Thaddeus and the Four Gospels erupted in cheers
at this news.

"Hush, boys," said Mrs. Wiggins, but trying to
quell their enthusiasm was like trying to stop a flood
tide. Beside me, Thaddeus wriggled with glee. To be

honest, I quite felt like wriggling myself.

The only thing to mar our anticipation of the trip was the fact that there was still no word from the *Morning Star*. My father's ship was now long overdue, and I could tell that even the adults were growing concerned, try as they might to make light of it.

"They've likely just had a string of greasy luck," Aunt Anne said repeatedly, echoing Captain Russell, but her cheeriness was forced. I saw the glances she and Fanny exchanged when they thought I wasn't looking, and the way Fanny's hand slipped unconsciously into the pocket where she now kept her treasured letters safe from prying eyes, and I knew they were as worried as I.

The day of our outing dawned fine and clear, and after breakfast and prayers we set off—all but Mrs. Wiggins, who chose to remain behind with Pali.

"I do wish you'd join us, Mama," said Charity.

Mrs. Wiggins shook her head and patted her protruding stomach. "No, dear, it's much too far of a walk for me these days. Besides, just think how peaceful it will be here without the boys!"

Promising to keep a close eye on her brothers, Charity kissed her mother on the cheek. Reverend Wiggins, who looked more like a chamber pot than ever in a wide-brimmed straw hat, followed suit, and we started off down the road to Wailuku.

Thaddeus and the Four Gospels were in tearing high spirits and raced ahead, shouting and shoving each other. Friday trotted along beside them, panting happily. The rest of us paired up demurely in a long double line with Reverend Wiggins at the head like a sober mother duck. Fanny Starbuck and Aunt Anne were directly in front of Charity and me, and the two of us pulled faces at each other as Fanny nattered on.

"One cause of thick ankles in ladies is want of exercise, Hester Halifax says," Fanny noted, pausing for a moment to poke one neat foot out from under her dress, a spring green confection embroidered with tiny daisies. Frowning, she inspected her ankle.

"Is that so?" said Aunt Anne absently, her gaze fixed on the acres of neat taro patches and rows of waving sugarcane that lined the road.

Behind them, I stuck out my own sturdy ankle, frowned at it, and clapped my hands to my cheeks in mock horror. Charity grinned.

At the rear of our line, Upa and one of his assistants carried the quilts and picnic baskets we would need at the shore, all of it piled on long, polished boards they balanced atop their shoulders.

At the Wailuku parsonage, we added Reverend and Mrs. Chapman and Dr. Phillips to our party, and another hour of walking brought us within view of the beach.

It was a perfect day for an outing, early enough that the air hadn't yet grown heavy with humidity, and with just a light offshore breeze to ruffle the tops of the waves. Later, the trade wind would whip them into whitecaps, of course, but for now it was a peaceful scene. I shaded my eyes and feasted on the sight of the sun glinting on the water, letting my gaze rest on the far reaches of the horizon—*kukulu-o-ka-lani,* as La'ila'i had taught me. The walls of heaven, where the sky meets the sea. Nary a sail was in sight, and for a moment I was gripped with renewed concern for the *Morning Star.* But it was impossible to be gloomy on such a glorious morning, and I resolutely pushed my worries away.

As Fanny and Charity and Aunt Anne and I began spreading the quilts out on the sand, the island girls whooped with glee and took off running down the beach.

"Young ladies!" called Reverend Wiggins, trotting after them and huffing and puffing in a vain attempt to restore order.

"Very well then, where's the food?" cried Reverend Chapman, rubbing his hands together in mock anticipation. He too wore a wide-brimmed straw hat, and it was cocked rakishly over his starboard ear.

His wife and Fanny both giggled obligingly.

"Now, Reverend Chapman, it's far too early in the

day to be thinking about eating," Fanny scolded.

"It's never too early to think about eating," he protested. "God's good bounty is here for us to enjoy!"

Dr. Phillips, whose bald pate was covered not with a hat but with a white pocket handkerchief knotted at each of the four corners, passed him one of the picnic hampers. "Mind you leave something for the rest of us," he warned, smiling broadly.

The change of scene had clearly lifted everyone's spirits, and as the adults settled in for a visit Charity and I stood apart and watched our fellow students galloping up and down the beach. Their *holokū* were hiked up, and with their bare legs and streaming hair, they looked like a herd of wild ponies. I envied them their freedom.

"Patience! Come and play with me!"

Thaddeus and the Four Gospels had stripped down to their Skivvies and were splashing about in the shallows. Friday ran up and down the shore, yapping and chasing the waves as they advanced and retreated.

Charity and I exchanged a glance.

"Go ahead, girls," said Aunt Anne, who had come up behind us. "I'll keep an eye on everyone."

I didn't need to be told twice. Plunking myself down on the sand, I tugged at my shoes. After a moment's hesitation, Charity did the same. Reverend Wiggins, who had given up trying to corral his students into something resembling decorum, caught sight of us and frowned.

"Girls!" he called, struggling back through the sand in our direction. Dr. Phillips wagged his finger at him reprovingly and Reverend Wiggins stopped. He put his hands on his hips. "Oh, very well," he panted crossly, then added, "but remember, you are young ladies, not hoydens!"

The sea here in the Sandwich Isles was nothing like it was at home. In Nantucket the water could be icy even in high summer. This was invitingly warm yet refreshing and slipped over my feet and ankles like silk. I waggled my naked toes ecstatically. Beside me, Charity did the same.

"Yaaaaaaaaahhhhhh!"

The boys descended on us, howling like cannibals, and I shrieked as Matthew and Mark began splashing us vigorously.

"Ambush!" I sputtered. Scooping up armfuls of water, I began to defend myself.

Charity hesitated a moment, glanced toward her father, saw that he was engaged in deep conversation with Dr. Phillips, then joined in with a war whoop of her own. Out of the corner of my eye I saw Thaddeus launch himself at me, but I wasn't quick enough and as we collided I staggered, then fell flat on my back. Laughing and choking, I struggled to regain my footing, then gave up and lay back in a heap and let the waves wash over me.

I flung my arms out and closed my eyes, floating on my back and basking blissfully in the sun.

"Oh my," said Charity.

I opened my eyes. "What?"

She pointed silently down the beach, wide-eyed in amazement. Thaddeus and the Four Gospels had stopped their skylarking as well and stood rooted to the sand, gaping like codfish.

"What is it?" I cried, struggling to sit up. I was hampered by the sodden, sandy mess of my petticoats, but I finally managed it, and turned in the direction toward which Charity was pointing.

"Thunder and lightning!" I breathed.

La'ila'i and Hi'iaka had abandoned their *holokūs* and were running straight toward us. Their classmates were quickly following suit.

"Merciful heavens!" said Aunt Anne as the girls streaked past in a blur of brown skin and laughter, clad in nothing but a blush, as Mama used to say.

Reverend Wiggins charged up to the water's edge, sputtering like Glum's old teakettle. Dr. Phillips was right on his heels, and before Reverend Wiggins could say a word he laid a restraining hand on his arm.

"Remember, Brother Wiggins," the doctor said. "'Judge not, that ye be not judged.' Matthew, chapter seven, verse one. It's simply their custom."

"But it's *kapu*—" sputtered Reverend Wiggins.

"Look at them!" Dr. Phillips said. "This time a fortnight ago we didn't know if they'd live or die."

But Reverend Wiggins would not look. Averting his gaze from the happy throng of bronzed mermaids who had swum out beyond the fringe of surf and were now leaping and diving in the waves, he channeled his fury toward Thaddeus and his sons. "You boys get on up to the trees!" he thundered. "Away from this heathenish rite! Charity and Patience, you two as well!"

As he hauled us a more seemly distance from the frolicking, I glanced back over my shoulder. Shocking a sight though it was, I had to admit it looked like fun.

"It doesn't appear that I'll be needed to watch over them," said Aunt Anne, heaving a sigh that made me suspect she, too, felt constrained by layers of petticoats and decorum. "Those girls are far better swimmers than I'll ever be."

As we seated ourselves on the quilts—backs toward the sea, by order of Reverend Wiggins—Upa and his assistant trooped past toting the long boards on which they had carried the day's provisions.

"What are they doing with those?" I asked.

"Have you never seen surf riding?" Dr. Phillips sounded surprised.

I shook my head.

"Well, that will never do," he said. "You simply can't visit the Sandwich Islands and then sail away without ever having seen surf riding. Isn't that right, Brother Wiggins?"

"If you insist," sniffed Reverend Wiggins, chagrined at having his authority undermined once again.

I turned and gazed out to sea.

"You too, Thaddeus," said Dr. Phillips. "You'll both have something to tell your grandchildren back on Nantucket someday."

Upa and his companion had shed their shirts and trousers and were now clad only in *malo.* They waded out, pushing the boards ahead of them through the incoming breakers. When the water was chest-deep, they paused, and as a large roller raised up above them, they dove into the heart of it, emerging on the other side still gripping their boards.

"The surf here is quite gentle, barely enough for a decent ride," said Dr. Phillips. "On the island of O'ahu, I've seen men ride waves nearly as big as one of your whaling ships."

"You speak as though you've attempted this heathen custom," accused Reverend Wiggins.

The Four Gospels were wiggling with frustration, clearly desperate to take a peek at the proceedings, but their father held them firmly in his grasp. Charity dutifully sat with her back to the sea, but I could tell by the set of her shoulders that she too was itching to turn around. Only Fanny, who was chattering away to Reverend and Mrs. Chapman, seemed oblivious.

"As a matter of fact, I have tried it," Dr. Phillips replied calmly. "And I can assure you it is not as simple as it looks. It takes a great deal of coordination and strength, but the effect is most invigorating, not to mention healthful. More visitors to these islands ought to try it."

Reverend Wiggins grunted.

Truly, the men made it look easy. They were now flat on their bellies atop the boards, and as a swell lifted them up they paddled furiously to match its pace. Then, as the wave carried the surfboard forward, they crouched, rose to their feet, and with arms flung out for balance rode the cresting wave triumphantly in toward shore.

"That looks almost as much fun as a Nantucket sleigh ride," said Thaddeus, referring to the fast clip at which whaleboats were sometimes dragged when fastened by a harpoon to a feisty whale.

"It does, doesn't it," I agreed.

"Is that Friday?" asked Aunt Anne, pointing to a

small white object struggling to rise above an incoming wave. It failed and was hurtled back into the shallows.

My brother took off after his dog like a shot. "Friday!" he called anxiously.

I raced after him. He paused at the water's edge and we watched as Friday's head popped back up out of the water. He shook himself vigorously and sneezed, then turned again into the surf.

"Friday!" Thaddeus cried again, wading out toward him. "Come, boy!"

The dog ignored him and attacked another wave. All four legs churned furiously as he propelled himself forward, finally managing to launch himself up and over and out into the calmer water where Upa and the girls were swimming. But the effort had taken all his strength, and his muzzle was barely visible above the water's surface.

La'ila'i heard us yelling, and grabbing the surfboard from Upa, she aimed it in Friday's direction and sped to his side. Plucking him from the water, she grinned at us and held him up in the air. Then she placed him in front of her on the board and began paddling toward shore. A swell lifted the board up and now it was La'ila'i who crouched, then stood, and, bending her knees, guided the board down the steep beachward slope of the wave toward shore.

Barking furiously, Friday was carried along for the ride.

"He's surf riding!" shouted Thaddeus, hopping up and down in excitement. "Thunder and lightning, Patience, Friday's surf riding!"

Reverend Wiggins's protests went unheeded as his children wriggled out of his grasp and tumbled down to the water's edge to watch. Dr. Phillips and the Chapmans weren't far behind, and even Fanny was mincing her way toward us to see this wondrous sight, her parasol clutched in one hand to shield her from the sun.

"Merciful heavens!" said Aunt Anne again.

"I'll be hornswoggled," said Dr. Phillips, and Fanny Starbuck and the Chapmans allowed as it was the most amazing thing they'd ever seen.

"I wish Friday was my dog," said Matthew enviously as Friday, clearly pleased with himself, hopped down off the board and bounded through the shallows toward Thaddeus.

"Me too," chimed Mark.

Luke and John got down on all fours and chased each other up and down the beach, barking. Reverend Wiggins came barreling toward us and nearly tripped over them.

"That's quite enough of this heathen foolishness," he boomed. "Thaddeus, take that beast and tie him to a tree so he can't get into any more mischief. And the rest of you children, return to the picnic area immediately."

My little brother's face crumpled at the stern rebuke, and a flare of anger surged through me.

"Why do you always have to ruin everything?" I said. "Why can't you ever let anyone have a little fun?"

Reverend Wiggins looked taken aback at my outburst, but he quickly recovered. "'The rod and reproof give wisdom,'" he boomed. "Proverbs, chapter twenty-nine, verse fifteen. You have had far too little of either, young lady, and I will not countenance your disrespect."

"Hester Halifax says that sweetness of temper is sunshine falling on the heart," added Fanny, her reprimand squashing the small tendril of admiration I had nurtured toward her in the wake of our school's epidemic.

Reaching out, Reverend Wiggins took my arm and tried to drag me back up toward the quilts in the shade. I pulled away and stalked off. Behind me, I heard him start to protest, but Aunt Anne cut him off.

"Leave her be," she said, and for once he did.

Where oh where was the *Morning Star*? I thought desperately. Would Papa never come back and take me away from this sour-spirited man?

I started down the beach, intent on getting as far away from Reverend Wiggins and Fanny Starbuck as possible. Small sand crabs scuttled out of my way as I skirted a rough outcropping of volcanic rock. It was nearly midday now, and the sun was hot on my shoulders. The bodice of my dress quickly soaked through with perspiration, and I stopped and looked out to where La'ila'i and Hi'iaka and the other girls were cavorting in the water.

I was so weary of decorum and refinement and respectability. Hardly anything I had done since arriving in this place had been fun. The best I seemed to be able to manage was skulking around behind the girls' privy with my sextant and sneaking under cover of darkness to meet with my fellow rebel female scholars.

Ducking behind a thicket of bushes, I peeled off my dress and the layers of still-soggy petticoats underneath, leaving only pantaloons and a chemise for modesty's sake. If Fanny Starbuck thought she could mold me into her silly notion of a lady, let her catch me first.

I peeked around the shrubs to see if anyone had noticed, but Reverend Wiggins and the rest of our party had settled onto the quilts again. The food hampers were open, and Fanny and Mrs. Chapman and Aunt Anne were setting up the picnic. Dashing across the sand, I ran straight out into the water and splashed my way through the shallows to the waves beyond. I dove in and came up laughing. Oh, how wonderful it felt!

La'ila'i spotted me and waved. I waved back, then swam over to join her.

"Will you teach me?" I asked, rapping my knuckles on Upa's board.

La'ila'i looked at me in surprise. *"Papa heé nalu?* Wave-sliding board?"

I nodded. She glanced toward shore. We had been spotted, and Reverend Wiggins was waving his straw hat vigorously, trying to get our attention.

"Pilikia," I said.

"Trouble," she agreed.

Our eyes met, and we both smiled. La'ila'i slid the surfboard toward me and held it steady as I flung my leg awkwardly over it. I pulled myself up onto my belly, and lay there panting as she took the other board from her sister and climbed onto it beside me.

I felt rather than saw the surge of water that came from behind and lifted me up, and watching La'ila'i, I tried to mimic her motions, flailing my arms and feet to propel the board forward.

She rose to a kneeling position and shouted to me, gesturing encouragingly with her hand. My knees were shaking wildly, and one of them slipped off the board, but I was able to draw it up under me again. I was being swept forward now at what felt like a terrific speed and had to half close my eyes to shield them from the spray.

La'ila'i stood upright and shouted to me again. I gripped the edges of the board and rose to a half crouch, hardly my friend's graceful posture but enough to set my heart pounding with the thrill. My toes gripped the wood beneath me for dear life as I teetered suddenly and almost toppled over, but by windmilling my arms I just managed to stay partially upright.

Side by side, La'ila'i and I surged toward shore. She veered off before the wave flung itself onto the sand, but I was not so adept, and as my board scraped bottom I was thrown forward into the shallows. I lay there, coughing and spluttering and spitting out sand, but every inch of me was alive with happiness. No wonder Friday had looked so pleased with himself!

My laughter faded, however, as a shadow fell across my face. I looked up. Reverend Wiggins was standing over me, and once again he looked most seriously displeased. Behind him were Aunt Anne and Fanny Starbuck. As I rose to my feet, a collective gasp went up from the three of them, and Reverend

Wiggins quickly averted his eyes. Fanny stared at me, her mouth a perfect O. Even Aunt Anne looked shocked.

"Patience Goodspeed!" said Fanny, her voice carrying clearly down the beach to where Reverend and Mrs. Chapman were gathered with Dr. Phillips, Charity, Thaddeus, and the Four Gospels. "You need a corset!"

Nineteen

A young lady should ever, whatever
pains it cost her, keep her temper.
—*Young Lady's Own Book, a Manual of
Intellectual Improvement and Moral Deportment*

November 12, 1836

*I shall never, so long as I live, forget the events of
this horrible day.*

*Every moment of it is etched in my memory,
from the humiliating discovery that the seawater
had rendered the thin cotton of my undergarments virtually invisible, to Reverend Wiggins's
instant and thunderous condemnation of my
actions.*

*"'Woe to the rebellious children!'" he boomed,
his chamber-pot ears trembling with indignation.
"Isaiah, chapter thirty, verse one."*

*Trust the old walrus to have a verse "suitable
for the occasion," as Mr. Macy would say. He
went on to denounce the "lax and unwise fashion"
in which Papa had raised me, said that he'd tried
to "make allowances when I stole Mrs. Starbuck's
diary," and even insulted Aunt Anne, calling her a*

"bluestocking" who had led me and his daughter astray in viewing what he called "that heathen dance."

This, however, my latest escapade, quite sent him over the edge, and he could hardly get the words out for glaring at me.

"This brazen act is beyond comprehension," he'd finished. "You are a deceitful, thieving, wicked hoyden of a girl!"

Even Aunt Anne's attempt to defend me (and herself, for that matter—she despised the term "bluestocking") couldn't allay the sting of those words.

Hoyden, was I? Brazen, was I? And a thief! It was all simply too much, and my anger, which had been simmering for months, boiled over. I had been dutifully holding my tongue since arriving at Wailuku, trying my best to honor Papa's wishes that I act befitting a Goodspeed, but I could no longer restrain myself.

"How dare you!" I had cried, my voice shaking with anger. "You—you are nothing but a fraud. Laʻilaʻi and Hiʻiaka and the other girls nearly died because of you and your stupid pigheaded nonsense—your endless list of kapus and 'thou shalt not's! And yet you dare judge me?"

Unwisely, Fanny had tried to intervene, quoting Etiquette for Ladies ("Anger hurts the woman who is possessed by it more than any other against whom it is directed"), and I'd turned on her as well and told her exactly what I thought of Hester Halifax—and of her.

"I do not value her opinions, nor do I value those of a simpleton like you," I had said. "You are not my mama and I hope you never will be!"

Any relief I might have felt at finally unburdening myself of these thoughts drained away at the sight of Fanny's face, however, and I instantly regretted my rash words.

She'd drawn back, stricken, her eyes filling with tears. "Is that what you think of me?" she'd said dully.

She looked as though I had slapped her, and truly, now that I think on it, I may as well have.

Once again my temper has gotten the better of me, and my sharp tongue tastes the ashen residue of remorse. It is all it is destined to taste today— for the seaside picnic was entirely ruined, and I have been confined here to my quarters with no prospect of dinner.

—P.

I closed my diary and stared off into space, brooding. Just thinking about the day's dismal conclusion brought a flame of embarrassment to my face. The walk back here to school had been accomplished in miserable silence, as Reverend Wiggins yanked Charity up to the front of the line beside him and relegated me to the very rear, behind Upa.

Aunt Anne had gazed at me sorrowfully over her shoulder several times, but her attentions were engaged in comforting Fanny, who wept nearly all the way back. The Chapmans and Dr. Phillips were quite speechless, and as they turned into their gate without a glance in my direction, Reverend Wiggins glared at me in triumph. My scalding words had confirmed his low opinion of me, and I was, for all intents and purposes, an outcast.

A shaft of sunlight fell on the table before me, breaking my remorseful reverie. I glanced over toward the door. Aunt Anne had pulled aside the *kapa* cloth and was standing there, regarding me silently. She crossed the room and took a seat on the edge of our bed.

"I remember when I was your age," she said quietly. "My heart felt too big for my body sometimes, overflowing as it did with such a wild rush of feelings. I yearned for so many things and felt tugged in so many directions that I was quite sure I would be torn apart! Wanting so desperately to find my place in the world, but not necessarily wanting the place that was set for me at the world's table."

"Oh, Aunt Anne, what's to become of me?" I blurted. "I've made such an awful mess of things. Papa was right—I do have much to learn!"

"We all do," she said, reaching out her arms to me. I ran into them and laid my head on her shoulder, words and tears tumbling out of me now in a rush.

"And I've gone and gallied Reverend Wiggins again and said such cruel things to Fanny, things I cannot erase, and even though I don't want her for a stepmama, she's not all that bad, only a little silly sometimes!"

"I know, dear heart." Aunt Anne stroked my hair soothingly, and my sobs slowly subsided. "There are two kinds of learning in this world," she continued. "There's book learning, and there's people learning. Of the two, people learning is by far the more difficult."

"You manage it, though—you keep your temper! Why is it that I can't seem to?"

"I've had a lot more practice," Aunt Anne replied, lifting my chin with her finger.

"The only thing I seem to be able to manage is mathematics," I said. "I know what to do with numbers. They're tidy and reliable, and when they're in a tangle I can always manage to untangle them again somehow."

Aunt Anne's lips quirked up in a smile. "Life is not a neat equation to be solved," she said. "It's messy and wild and unpredictable. That's the heartbreak of it, but that's also the glory of it."

"It's all well and good for me to learn to dance, and to hold a teacup properly, and even to curtsy," I continued, "but if I can't learn to curb my tongue, I'll never become the proper lady that Papa sorely wants me to be."

"You'll become the woman you were meant to be," Aunt Anne assured me. "And as for curbing your tongue, did you ever think when you were first learning how to add that you would some day master navigation?"

"That's hardly the same thing," I protested.

"Is it not? Be patient with yourself, dear heart. You're just growing up, that's all."

"And out and every which way," I said ruefully, tugging at the bodice of my dress. My body had grown as lumpy as my moods of late.

Aunt Anne laughed. "That at least can be easily remedied," she said. "Fanny is correct for once—you do need a corset."

And standing up, she reached for my hand. "Come along now. Reverend Wiggins wishes to see you."

November 13, 1836

My fate has been decided.

    For my act of defiance, as well as what Reverend Wiggins calls my "rude and romping behavior," I will not be allowed to attend the quarterly examinations in Lahaina next week.

    This is a most grievous punishment. My heart was set on testing my mathematical skills against the vaunted scholars of Lahainaluna. Even Aunt Anne feels the sentence is too harsh, but Reverend Wiggins is as fixed and unmovable as the firmament, he says.

    I will be left behind here in Wailuku with Mrs. Wiggins and Pali. Aunt Anne seems regretful but says there is nothing she can do. Charity, who is barely allowed in my disgraced presence, looks at me pityingly. Today during our French lesson, when her father left the room for a moment, she pressed my hand and whispered that she would try doubly hard on the geometry exam in my honor. "Be brave and remember Sophie Germain," she says. That is cold comfort, but at least she's speaking to me.

    Fanny, on the other hand, is not, despite my repeated attempts to apologize. Not that I blame her. She might be giddy and foolish at times—and certainly we could all do with a little less from Hester Halifax—but she didn't deserve such a scathing set-down as I gave her.

Papa's choice of a wife is none of my business, Aunt Anne told me. Is she right?

"What can't be cured must be endured," Papa always says. If he indeed marries Fanny, could I learn to endure it with good grace? Am I cutting my nose off to spite my face by being so unkind to her?

—P.

P.S. Aunt Anne is going to buy me a corset in Lahaina. I don't want a corset, I tell her, but she says even Mama would insist that I wear one.

P.P.S. I wish Mama were here.

P.P.P.S. Still no news from the Morning Star, and the weather has turned as gloomy as my spirits.

Twenty

It is proof of attention and politeness on
the part of a lady, always to be in readiness
to receive unexpected guests.
—*Etiquette for Ladies, or The Principles of True Politeness*

By the fifth day of my exile, I was bored to extinction.

The schoolgrounds were unnaturally quiet with everyone away. Dr. Phillips and the Chapmans had accompanied the group to Lahaina, and Mrs. Wiggins and Pali and I rattled around in the silence like three dried peas in an empty whale-oil barrel.

Mrs. Wiggins had been noticeably cooler toward me since my escapade at the seaside, so much so that I had made myself scarce and holed up for much of each day in our quarters with only my books and my doll Miranda for company.

Today was particularly warm, however, with less of a breeze than normal, and the air inside the small room had grown so stuffy that by late morning I could hardly breathe. I wandered out into the garden thinking to do a little weeding in my plot, but the sun's glare soon drove me to take refuge under the lanai instead. Pali found me there a short time later.

"Mrs. Wikkins like to see you," she said in her soft voice.

When I entered the parlor, Mrs. Wiggins patted the horsehair sofa beside her.

"Why don't you come and keep me company," she said. "It's far too quiet around here. Don't you have some knitting you can work on?"

Whether I had been forgiven or whether Mrs. Wiggins was just lonely, I didn't know, nor did I care, as I was feeling a bit lonely myself.

"Very well," I replied, and returned a few minutes later—not with my misshapen sweater, which looked more suited for service as a try-pot cozy than anything a human being might actually wear—but with a letter I had started to Miss Mitchell.

I had just finished describing my surf-riding adventure—hoping all the while that Mrs. Wiggins wouldn't ask me to read a portion of it aloud—when Pali entered the room.

"Luncheon is ready," she said.

"Thank you, Pali," Mrs. Wiggins replied. "I hope you have a pleasant afternoon."

Pali glided away.

"Where is she off to?" I asked.

"The market in Wailuku, and then for a visit with her sister," said Mrs. Wiggins. "She'll be back after supper."

We ate our meal in companionable silence, Mrs. Wiggins tucking into her baked chicken and sweet potatoes with gusto. She saw me eyeing her stomach and laughed.

"I'm a buster, aren't I?" she said, patting herself contentedly and not sounding displeased at all.

Mrs. Wiggins was no longer the pale creature I had first met in Lahaina last July. Expecting a small messenger from heaven clearly suited her, for her countenance had bloomed along with her belly. She would never rival Fanny in looks, but the added weight from the baby and the school's new schedule were doing her good. Even though, like Fanny, she carefully shielded her fair complexion from the island's fierce sun under a poke bonnet or parasol, our out-of-doors activities had rendered her rosier than ever before. She certainly no longer resembled a rabbit.

It suddenly occurred to me that with Pali gone for the day and Fanny in Lahaina, I had the run of the kitchen.

"Would you mind if I made cookies?" I asked, gripped by an overwhelming desire to treat myself to a baking spree.

Mrs. Wiggins's eyes lit up. "What a splendid idea! We'll have a tea party this afternoon, just the two of us. I'll get out the Spode teapot and my apostle spoons."

As I cleared the dishes from the table, she yawned and stretched. "I do believe I'll go upstairs and take a nap first," she said. "Will you be able to manage by yourself?"

I nodded. "Of course," I said. The crusts on my pies might not be as praiseworthy as Fanny's, nor my humble gingersnaps a match for her superior shortbread, but if there was one thing I knew how to do, it was cook. I was Glum's right-hand helper in the *Morning Star*'s galley, was I not? When Fanny wasn't aboard, at least.

I had just popped the first batch of cookies—I'd decided to try Fanny's shortbread recipe for myself—into the oven when I heard a cry from the house.

"Mrs. Wiggins?" I called.

There was no reply.

I wiped my hands on my apron and went inside. I paused at the bottom of the stairs. "Mrs. Wiggins?"

Again there was no reply.

I ran upstairs. The shutters in Mrs. Wiggins's room were closed, shrouding it in gloom, and for a moment I didn't see her. Then I spotted her. She was crouched on the floor, clutching the bedpost, a look of sheer terror on her face.

"What is it?" I asked in alarm.

"The baby," she whispered. "The baby's coming."

I stood there, rooted to the spot, staring at her

in disbelief. "I'll run for Pali," I said.

Mrs. Wiggins shook her head. "There's no time. The baby's coming *now*."

"But this wasn't supposed to happen until next month!" I cried, panic rising in me like a tidal wave.

Mrs. Wiggins attempted a smile. "Babies can't read timetables."

"What shall we do?" My knees were starting to shake.

"You'll have to help me, Patience."

"Me?" I gaped at her, stunned. My heart was racing so fast I could scarcely breathe. What could I do? I was not quite seven the day Thaddeus was born, and all I remembered was Martha whisking me next door after breakfast to stay with old Mrs. Starbuck, Fanny's mother-in-law. That and creeping back into Mama's room at dusk, where the sight of her wan, exhausted face as she cradled the bundle in her arms that was my new brother left me limp with terror.

"I can't," I said weakly.

"You must."

Mrs. Wiggins gripped the bedpost again. Her knuckles whitened. I stared at them, overcome by a feeling of complete helplessness. Surely there was some other way—someone else we could fetch.

Mrs. Wiggins saw the expression on my face. She took a deep breath. "Do you know anything of this?" she asked.

I shook my head. "No."

Mrs. Wiggins was breathing heavily now. "Well, I likely know enough for the both of us," she panted. "This is hardly my first. Help me into bed."

Making an effort to remain calm, I helped her swing her legs up atop the mattress. She grasped my pinafore as I plumped up the pillows behind her.

"There's a book in my husband's study," she whispered urgently, "in his doctoring bag. A medical book. *Dewees's System of Midwifery*. Bring it to me— and the bag."

I nodded, dazed.

"We'll need other things as well," she continued, and I listened as she rattled off a list of items I would need to gather and prepare.

When she finished, I bolted from the room. I ran to the cookhouse and set a large pot of water on top of the stove, paused long enough to pull the shortbread— cooked to golden brown perfection, by a stroke of miraculous luck—from the oven, gathered twine and a clean, sharp knife from the cupboard and tucked them in my pinafore pocket, then skittered back into the house to Reverend Wiggins's study to fetch his doctoring bag. Once I had retrieved it, I pelted back upstairs.

Mrs. Wiggins's breathing was deep and laborious, and her face dripped with perspiration. I opened the shutters, letting in the breeze that rustled through the kukui nut tree outside, and picked up a whale-bone fan from her dressing table.

"Bless you," Mrs. Wiggins whispered, smiling feebly at me as I waved it back and forth over her head. "Poor Patience. I'm sure you're wishing you were in Lahaina right now or back aboard the *Morning Star* with your father."

I made no reply, only offered her a feeble smile of my own in return.

"Well, I for one am most thankful you are here. Give me the book, would you?"

I rummaged through Reverend Wiggins's doctoring bag, which was nearly identical to Papa's, right down to a blue glass bottle of laudanum just like the one I had used to dose the biscuits for the mutineers. My thoughts turned briefly to our ship's treacherous former first mate and his two cohorts, and I wondered if they had been brought to justice in Honolulu yet. That episode seemed like another lifetime ago just now, however. I found the book and handed it to Mrs. Wiggins, who flipped it open to a well-worn passage.

"Read this," she said, handing it back to me.

Moving to the window, I held the book to the light and traced the paragraphs in question with my forefinger. I frowned when I reached the end. Surely this couldn't be right! I must have misunderstood. I squinted closely at the pages and scanned them a second time.

"But this is— It's— Why, it's hardly any different from our barnyard back on Nantucket!" I burst out, indignant to learn that nature hadn't arranged something more dignified for women.

Mrs. Wiggins laughed, a short bark that quickly changed into an entirely different sound. "Not long now," she gasped.

Indeed, she was right, though the hour that followed was the longest of my life. Battling mutineers and cannibals paled in comparison to playing midwife. Holding Reverend Wiggins's medical book in one hand, I tended to his wife with the other, gritting my teeth when Mrs. Wiggins gritted her teeth, sweating when she sweated, crying when she cried, and trying to offer what encouragement I could, which hardly seemed enough.

Under Mrs. Wiggins's direction, I tied sheets to each bedpost, twisting them into ropes. She clung to those ropes and alternately to my hands—bone-crunching grips that left me gasping for breath—as each fresh wave of exertion overtook her.

Finally, after one last monumental effort on my laboring companion's part, when it seemed surely she would split in two—

"It's a girl!" I said in astonishment, catching the unexpectedly slippery babe who emerged into the world.

I stared down at the little creature in a tangled welter of emotions—wonderment and awe and gratitude and amazement, all tumbled together with happiness and an enormous sense of relief. A sob burst forth from deep within me, and I looked up at Mrs. Wiggins, smiling through my tears. "Oh, Mrs. Wiggins, it's a girl!"

"Oh, joy!" she cried, reaching for her daughter.

Exhausted, drenched in sweat, my heart still pounding, I sat down on the edge of the bed beside the two of them. I looked at the brand-new child, a perfect girl baby whose impossibly small fingers clung to her mother's and mine with surprising tenacity.

She was flawless; a tiny miracle. As I gazed at her, one of Mama's favorite Bible verses floated into mind unbidden. "When I consider thy heavens, the work of thy fingers, the moon and the stars, which thou hast ordained; what is man, that thou art mindful of him?" Psalms, chapter eight, verses three and four, I whispered to myself, smiling ruefully. Wouldn't Reverend Wiggins be flabbergasted if he could hear me now!

"Her name will be Joy," said Mrs. Wiggins, her face shining with contentment. "For what a delight it is to have another daughter. And won't Charity be pleased to finally have a sister?"

I nodded, wondering if Mama's face had shone thus when she first gazed at me and wondering at the strength that lay in ordinary women such as Mrs. Wiggins, strength that enabled them to endure such an extraordinary experience as the one I had just witnessed.

As I severed the cord that anchored mother and babe together and tied both ends off with twine, it occurred to me that I, too, would be very pleased to have a baby sister of my own someday. Perhaps even pleased enough to resign myself to a stepmama, much as I hated to admit it.

"We'll bathe her in a bit," Mrs. Wiggins murmured. "After I sleep."

And leaning back against the pillows I plumped up behind her, she closed her eyes, cradling the baby against her. I tiptoed out and shut the door, leaving the two to rest.

Word of Joy's birth—and of my part in it—spread quickly throughout Wailuku, and by morning the parlor was crowded with women from the village, bearing food and gifts. I was much fussed over, the baby much admired, and Mrs. Wiggins much doted upon. In the midst of all the activity, Reverend Wiggins walked in the door. Charity and Aunt Anne and

Fanny and the boys were right behind him.

"What is the meaning of this throng?" he cried crossly. "After such a tiring journey, I had hoped to enjoy a little peace."

Mrs. Wiggins held up the bundle in her arms. "We've had an unexpected visitor," she said, quite unruffled by his fretting.

Reverend Wiggins stared at the baby. "Is that our— Do you mean—"

"Yes, dear," said Mrs. Wiggins, nodding happily. "'For unto us a child is born.' Isaiah, chapter nine, verse six."

Charity and the Four Gospels crowded around their mother, eager to inspect their new baby sister.

"Her name is Joy," Mrs. Wiggins continued. "And Patience here helped bring her into the world."

"Merciful heavens!" whispered Aunt Anne, and even Fanny looked impressed.

Reverend Wiggins frowned. "Patience Goodspeed?"

His wife laughed. "Do you know another? A veritable angel of mercy she was too. I don't know what I should have done without her."

"But where was Pali?"

"In the village, visiting her sister."

Reverend Wiggins seemed quite flummoxed. His round face grew pink, and he tugged awkwardly at his collar. I had to admit it wasn't entirely unpleasant watching him squirm.

"Well," he said finally, the words emerging with audible reluctance as he turned to me and offered a stiff bow. "It seems I am in your debt. It seems perhaps that I even owe you an apology. It seems perhaps I was a bit hasty in my assessment of your character and that there may be hope for you after all."

Aunt Anne's eyes twinkled merrily at me over Reverend Wiggins's shoulder. Apparently she enjoyed seeing him eat crow as much as I did. I arched an eyebrow at her in response and inclined my head graciously toward Reverend Wiggins, just as Fanny—and Hester Halifax—had taught me. It wasn't the most satisfactory of apologies, but I was determined to accept it as befitting a Goodspeed.

That wasn't the end of it, however.

"It also seems I owe you—or our school owes you—another debt of gratitude," Reverend Wiggins continued, much to my surprise, tugging at his collar again.

"You do?" I said, mystified.

Charity grinned. She reached in her pinafore pocket and pulled out a scroll tied with a bright red ribbon. "I won the geometry prize!" she said triumphantly.

I threw my arms around her and kissed her on the cheek. "I knew you could do it!"

"I, ah, understand you were my daughter's tutor," Reverend Wiggins continued, torn between chagrin and pride.

I smiled modestly, trying not to appear too pleased that his pet theory about the limits of female brains had been proven entirely false. "The talent was entirely Charity's," I replied.

Reverend Wiggins looked at his daughter. "Is that so?" he said. Pride finally won out, and a smile spread across his broad face. "Well now, what do you know about that."

"My sister is a capital teacher," said Thaddeus with equal pride. "She's going to teach me mathematics when I get good enough with my sums, and then I'll win a prize too."

"She's a Goodspeed, all right," added Aunt Anne, putting her arm around my shoulders and giving me a squeeze. "Through and through."

November 20, 1836

In the wake of these fortuitous events, I am no longer an outcast.

Although the recitation prize slipped through the Wailuku Female Seminary's fingers—lost to the diligent scholars of Lahainaluna—Charity's unexpected triumph in the mathematics competition has brought a share of glory to our small school, and that, coupled with my "exceptional bravery" as a midwife, as Mrs. Wiggins insists on calling it, has redeemed me in everyone's eyes.

Dr. Phillips jokingly says that he plans to inform the missionary board of my abilities and that perhaps I might consider adding assistant midwife to my qualifications as assistant navigator.

I thanked him kindly for his suggestion but hastened to inform him that I have had quite enough of midwifery for the time being.

—P.

The newest little Wiggins was christened the following Sunday in a ceremony at the Wailuku church.

"Our cup of domestic blessing runneth over," announced Reverend Wiggins pompously to the congregation, along with his daughter's official name: Thankful Joy.

For just plain Joy was far too frivolous a name for a missionary's child, he decreed, and affixed Thankful to the bow of it. But just plain Joy was what the rest of us called her, for just plain joy was exactly what she brought to our school.

Charity and I and all of the other students hovered around Mrs. Wiggins night and day, ready to cuddle Joy at the first sign of a quivering lip. Fanny clung to her like a barnacle to the bottom of a ship, and Aunt Anne changed diapers with her usual efficiency. Thaddeus and the Four Gospels set to work building a toy of shells and feathers to dangle over the crib, and even Friday was smitten, his crossed eyes watching vigilantly in both directions as he guarded the basket where Joy slept at Mrs. Wiggins's feet during lessons in the parlor.

Reverend Wiggins occasionally tried to disapprove and scold us for spoiling "young Thankful," as he called her, but even he could not hide his delight with the newest addition to his family and had hardly stopped beaming since arriving home from Lahaina.

There was only one cloud hanging over us now, and that was the fact that the *Morning Star* was seriously overdue.

She was the only remaining ship that hadn't returned yet from her summer cruise. All the rest of the whaling fleet was present and accounted for. Thaddeus asked me daily when Papa would return, and daily my reply was the same—soon. But doubt had sown its dark seed in my heart, and I was beginning to wonder if I'd ever see my father and my shipmates again.

Twenty-One

Never talk or laugh loud; giggling and
tittering must also be avoided.
—*The Ladies' Pocket Book of Etiquette*

"Thunder and lightning!" I cried, throwing the tangled
ball of yarn across the lanai in frustration.

Friday lifted his head off his paws, peered into the
basket beside him to be sure that Joy hadn't vanished
in the thirty seconds since he'd last checked on her,
then took off after it like a shot.

La'ila'i glanced over at me and smiled. She knew
how much I despised needlework.

"Patience!" clucked Mrs. Wiggins. "You know
what Hester Halifax says: 'Heaven did not give
woman a sweet voice to be employed in scolding.'"

Even Mrs. Wiggins was quoting *Etiquette for
Ladies* now.

"Hang Hester Halifax," I muttered, throwing my
knitting needles down with a clatter. I was in a foul
temper, gnawed raw with worry about the fate of the
Morning Star.

If I was in no mood to be lectured on my manners, I was certainly not in the mood for needlework. We had finished our straw bonnets—mine so

misshapen it looked as if it had been sat upon—and returned to knitting. I had long since abandoned the sweater in favor of a baby blanket for Joy, but although it was a much simpler project in theory—no sleeves, no worrisome buttonholes, just a simple square—in practice it was proving equally fruitless. The sides weren't even and the rows were so full of holes from dropped stitches that I was tempted to try to pass it off as lacework. Either that or blame the damage on moths.

Friday returned, wagging his tail proudly, and dropped the ball of yarn at my feet. I regarded the slimy object with distaste, then picked it up gingerly and dropped it into my knitting basket along with the misbegotten blanket.

Music wafted out the window of the house toward us. Charity was at the melodeon, practicing for tomorrow's Thanksgiving service. Her musical talents had not gone unnoticed, and Mrs. Chapman had gladly handed over her role as church accompanist. I was in no mood for Thanksgiving, either. What did I have to be grateful for? Thaddeus and I would probably be declared orphans any day now.

I excused myself from the circle of busy needleworkers and scuffed my way to the cookhouse. Fanny and Pali were making pies for the holiday meal. It was clear from Fanny's tone of voice that I wasn't the only one in a black mood.

"Not like that, Pali," she said in exasperation, plucking the wooden spoon out of her assistant's hand. "Like this," and she began expertly beating a bowl of eggs.

I breathed in the familiar blend of spices—cinnamon and nutmeg and ginger, their pungent scent a balm to my battered spirits—and sat down at the table. Picking up a knife, I began hacking at a pumpkin.

The music stopped and Charity wandered in. "May I help too?"

Fanny pushed a stray ringlet off her face, streaking her forehead with flour, and nodded shortly. "Just mind you girls don't cut yourselves."

"Look what Friday can do!" Thaddeus ran into the kitchen with the Four Gospels close on his heels. They all snickered as my brother's dog scampered in. Thaddeus snapped his fingers, and Friday raised up on his hind legs and proceeded to hop around the room. One of Joy's bonnets was tied on his head.

"Take that ridiculous thing off him, Tad," snapped Fanny. "That dog is too ugly for Joy's pretty things. Besides, she might get fleas. You boys get out from underfoot now."

The five of them thundered out again, followed by the now-bonnetless Friday, and a minute later Reverend Wiggins and Aunt Anne entered.

"How's the baking coming, ladies?" asked Reverend Wiggins, sniffing the air appreciatively.

"How can I be expected to finish with so many interruptions!" cried Fanny. She threw down the rolling pin with a bang and ran from the room.

Reverend Wiggins looked startled. "Was it something I said?" he asked.

Aunt Anne shook her head. "Fanny's a bit testy these days, that's all," she replied, with a cautious glance toward me. "She's worried about things, you know."

I looked down at the table and stabbed my knife into another wedge of pumpkin. Aunt Anne meant worried about the *Morning Star*. I could feel Charity watching me out of the corner of her eye.

"I go to her," said Pali softly, and padded out of the room.

"Perhaps I should go to her as well," offered Reverend Wiggins. "Mrs. Starbuck should take comfort in the Psalms. That is what I always do." With a glance in my direction, he lowered his voice and continued, "Does the, ah, delay bring back memories of her worries for her own dear departed husband?"

"I believe she has a sweetheart aboard," whispered Aunt Anne.

Reverend Wiggins waggled his chamber-pot ears

thoughtfully. "I see," he said. "I had not been advised of that fact."

He looked regretfully at the array of half-finished pies on the table. His stomach rumbled. "Well, I do hope Mrs. Starbuck is able to finish these delectable-looking confections and join us at the service tomorrow."

Fanny was indeed able, thanks not to the comforts of the psalmist but rather to her desire to show off the new dress she had sewn. She made her entrance as we were all lining up in our Sunday best for the walk down to Wailuku, a picture in rose pink, with a spray of matching silk ribbons on her new braided bonnet (which did not look sat upon, naturally). Hi'iaka and the younger girls vied for the privilege of walking nearest her.

I had not bothered to decorate my misshapen bonnet, nor had Mrs. Wiggins. Pali had been able to spare enough time from taking care of Joy to help make me a new dress, so I had to make do with my old Sunday muslin. At least the seams had been let out enough so I could breathe. What passed for breathing these days, now that I was squeezed into a corset, vile thing.

An overflow crowd was gathered at the church, where Reverend and Mrs. Chapman greeted us and ushered us to the rows of benches in the front that were always reserved for the school.

Thaddeus and the Four Gospels took their seats beside me, poking and prodding each other and try- ing to stifle their giggles.

"What are you up to?" I asked suspiciously.

Thaddeus wouldn't meet my gaze. "Nothing," he said innocently.

Matthew's and Mark's faces were wiped clean of expression too, and the freckle-faced twins offered me their best cherub smiles. Something was most definitely afoot.

Before I could investigate whatever mischief they had up their sleeves, however, the service began. Charity struck up a chord on the organ, and we joined our voices to those of the native choir in a hymn of thanksgiving and praise. As the final notes died away, Reverend Chapman rose to his feet, and from the pulpit he reminded us of the importance of counting our blessings. He numbered Wailuku's own blessings in the past year, from the successful launch of the new female seminary to the arrival of Thankful Joy. Tears pricked my eyelids as he offered a prayer for the safe return of the *Morning Star*. We sang another hymn, and then it was Reverend Wiggins's turn to preach.

As he swept up toward the pulpit with his usual pompous flourish, I heard Thaddeus snap his fingers.

I looked over to see Friday scoot out from under the pew. My brother pulled something out from underneath his jacket and bent down over his dog. When he sat up a few seconds later, I gave a small squeak of surprise.

Perched on Friday's head was a miniature stovepipe hat, just like the one Reverend Wiggins was wearing, only Friday's was made of black paper. Around his neck, a stiff white collar was held into place by a knotted black silk cravat, also just like Reverend Wiggins's own.

Thaddeus snapped his fingers again, and Friday raised up on his hind legs and hopped down the aisle behind Reverend Wiggins, who had paused at the steps to the pulpit to fish his reading spectacles out of his pocket. Placing them carefully on his nose, he climbed up and took his place. Below him, Friday stopped, turned around, and rested his paws on a small box that had been placed on the floor. The front rows dissolved in giggles, for perched on Friday's muzzle was a pair of wire-rimmed spectacles.

"Thaddeus Goodspeed, are those Aunt Anne's?" I whispered furiously.

My brother, who was not a hardened sinner, had the grace to look guilty. Meanwhile Reverend Wiggins, who couldn't see the dog from his vantage point, glared down at the front pews.

By now half the congregation had caught on, and the other half were craning their necks to see what all the fuss was about. Beside me, the Four Gospels shook with suppressed laughter. Although I knew I should scold the boys, I couldn't help smiling myself.

Aunt Anne leaned forward in her seat at the opposite end of our row and scowled at us. Fanny elbowed her and nodded toward the podium. Aunt Anne turned and looked, and when she caught sight of Friday, her eyes widened in disbelief. Shaking her head, she sat back in her seat and closed her eyes. Her hand crept up and covered her mouth as she too tried to suppress a smile.

Still puzzled as to what was causing the hilarity, Reverend Wiggins cleared his throat and pressed on. As he began to speak, Friday's pink tongue lolled out. He panted happily and wagged his tail. A fresh wave of giggles swept through the church. Reverend Wiggins stopped. He looked up. His broad face reddened. He was not accustomed to being laughed at—especially not in church. He looked over at Reverend Chapman, who hastily wiped the grin off his own face and rose to his feet.

"Let us sing," he said.

Smiling from ear to ear, Charity sounded the first chord of another hymn, and as we once again raised our voices in song Friday lifted his muzzle and began to howl. Quicker than Jack Flash, as Sprigg would have said were he with us, we were all howling along with him, holding our aching sides and wiping away the tears.

Reverend Wiggins finally spied the source of the disturbance. Wadding up the pages of his sermon, he leaned over the edge of the lectern and threw it angrily at Friday. The dog dodged it neatly, then trotted up the aisle and sat down beside Thaddeus. His hat and tie were askew, and I reached out and plucked Aunt Anne's spectacles off him lest they come to harm. The congregation was helpless with laughter by now. Even Mrs. Wiggins was gasping and wiping her eyes. Only Reverend Wiggins was not amused at the trick that had been played on him.

And then, above the commotion, something caught my ear. Something familiar. A long, loud, hearty laugh that I hadn't heard in many months. I whipped around in my seat, scanning the crowded pews. My heart was in my throat. Could it be? There, by the door— It was!

"Papa!" I cried joyfully.

He caught sight of me and waved, grinning. With him were all of my shipmates, Sprigg and Glum, Charlie Fishback, Chips, Big John, and Mr. Chase and Mr. Macy too. They all waved, and the cold fingers of dread that had wound themselves around my heart these many weeks finally loosed their hold. I grabbed my brother.

"Look, Thaddeus!"

The *Morning Star* was back.

Twenty-Two

Most blunders are a result of haste.
—Etiquette for Ladies, or The Principles of True Politeness

Fanny Starbuck rose to her feet. Her face was shining with joy.

Papa! I thought. She means to go to Papa! All of my good intentions, all of my resolve to mind my own business and not interfere with Papa's affairs, promptly flew out the window, and I leaped to my feet as well.

Pushing past Thaddeus and Friday, I had only one aim in my mind as I ran up the aisle of the church: I had to get to Papa before Fanny did! I had to stop him somehow, stop them both, stop this mismatch of a marriage.

I could hear the rustle of silk behind me, and Fanny's quick steps as she followed me toward the door where my father and shipmates stood. Or had stood. The congregation had finally quieted down after the ruckus with Friday, the Thanksgiving service was over, and people were filing out of the church. The aisles were thronged with bodies, and I strained to see my father through the crowd. There he was! He was waiting for me. Or was he waiting for her?

Directly in front of me, Reverend Wiggins's walrus-like bulk blocked the way. I pushed past him, heedless of decorum or of his indignant "Well!" and flung myself at my father.

"Papa!" I cried. "Papa, you can't—"

My father hugged me so hard my ribs nearly cracked. His embrace left me more breathless than my corset, and as I struggled to catch my breath and speak again, he inspected me up and down.

"Patience, my girl, look at you!" he said, beaming. "You're nearly as tall as Anne! And there's something else that's different about you, though I can't quite put my finger on it."

The corset most likely, I thought sourly, but decided against announcing the fact—particularly since my shipmates were looking me over with equal curiosity.

Papa took my hands. "I received your letter," he said in a voice meant just for the two of us. "And I wanted to apologize as well. We Goodspeeds are known for our stubborn streak, and—"

"Papa, you can't marry Fanny Starbuck!" I blurted out.

The conversation around me suddenly ceased. As the crowd fell silent I realized that not only was Fanny right on my heels, but so also were Aunt Anne and Thaddeus, the Wiggins family, the Chapmans, and even Dr. Phillips. They all stared at me, shocked. So did Papa and my shipmates. Fanny's face, which had been radiating joy just a moment ago, turned as white as the altar cloth.

And then Mr. Macy stepped forward. "That's exactly right, Miss Patience," he said firmly. "Your father cannot marry Fanny Starbuck, because she is engaged to marry me."

Now it was my turn to stare in shock.

Mr. Macy held out his hand, and Fanny took it. A little of the color returned to her cheeks as he smiled down at her. "Your letter was waiting for me yesterday when we reached Lahaina," he said. He raised Fanny's hand to his lips and kissed it. "You've made me the happiest of men."

Fanny turned to me, her face pink with both pleasure at being reunited with her sweetheart and anger at me for spoiling this moment for her. "I couldn't tell you," she said softly, but her voice had an edge to it and she wouldn't meet my gaze. "I couldn't tell anyone until I knew that Mr. Macy—that John— had received my acceptance to his proposal."

This was all wrong, I thought, aghast. Fanny Starbuck was apologizing to me, and I was the one who should be apologizing to her! Once again I'd said exactly the wrong thing. Once again, my impetuous tongue had gotten the better of my good judgment.

And though I should have felt relief at this revelation, relief that she was not to be my stepmama after all, all I felt was shame and disgrace.

Papa looked from me to Fanny and back again. He frowned. I took a deep breath. This time I'd make things right, I decided. This time I'd show my father and everyone that I had manners too—manners befitting a Goodspeed and a real lady.

"No, Fanny," I started, "I shouldn't have—"

"Huzzah!" cried Charlie Fishback, and my words of apology were lost in a chorus of cheers as my shipmates hastened to offer the betrothed pair their hearty congratulations and much joy.

November 27, 1836

Fanny is to marry Mr. Macy! Imagine! My head still swims at the thought of it.

How I misjudged poor Fanny. I was so certain that Papa was her suitor, but our young second mate was her secret sweetheart this whole time. It was his letters she guarded so carefully, not Papa's at all, and his blue eyes of which she wrote in her diary. Mr. Macy's poetry won her heart, Fanny informed us at the Thanksgiving feast, and I had to smile at that, for Papa is most decidedly not the poetical type.

The wedding has been set for Christmas Day and will take place in Lahaina, where Papa and the crew, who are anchored here in Wailuku, will return shortly for repairs. Their long delay was due to a sprung foremast, which toppled in a gale off the coast of Kamchatka. They were able to limp into a remote harbor, where Chips jury-rigged a replacement sturdy enough to carry them back here.

Now the Morning Star must be thoroughly refitted and repaired before we leave for our Christmas cruise to New Zealand. Fanny and Aunt Anne and Thaddeus and I will remain here in Wailuku for the time being, and then join Papa and our shipmates for the wedding.

Meanwhile, I am convinced that love truly is blind.

There is no other explanation for the appalling manner in which Mr. Macy is acting. I know him to be possessed of a fine wit and a competent intellect, but we've seen scarce evidence of either since the announcement of his engagement. He gazes upon Fanny as if he can't believe his good fortune, indulging her every whim, laughing at her silliest remarks, and following her every move with great cow eyes. It is quite a pitiful display.

If this is love, I want none of it, for watching the two of them, I cannot imagine that I would ever wish to have someone mooning over me in that manner. Although I admit I would not object to having my shortcomings overlooked.

Of which there are many, Papa reminded me just this morning when I made the mistake of confiding my observations to him.

I am not to find fault with Mr. Macy, he says. He is a hard worker and a splendid second mate. Mr. Macy is soon to be wed, and thus entitled to be twitter-pated, he says. You should have seen your mama and me, he says. Ignorant misses should hold their tongues about things they do not understand, he says.

Apparently I still have much to learn.

—P.

"Fanny!" I called, picking up my skirts and sprinting over the grass toward her.

She was headed back from the privy, and for once Mr. Macy was not at her side. The two of them had scarcely been out of each other's sight since Thanksgiving Day, and I had not had the opportunity for a word alone with her.

Fanny paused. "Yes?" she said coolly.

I took a deep breath. It was now or never.

"Fanny," I replied, "I am so sorry, so deeply sorry for my behavior in church on Thanksgiving."

It was true. Fanny's brain might not be in danger of overheating, but Aunt Anne was right; she had a warm and generous heart, and she certainly hadn't deserved me spoiling what should have been a treasured moment for her.

"I'll understand if you don't feel you can forgive me," I continued, "especially in light of all the other unkind things I've said and done these past months, but I just want you to know how truly sorry I am and how truly happy I am for you and Mr. Macy."

Fanny couldn't help herself. A dimple appeared in her cheek at the mention of her beloved's name.

"He is wonderful, isn't he?" she gushed.

I nodded, for it was true. Mr. Macy was one of my bravest and dearest shipmates, and Fanny obviously adored him.

Fanny sighed and gave me a rueful smile. "There's so much joy in my heart at the moment that there's scarcely room for grudge holding," she said. "And if truth be told, there are things I've said and done these past months for which I should be asking your forgiveness."

"There are?" I said, surprised.

She nodded. "I admit I did have my cap set for your father at first—until I realized that it was not his blue eyes that kindled my affection, but John's. Of course, the way you looked at me all the time, as if you wished the earth would open up and swallow me, that was hurtful, I will admit. But I was jealous of you too."

"Jealous of me?" I was incredulous.

"Everywhere I turned, all I heard was 'brave Patience, clever Patience.' Saving the ship from mutineers! Outwitting cannibals! Delivering a baby!" She shook her head sadly. "The only compliments I ever received were for how I looked or what I wore."

"But you're brave too," I protested. "Why, I thought you were perfectly splendid, standing up to Reverend Wiggins after La'ila'i and the others fell ill."

"You did?" Now it was Fanny's turn to look surprised. She dimpled again at the thought of Reverend Wiggins. "You must admit, he is quite a pompous . . . a pompous—"

"Walrus?" I offered.

Fanny giggled. "Exactly!"

We looked at one another and smiled.

"Friends?" asked Fanny.

"Friends!" I replied.

"By the way," she added, linking her arm through mine and drawing me across the lawn back toward the parsonage. "It occurs to me that I'll be needing a maid of honor at my wedding. Do you suppose you might be up to the task?"

A great weight lifted from my heart then, carrying with it every last shred of remorse and leaving in its place only a sweet surge of affection for Fanny Starbuck-soon-to-be-Macy.

"Nothing would make me happier," I replied, and I meant it.

Twenty-Three

Great taste ought to be exerted on the
arrangements of the wedding breakfast.
—*Etiquette for Ladies, or the Principles of True Politeness*

We were in a flutter of preparations for the wedding.

The day after the *Morning Star* set sail for
Lahaina, Fanny produced a bolt of dove gray satin
and one of matching French lace that she just happened to have stashed in the bottom of one of her
trunks.

"'A lady is always prepared for every eventuality,'"
she said brightly.

"Hester Halifax?" I ventured.

Fanny looked at me and winked. "Martha, actually," she said, referring to our housekeeper back
home on Nantucket.

Reverend Wiggins had volunteered to perform the
ceremony "to thank dear Mrs. Starbuck for all she has
done to bring the sunlight of refined womanhood to
these dark shores," as he pompously put it, and Mrs.
Wiggins said that if he was going to Lahaina, so was
she, and she intended to take all the children with her.
We had a great deal of sewing ahead of us to ensure
everyone was properly turned out for the wedding.

Every morning during the weeks that followed, Mrs. Chapman made the trek up from the village to lend her needle to the task of making Fanny's wedding dress and new dresses for all of us—except the boys, of course, who would receive new trousers and shirts instead.

Although Papa had brought me a bolt of turquoise silk as a belated birthday present—"Your Mama's favorite color," he told me, adding that he'd always liked the way it set off her hair—I was the only one not allowed near a needle. They would have had to undo anything I tried to stitch anyway. Instead, I was put in charge of baby Joy, which suited me just fine.

Reverend Wiggins was delighted by the sudden burst of domestic industry.

"'She maketh herself coverings of tapestry; her clothing is silk and purple,'" he said, rubbing his hands together and fixing us all with a benign gaze. "Proverbs, chapter thirty-one, verse twenty-two. What we need here at this school is more weddings."

Mrs. Wiggins poked her husband in the leg with the handle of her scissors and shooed him out of the lanai.

Two days before Christmas, the wedding dress and other new garments were finally complete, and we packed up all our things and bid good-bye to Wailuku.

"I shall miss this place," said Aunt Anne.

"As will I," I said, surprised to find that it was true.

Saying good-bye to La'ila'i was the most difficult part, for she and the other students were to remain behind with Pali and Upa.

"Promise me you'll keep up your English studies?" I asked, as we bid each other a tearful *aloha*.

"*Ae*," she said sadly, pressing her cheek to mine. "Yes. Come back *awiwi*."

"Quick?"

She nodded.

"I will," I said. Papa had told us we'd return to the Sandwich Islands in the spring.

With favorable winds to speed our voyage, the passage to Lahaina was swift. By nightfall Fanny had been installed at the hotel in town, the Wigginses and Chapmans and Dr. Phillips parceled out amongst local missionary families, and Thaddeus and Aunt Anne and I were back aboard the *Morning Star*.

"Where's Jocko?" my brother asked the moment he set foot on deck.

Papa sighed dramatically. "What, not even a howdy-do? Have I been so quickly replaced in your affections, and by a monkey?" He shook his head sadly.

Thaddeus looked guilt-stricken, then realized

Papa was only teasing and launched himself at him with a happy squeal.

"Oof, Tad, you're a buster," said Papa, swinging him up for a big hug. "What has Mrs. Wiggins been feeding you?"

He drew me toward him too, and I buried my face in his coat.

"Papa, I'm so glad to be back," I said, feeling a bit shy.

"And I'm so glad to have you back," he replied, kissing me soundly. "Things just weren't the same around here without you two."

Charlie Fishback was standing by the mainmast, and he stepped forward and pulled off his cap. His coppery red hair shone in the bright Hawaiian sun like a new penny.

"Welcome back, Miss Patience," he said with a smile.

"Mr. Fishback," I replied, inclining my head regally just as I had been taught.

"Your father advanced me part of my wages, and look what I purchased at the mercantile!" He reached into his pocket and pulled out a brand-new sextant.

I dropped my air of refinement instantly. "Oh, Charlie, that's capital!" I cried in excitement, rushing forward to take a closer look.

Daisy the goat caught sight of my brother and

hurtled across the deck to butt him happily. Ishmael twined himself around my ankles as Sprigg appeared and began to chatter—or so I thought until I looked closer and realized that the sound was coming from the bright-eyed monkey peeping out from underneath his gray pigtail.

"Jocko!" cried Thaddeus in delight.

"None other," rasped Sprigg proudly.

The monkey was very small, about the size of a squirrel, with a cunning little face that wrinkled in alarm as Friday advanced toward him, barking.

"This is Friday," said Thaddeus, with equal pride. "He's my dog and he's very clever."

"If we keep this up, I'll be forced to rename my ship the *Noah's Ark*," grumbled Papa.

Sprigg peered at Friday over his spectacles. "What's wrong with his eyes?" he asked.

"Ill-favored beast, isn't he?" Papa agreed, springing lightly aside as Aunt Anne aimed a kick in his direction.

"Hush, Isaiah. Thaddeus thinks he was a birthday present from you," she whispered.

"From me?" said Papa in astonishment.

While my brother got introduced to Jocko, Aunt Anne and I quickly outlined the events of his birthday and how we had pulled the wool over Reverend Wiggins's eyes. Papa laughed uproariously at the tale.

"No wonder poor Titus looked so pleased when I gave him something for the school's coffers to make amends for any trouble my young scamps might have caused," he said. Papa placed his forefingers behind his ears and waggled them at us in a perfect imitation of Reverend Wiggins. "'The Lord loveth a cheerful giver. Second Corinthians, chapter nine, verse seven.'"

Aunt Anne and I laughed.

The following day was Christmas Eve, and as soon as breakfast was over I made a beeline for the *Morning Star*'s galley.

"I want every detail to be perfect," I told Glum.

I had been racking my brain for an idea for a wedding present for Fanny and Mr. Macy and had finally come up with the perfect one. I would bake their wedding cake—a surprise wedding cake.

I swore Glum to secrecy, and we sent Sprigg to town for fresh flowers with which to decorate it. Aunt Anne had joined him in the whaleboat to see if Fanny had any last-minute needs, and meanwhile Papa had set the crew to work scrubbing the *Morning Star* from stem to stern. With her fresh paint and new foremast, she looked nearly as shipshape and Bristol fashion as she had the day we left Nantucket, and I could tell Papa was pleased. We were all eager to show our ship to her best advantage, for our friends from Wailuku had been invited back aboard to celebrate after tomorrow morning's ceremony and the wedding breakfast that would follow.

"You and Friday stay out of the galley," I told Thaddeus sharply as he and his dog wandered in, lured by the scent of Mama's best spice cake that had begun to waft across the quarterdeck.

"But I'm hungry," whined my brother.

"Sprigg will be back soon, and he'll fix you something," I told him. "And leave Jocko alone!"

Thaddeus wandered off reluctantly, and Friday trailed behind, casting a reproachful, cross-eyed glance back in my direction. I turned my attention back to the cookies I was readying to go in the oven as soon as the cake was done.

Not five minutes later Friday began barking excitedly, and I poked my head out of the galley to see Jocko now perched on the deckhouse roof.

"Friday, come here!" I called.

The dog ignored me.

"Hound shows good sense," said Glum approvingly. "Pesky monkey."

"Oh, Glum, do stop a clapper to it and fetch me some more sugar, would you?" I said peevishly.

Glum ambled off and I squinted at Jocko more closely.

"Thaddeus Goodspeed!" I hollered. Jocko was

wearing one of my doll Miranda's dresses. My brother was nowhere to be seen, of course.

Chips and Charlie rounded the mizzenmast just then.

"How about I find your brother and put him to work?" said Chips.

"Oh, Chips, could you?" I replied, pushing my hair back off my perspiring face. I'd forgotten how hot the *Morning Star*'s small galley could be, especially in these latitudes. "And tie Friday up while you're at it, please. Charlie, if you could get that dress off Jocko and put him in his cage—"

"Sprigg doesn't like him to be shut up in there," Charlie said. "I'll get thumped with his thimble for sure."

"Bother Sprigg!" I said crossly. "These animals are driving me to distraction."

Glum shouldered his two shipmates aside and squeezed into the narrow space alongside me. In his skinny arms he held a sack of sugar.

Chips sniffed the air appreciatively. "You two still at it, eh?" he said, eyeing the mounds of cookies Glum and I had already produced.

"Here, try one and tell me if it's as good as Fanny's," I said, passing him and Charlie each a piece of shortbread.

Between the two of us, Glum and I had baked not

only shortbread but also a plum pudding, since tonight was Christmas Eve. After the cake was done, we would finish up with gingersnaps and pies—an even dozen of them, apple, pumpkin, and mince-meat.

Although tomorrow's guests would be well fed at the wedding breakfast—in actuality it would be a mid-day Hawaiian-style feast, but Hester Halifax insisted on the term *wedding breakfast*, and thus so did Fanny, of course—we were still anxious to ensure that no one went hungry while here aboard the *Morning Star*. Glum was planning a simple collation of cold meats, fresh fruit, and pineapple punch for supper, but we also wanted to be sure there were plenty of sweets with which to celebrate the newly wed sweethearts.

"Very good," mumbled Chips, and Charlie nodded his approval as well. Trailing crumbs, they wandered off to corral Thaddeus and the pets.

The cakes emerged from the oven a short while later. There were four of them, a quartet of fragrant layers that I planned to stack into a lofty tower twined with blossoms. Glum sniffed at each one, then looked at me suspiciously.

"No laudanum in them, is there?" he said gruffly.

Taken aback at this accusation, I started to sputter, then caught the glint in his eye. Whether it was the prospect of his favorite gingersnaps, the anticipation of the wedding, or simply a dose of the Christmas spirit, our doleful cook was in an unusually good mood. I smiled at him. "No, Glum, no laudanum. That's strictly for mutineers."

He nodded sagely and, pulling his pocketknife from his trousers, sat down on a stool and began to pick his teeth.

"'No lady, having any pretension to the name, will be guilty of picking her—'" I stopped. I was blasted if I was going to start quoting Hester Halifax. Especially not to Glum.

My shipmate raised his eyebrows inquiringly.

"Never mind," I said.

He shrugged and went back to his dental ministrations, watching carefully as I whipped the icing and smoothed it over each layer. Finally, the cake was done. We'd add the flowers—red hibiscus twined with green ferns to give it a festive Christmas air—right before the ceremony.

"Not too shabby," he said after inspecting it closely—high praise from Glum.

We carried it carefully down below to the small pantry off the main cabin. This was Sprigg's private domain, but it was cooler here than on deck, which would help keep the cake from wilting before tomorrow's celebration. Plus, the door had a lock, which would keep out inquiring noses—and fingers. I wouldn't put it past my brother to take a swipe at the icing. I felt like taking a swipe at it myself, for that matter, for it looked and smelled delicious. Fanny would be pleased, I was sure.

With all of our attentions focused on the morrow, our Christmas Eve festivities were modest. Glum rustled up one of his fish chowders, I supplied biscuits, and Papa ordered up an extra round of grog for the crew to accompany our plum pudding.

"Nervous about tomorrow?" he said to Mr. Macy, who had indeed been acting a bit jumpy all day.

"Not at all," Mr. Macy replied, promptly dropping his knife into his chowder bowl. He blushed.

Papa and Charlie and Mr. Chase grinned.

Suddenly there was a shriek from the pantry.

"Naughty, naughty Jocko!" Sprigg croaked, as a small dark blur shot out between his feet and whisked up the stairs past where Glum sat, as was his habit, dourly observing us eat. Friday, who had been napping under the table at Thaddeus's feet, lunged after him.

Our cook unfolded himself, the top of his bald head scraping the companionway entrance.

"What did that wicked animal do?" he demanded.

Sprigg took a step backward. "Nothing," he said, peeling his lips back in an unconvincing smile. It faltered as Glum advanced toward him. Our steward flung out his wizened arms to bar the entrance to the pantry, but Glum plucked them aside with ease. Although as thin as a whisker, Glum was strong.

"I knew it!" he cried.

My heart sank. I pushed back from the table and ran to see. "Oh, no!"

"What is it?" said Papa and Aunt Anne at the same time.

Jocko had gotten into the wedding cake.

Twenty-Four

When a gentleman who has been properly
introduced requests the honor of dancing with you,
etiquette requires that you will accede, unless
prevented by a previous engagement.
—*The Ladies' Pocket Book of Etiquette*

"Sprigg, did you let Jocko out of his cage?" I cried,
transfixed in horror at the trail of tiny paw prints
running up and down one side of the cake. From
the looks of the damage, the monkey had perched
boldly on the top layer and had himself quite a
feast.

Papa, Aunt Anne, Mr. Macy, Mr. Chase, and
Charlie crowded in behind Glum and me and peered
over our shoulders. Thaddeus wormed his way
between our legs. We stared first at the cake, then at
Sprigg, who squirmed uncomfortably.

"I never meant— I didn't— I mean I— Hang it all,
you know how much he hates being cooped up!" he
burst out.

His words were met with grim silence.

Glum shook his head. "Nothing but trouble since
you brought that little beast aboard," he said mourn-
fully. "And now look what he's done." He patted me

on the shoulder. "Don't cry, Miss Patience, we'll soon have it back to rights again."

"It's just that—oh, I wanted so much for it to be perfect for Fanny!" I wailed.

"You made this cake?" said Aunt Anne.

I nodded tearfully. She and my father exchanged a glance.

"That was most generous of you, Miss Patience," said Mr. Macy.

"I wanted it to be a surprise!" I sniffled. "It was meant to be your wedding present, yours and Fanny's."

Aunt Anne passed me her handkerchief. "Glum is right," she said. "It's just the top layer that needs seeing to, and some of the icing."

"We'll take off the part the little wretch et and bake a new one, see if we won't," Glum continued. "Have her looking shipshape again quicker than—"

"Jack Flash?" Thaddeus finished.

We all looked over at Sprigg again. He glared back reproachfully, but the wind had clearly been taken out of his sails.

"Can I have the bits you don't want?" asked my brother.

"May I," I said automatically. "And no, you can't. Who knows where those nasty paws have been."

A smile tugged at the corner of Papa's lips. "Did

you see the look on that little rascal's face?" he asked. "His tail covered with icing and fleeing the wrath of Pardon Sprigg."

Mr. Macy guffawed, and in spite of myself I started to giggle. Jocko had looked comical.

Sprigg perked up at the laughter but cowered again as Glum grabbed him by his scrawny gray pigtail and hauled him up the companionway onto the quarterdeck. We could hear them through the skylight above, Sprigg screeching in protest as Glum took him to task for his carelessness.

"And if I hear so much as a peep out of that blasted monkey before we set sail again," bellowed our cook, "I'll see to it that the both of you are tied to the next whale we meet and sent on a Nantucket sleigh ride you won't forget!"

Sprigg kept a low profile for the rest of the evening. He didn't even venture up on the foredeck later when Glum and I, after we'd finished repairing the ravaged wedding cake, joined the rest of the crew for Christmas carols.

Charlie Fishback smiled at me as we launched into "Deck the Halls," and I smiled back, thinking how odd it was to sing of "boughs of holly" and "the blazing yule" while we lay here at anchor in the Sandwich Isles, with nary a holly berry or a yule log in sight.

I thought of our Christmases back home on Nantucket, with her cozy gray houses wreathed in evergreen. I thought of the snow crunching on the cobblestones beneath my feet as we went caroling door to door, and the cheery glow of hearth fires shining through our neighbors' windows. I thought of the mulled cider that always awaited us when we returned home and of Martha bustling about with preparations for our holiday dinner and of Mama lighting the candles on our tree in the parlor. How I missed her still!

My heart grew warm at the thought of my mother and at the sight of my family and friends gathered about me. And as I gazed out across the harbor at the other whaling ships swinging gently at anchor, I thought that this exotic place was festive in its own way too.

I could hear singing on other foredecks, and laughter, too. And if we had no tree and no candles, we did have a sky flung wide with stars, their light reflected in the still waters of the harbor. If I couldn't be home on Nantucket tonight to celebrate Christmas, there was no place I would rather be than right here on the deck of the *Morning Star.*

Christmas Day, 1836

We leave for the wedding in a quarter of an hour!

Everyone is in a dither getting ready. Papa is bellowing for his top hat, which he seems to have misplaced, though Sprigg bellows back that he set it out for him on his desk last night. Thaddeus is bellowing because Aunt Anne is brushing his hair, and Aunt Anne is bellowing because Thaddeus won't sit still. Up on deck, Mr. Chase is bellowing at the crew to "spring to it, then!" and put on their best bib and tucker if they don't want to be late.

I am the only one not bellowing, except for Mr. Macy, who is pacing the quarterdeck instead. I can hear him up above us right now, back and forth, back and forth he goes. He is composing a poem "suitable for the occasion" for his beloved. I know this because snatches of it are blowing in through Papa's day cabin window. What I have heard so far is very fine, and I am sure Fanny will be pleased.

I too am "suitable for the occasion," trussed up like a holiday turkey in my corset and resplendent in my new turquoise silk, with my hair pinned up to boot. Aunt Anne says I look a picture, and in truth so does she, in an elegant sweep of navy that sets off her black hair and snapping eyes.

Glum and Chips have transferred the wedding cake to Papa's whaleboat, where Glum is seated now, guarding it carefully from monkeys and hungry shipmates. Chips, Owen Gardiner, and Sprigg—who is still in disgrace—will remain behind as shipkeepers, and Chips has promised to keep an eye on the other baked goods for me. Friday and Jocko are both prisoners for the morning, just in case—the one tied to the taffrail, the other in his cage below in steerage.

Sprigg flies in and announces that it's time to depart. We are slower than ten possums on a dark night, he says.

I notice that he has woven scarlet ribbons through his pigtail. I like the festive touch, I say. May I borrow them sometime? Sprigg peers at me over his spectacles. Certain young ladies have grown too big for their britches, he says, and threatens to thump me with his thimble.

—P.

Lahaina had never seen a wedding such as that of Fanny Starbuck and Mr. Macy. The streets were thronged with curious onlookers who followed our procession from the *Morning Star* to the church, many of them crowding right up to the windows, where they peered in to catch a glimpse of the ceremony.

The church itself was stuffed to the gills, and I

spotted the Wiggins family and Reverend and Mrs. Chapman and Dr. Phillips amongst the guests. All the whaling captains in port had turned out to honor one of their own, and those who had carried their wives to sea were accompanied by them as well. Everyone sparkled in their Christmas finery.

Charity, whose pale yellow dress brought an unaccustomed luster to her brown hair and eyes, preceded me up the aisle with a basket of petals, scattering them on the carpet as she went. She joined Mr. Macy, who was waiting alongside Reverend Wiggins at the front of the church, his Adam's apple bobbing nervously. Beside Mr. Macy stood Mr. Chase, his best man, whose round face was shiny with perspiration. I moved into place beside him. The music swelled, the doors opened, and every head swiveled as Fanny Starbuck floated in on my father's arm.

A sigh went up from the gathered guests, for she was truly lovely, a fairy tale beauty in a fairy tale dress. The collective efforts of her friends and students in Wailuku had produced a resplendent gown, and the dove-gray satin and cascades of matching lace set off her china-doll loveliness to perfection.

Papa looked very fine too in his best black dress coat with its gleaming silver buttons, and I had to admit that the two of them made a handsome couple as they proceeded to the front of the church. But

Fanny's gaze was fixed on her Mr. Macy and, beaming, she took her place beside him in front of Reverend Wiggins.

The church was silent as they repeated the time-honored marriage vows. Baby Joy didn't make a sound, and even Thaddeus and the Four Gospels, who had scuffled briefly outside in excitement at being reunited once again, sat up straight and paid attention. A few of the ladies sniffled quietly into their handkerchiefs, and Papa's eyes glistened. I wondered if he was recalling his own wedding day.

After the final "I do," Mr. Macy placed a slim gold band on Fanny's finger, then leaned down and kissed his new bride.

"Huzzah!" cried Charlie Fishback, and the *Morning Star*'s crew took up the cheer. Mr. Macy blushed, then grinned. Proudly offering Fanny his arm, he swept her down the aisle and out into the sunshine.

The wedding breakfast at the hotel was a resounding success as well, and after stuffing ourselves with roast pig and all the trappings, it was time for the cake.

I signaled to Glum, who nodded and left the room, returning a moment later bearing the platter. The cake was perfect, a soaring, flower-strewn confection that drew a collective gasp of admiration from the wedding guests. But dressed as he was in a sober black coat and wearing his customary funereal expression, Glum looked like an undertaker who'd wandered into the wrong reception.

"Smile," I hissed at him between clenched teeth. Startled, he produced a rusty grin and set the cake down in front of Fanny Starbuck—Fanny Starbuck Macy now.

"Why, Mr. Glumly, what a surprise!" Fanny said, dimpling at him. "Did you bake this?"

Our cook shook his bald head and pointed at me. "It was all Miss Patience's idea."

Fanny turned to me. "It was?"

I pressed my lips together nervously. "I wanted to do something special for you, for a wedding present," I explained. "I wanted to make you happy."

Fanny looked at the cake for a long time—so long that I began to worry that she didn't like it. Then she looked at her new husband, who beamed at her, and finally she looked at me. Her eyes shone with tears. "Oh, you have made me happy, Patience!" she said, leaning over the table to embrace me. "You have! It's beautiful—the best and most beautiful wedding cake I have ever seen, and the best wedding present that I—that we—could ever ask for."

"Hear, hear!" agreed Mr. Macy.

Papa tapped his glass with his knife to get everyone's attention, then stood up and raised it to the newly married couple.

"A toast!" he cried. "To Fanny and John, or Mr.

and Mrs. Macy, as you shall be known from this day forward. May your lives be happy, your children many, your home and hearth blessed with prosperity and peace, and may you always have greasy luck!"

We applauded and cheered again, and then Mr. Macy rose to his feet.

"I've written a poem suitable for the occasion," he said, his voice cracking ever so slightly.

Fanny blushed and smiled shyly at her new husband, who cleared his throat and continued in a more manful tone:

I find myself this Christmastide
In possession of a brand-new bride.
How this wonder came to pass
I truly cannot say, alas.
She says my rhymes have won her heart,
But surely that's just one small part.
I say the fates have had a hand
In making me a happy man.
I offer her to you this day
The loveliest flower to come my way.
Sweet and gentle, with disposition pure,
There's just one thing I know for sure—
For this love-struck husband there is no cure!

We applauded and cheered again, and as Mr.

Macy and Fanny cut the cake, Glum and I supervised its distribution. Reverend Wiggins accepted his piece from me quite graciously and didn't even make a fuss over the flowers this time.

We lingered at the hotel until midafternoon, and then it was time to return to the *Morning Star*. It took several trips in the whaleboats to ferry all of our guests aboard, and as Reverend Wiggins clambered up on deck, huffing and puffing, I saw Sprigg nudge Glum.

"You could hang a set of dish towels on them ears," he remarked in a low voice, nodding in the good reverend's direction.

I smiled.

The first thing Thaddeus did was untie Friday and let Jocko out of his cage, and soon the dog was chasing the monkey, the boys were chasing the dog, and Sprigg was chasing the boys, wheezing loudly and threatening them all with his thimble.

Papa offered a tour of the ship to all the men, after which it was time for dancing. Our shipmates struck up a merry tune on fiddle and flute and squeezebox, and thanks to Fanny's persistent tutelage, I didn't disgrace myself this time.

"Seems as though you learned a bit at Wailuku," Papa said, raising his eyebrows in surprise as he whirled me around the mainmast.

"I don't know what you're talking about," I replied loftily, but I couldn't help smiling at his approval.

Over his shoulder, I caught sight of Reverend Wiggins. He was frowning, and his movements were as stiff as a broom, but there was no question about it—Reverend Wiggins was dancing.

"'To everything there is a season,'" he said piously, steering Mrs. Wiggins carefully around us. "Ecclesiastes, chapter three, verse one."

In all I danced with Papa, Mr. Macy, Mr. Chase (who sweated profusely throughout the quadrille), Captain Russell and several of the other captains whose names I did not recall, and finally Charlie Fishback, whom Papa permitted one dance each with Charity and me.

"Just one, mind, Mr. Fishback," he said sternly.

"Aye, sir," Charlie replied, as he placed his hand gingerly on my waist and swept me off.

"You look different," he said after a minute.

"So do you," I replied, eyeing him critically. He'd slicked his red hair back, and I was sure he'd grown taller since last summer.

"No, I mean—nice," he mumbled, looking away.

"Oh." I was flustered. Charlie had paid me a compliment! I knew it was polite to offer a response and frantically tried to recall Hester Halifax's counsel for situations such as this, but all that came to mind was something about fish forks, which didn't seem to suit.

While I was considering what to say, a pebblelike object struck the top of my head.

"Ouch," I cried, pulling away from Charlie. I rubbed my scalp and looked up. My brother and the Four Gospels had climbed up into the mainmast rigging and were seated on the crosstrees, aiming kukui nuts at the dancers below. "Thaddeus Goodspeed, you come down from there this instant!" I called furiously.

Thaddeus just grinned and started for the lookout.

"I'll get the rascals down, Miss Patience," said Charlie. Leading me to the safety of the refreshment table, he took off his jacket and swung lightly up into the ratlines as the music ended.

Fanny rustled over in her dove-gray gown. "He seems a very pleasant young man," she said, picking up a gingersnap.

"Charlie?" I replied. "I suppose so. I'm teaching him to navigate."

"Are you indeed?" said Fanny. She flashed her dimples at me mischievously and nibbled at the cookie. "Well, be sure and steer him to one of these. You know what they say after all—'The way to a man's heart is through his stomach.'"

What did she mean by that? I wondered. Before I could give it further thought, however, Charity found me.

"Father says we must go," Charity said sadly. "He says he wants us all safely ashore before dark."

The sun was indeed dropping low in the sky, and I realized that all of our guests would soon be departing.

"But surely it's too soon!" I cried, thinking how much I was going to miss my friends from Wailuku. "I wish you could come with us!"

"Me too," said Charity, embracing me. "But I promise to write."

"As will I," I replied. "And it's not for that long. We'll be back again in a few months."

I accompanied her to the whaleboat and bid good-bye to Mrs. Wiggins.

"I'll always think of you as another daughter," she said, pressing me tightly to her.

I couldn't help welling up at this, and when it came time to bid baby Joy farewell, my tears spilled over onto her plump little cheeks. I kissed her tenderly, and she gave me a toothless grin, which made me cry even harder.

As Reverend Wiggins thanked Aunt Anne and Fanny for all they had done for the school—"and most particularly for your generous gift of the melodeon, Mrs. Macy"—I drew out my handkerchief and blew my nose vigorously. I managed a less emotional parting from Captain and Mrs. Russell, whom we would see soon enough at the winter rendezvous in New Zealand, and from Reverend and Mrs. Chapman and Dr. Phillips, who confided that Wailuku would be a much duller place without Thaddeus and me around to keep them all on their toes.

Charlie reappeared towing Matthew and Mark by the scruffs of their necks, while Luke and John skulked along behind. As my friend began handing the boys to Kanaka Jim to stow into the whaleboat, I grabbed his arm.

"I almost forgot!" I said. "Wait just a minute, would you?"

Running down to my cabin, I plucked *Robinson Crusoe* from the bookshelf and hid it in the folds of my gown, then ran back up on deck again.

"Here," I whispered, stuffing it into Matthew's pocket. "Merry Christmas! Don't let your father find out."

Reverend Wiggins surveyed his woebegone brood. He withdrew his handkerchief from his pocket and passed it to Mrs. Wiggins, who was already seated in the whaleboat. "'Weeping may endure for a night,'" he boomed, taking the baby from Fanny, who relinquished her reluctantly, and handing her to her mother, "'but Joy cometh in the morning.' Psalms, chapter thirty, verse five." He chuckled at his little joke. "Come now, my dears, no more tears. We shall meet again, in this world or the next."

Then he turned to Thaddeus and me. "I hope that your time at the Wailuku Seminary has been profitable, children, and that you are returning to your father with an invigorated sense of duty and obedience," he began pompously, then paused, harrumphed, and unbent slightly. "I believe 'greasy luck' is the appropriate phrase at this time, Thaddeus," he said to my brother, clasping him warmly by the hand. Then it was my turn. "And I owe you an eternal debt of gratitude for all you did for Mrs. Wiggins and young Thankful." He harrumphed again. "And for helping Charity with her mathematics."

"Does your daughter have a head for figures as well?" asked Papa.

"So it would seem." Reverend Wiggins hoisted himself into the whaleboat. "Mind you, don't neglect your French, now, Patience."

"*Non, monsieur,*" I reassured him, not bothering to add that *Willis's Guide to Conversational French* was already buried deep in a trunk in the hold.

We bid a bittersweet farewell to all of our friends—and to Fanny and Mr. Macy as well, who were returning to the hotel in Lahaina and who would rejoin us first thing in the morning—and went below to pack. Our days here in the Sandwich Islands would soon be but a memory, for the *Morning Star* was due to sail with the forenoon tide.

Epilogue

To render a young woman wise and good,
to prepare her mind for the duties and trials of life,
is the great purpose of education.
—*Young Lady's Own Book: A Manual of*
Intellectual Improvement and Moral Deportment

January 1, 1837

What a whirlwind this past week has been!

I wish I could relive the wedding all over again, every moment of it, from putting my hair up, to the ceremony itself, to the look on Fanny's face when she saw the cake. And the dancing! Especially the dancing. . . .

But I have packed those memories away now, along with my turquoise silk dress, and as we return to whaling life, I have donned my worn and mended everyday gray calico, along with my role as assistant navigator.

We are bound for the Bay of Islands, heading southwest with a fair wind and a following sea— an idyllic cruise that Papa says he ordered specially for our honeymooners.

It is noon, and up on deck this New Year's

Day, Aunt Anne and Charlie Fishback are taking turns shooting the sun with their sextants. They are growing daily more skillful, and I am proud of them both. Here in the main cabin Fanny and Mr. Macy are seated at the table beside Ishmael and me, holding hands. The only stars they see are the ones in each other's eyes.

I can hear Sprigg and Glum quarreling in the pantry, and Jocko scolding Friday from the mizzenmast crosstrees above. From the sounds of it, Thaddeus is hard at work with Chips at the carpenter's bench, hammering on scraps of wood.

I think of what Aunt Anne told me once, that people learning is more difficult than book learning. I have certainly seen the truth of that these past months. I misjudged Fanny cruelly, and possibly Reverend Wiggins as well, though I still think he's a pompous walrus.

Aunt Anne also once said that life is a voyage and that we never know where its currents will carry us. I think perhaps I understand now what she meant by that as well, and as the winds and tides carry us toward New Zealand I can't help but wonder what other adventures lie ahead.

Aunt Anne says that I have a natural talent for teaching and that I might wish to consider attending the college she told Reverend Wiggins *about*—Mount Holyoke Female Seminary, I believe it was called. Perhaps I will investigate it after we return to Nantucket.

Or perhaps I will ship out again aboard the Morning Star and sail the seven seas with Papa and Thaddeus, hunting for whales. Or perhaps some other adventure altogether awaits.

Papa taps on the skylight and I look up. He waves at me and smiles. I smile back. For now, I don't need to know what lies ahead. For now it's enough just to be here, safe aboard the Morning Star with my family and friends.

For now, it's enough to be home.

Author's Note

One of the most delightful things about writing historical fiction is that you never know what you'll discover that may alter the course of your story.

When I left Patience at the end of her first adventure (*The Voyage of Patience Goodspeed*), I had only a vague notion that, true to the route followed by nearly all nineteenth-century New England whaling ships, she'd be spending a bit of time in the Sandwich Islands, as Hawaii was then called. After I began my research, however, I stumbled across a mention of the Wailuku Female Seminary. The minute I read this, there was no question in my mind but that Patience would be shipped off to boarding school.

Founded by Christian missionaries on Maui in the summer of 1837 (the same time that the wharf in Lahaina was built, but for the purpose of this story I pushed that date up a year), the school began with just six girls, a number that swelled to as many as seventy during the twelve years of its existence. The Wiggins family and their colleagues are fictitious characters, of course (Reverend Jonathan Green, his wife Theodosia, and what the Missionary Board termed a "dedicated spinster" by the name of Maria Ogden were the school's original teachers, followed by Edward Bailey and his wife, Caroline), but sadly, the seminary really was struck by an epidemic of "bilious fever," and five of the students died (another benefit to writing fiction is that a tenderhearted author can tweak the outcome).

This incident points to some of the difficulties that faced the two cultures—Western and Polynesian—as they encountered one another, for the cause of the epidemic was traced in part to the sedentary life that the girls led at the boarding school. While this life may have seemed normal to the New England missionaries, it was vastly different from the active one the native students were used to leading, and in the wake of the tragedy, the school's curriculum was changed to include gardening, physical education, and frequent trips to the mountains and the seashore.

Today visitors to Maui can tour the site of the Wailuku Female Seminary at the Bailey House Museum. Although the buildings that housed the schoolroom and dormitories are no longer standing, the parsonage and its outbuildings are still there, and they offer a vivid peek at what life was like at that point in history for the missionaries and their families, as well as for the native Hawaiians.

Something else I learned from my research was that surfing is an ancient Polynesian sport (embarrassingly, I thought it was invented in Southern

California by the Beach Boys). Almost without exception, nineteenth-century visitors to the Hawaiian islands exclaimed about surfing (some of them, including a few of the more adventurous missionaries, even attempted it themselves), and the fact that it was practiced with skill by men, women, and children alike. When I learned this, I knew Patience would somehow have to try "surf-riding" too.

The battle of *Kepaniwai* really took place, and if you ever go to Maui, be sure to drive up the 'Iao Valley to where the 'Iao Needle broods eerily over a verdant, mist-shrouded ravine. It doesn't take a great stretch of the imagination to envision Kamehameha's warriors streaming up this narrow slash in the mountains in a bid to trap their enemies, or the fierce clash and massacre that followed. The hula that Patience, Aunt Anne, and Charity witness La'ila'i dance to commemorate the battle, however, is a figment of my imagination.

So too is Hester Halifax, though all the quotes that I've attributed to her, as well as the ones that begin each chapter, are taken from real Victorian etiquette books. I couldn't resist using them—many are quite hilarious when viewed through twenty-first-century eyes, for one thing—and, too, they provide an authentic glimpse of the roles girls and women were expected to play throughout the 1800s.

Finally, although it seems far-fetched today, cannibals presented a very real danger to early nineteenth-century seafarers, and I drew from numerous eyewitness accounts in whaling journals and literature of the period in creating the "Dark Isles" and their inhabitants.

As for what surprises await Patience and her shipmates as they sail off toward New Zealand and the final leg of the *Morning Star*'s three-year voyage, all I can say is that I can't wait to see what history has up its sleeve for them next!

RECIPES

A Christmas Wedding Cake

"The cake was perfect, a soaring, flower-strewn confection that drew a collective gasp of admiration from the wedding guests."

2 1/2 cups flour
2 1/2 teaspoons baking powder
1/4 teaspoon salt
1 teaspoon cinnamon
1/2 teaspoon nutmeg
1/4 teaspoon cloves
1/2 cup butter
1 cup sugar
2 eggs
1/3 cup molasses
3/4 cup milk

Preheat oven to 350 degrees F. Cream butter and sugar together, then add eggs one at a time, beating thoroughly after each. Beat in molasses. Add baking powder, salt, and spices, then add flour alternately with milk, beating until smooth.

Bake in two greased and floured layer pans for 25–30 minutes. Cool. Frost with buttercream frosting.

Buttercream Frosting

1/2 cup butter
1 teaspoon vanilla
3 Tablespoons milk
3–4 cups confectioner's sugar

Cream butter and sugar until smooth; add vanilla and milk. Add desired amount of confectioner's sugar to make a smooth, spreadable frosting.

Fanny Starbuck's Shortbread

"'Mrs. Starbuck's shortbread!' is now the cry from fo'c'sle to quarterdeck."

> 1 cup butter
> 1/4 teaspoon salt (only if unsalted butter is used; otherwise omit salt)
> 1/2 cup sugar
> 2 cups flour

Preheat oven to 325 degrees F. Cream butter and sugar. Mix in flour; knead gently until soft. Roll dough out 1/4- to 1/2-inch thick with floured rolling pin and slice into rectangles or cut into shapes with cookie cutter (hearts look nice, and Fanny would approve).

Bake for 15–20 minutes until just barely golden brown, turning cookie sheet halfway through baking period for evenness.

Glossary

ae: (Hawaiian) yes

alii: (Hawaiian) chief

archipelago: a group or chain of islands

aūe: (Hawaiian) alas! Oh no!

awiwi: (Hawaiian) hurry

binnacle: the wooden base of a ship's compass

blubber gaff: a pole with a hook on the end for securing and lifting whale blubber

blubber spade: a sharp instrument for cutting whale blubber

collywobbles: upset stomach

cutting in: the process by which a whale is butchered and rendered into oil

fo'c'sle: abbreviation for "forecastle," the crew's quarters at the bow of the ship below the main deck

foredeck: the front part of the ship's deck, forward of the mainmast

gally: to irritate or annoy

gam: a social visit between crews of whaling ships

greasy luck: whaleman's term for good fortune

gurry: whaleman's term for the noxious mixture of whale innards that sloshes over the deck during the cutting in process

halakahiki: (Hawaiian) pineapple

haole: (Hawaiian) foreigner; non-Polynesian

holokū: (Hawaiian) a loose-fitting dress

ho'o kala kupua: (Hawaiian) magic

huhū: (Hawaiian) in a huff
hula: (Hawaiian) a traditional Hawaiian dance
imu: (Hawaiian) ground oven
jury-rigged: to build something in a makeshift way
kāhuna: (Hawaiian) priest
kanaka: (Hawaiian) man; nineteenth-century whaleman's term for Hawaiian islanders
kapa: (Hawaiian) cloth made from the inner bark of a paper mulberry tree
kapu: (Hawaiian) forbidden
kohola: (Hawaiian) whale
laudanum: a sedative, used in the nineteenth century as a painkiller
mai'a: (Hawaiian) banana
makamaka: (Hawaiian) friend
malo: (Hawaiian) a loincloth made from kapa cloth
merchantman: a merchant ship; a ship that carries goods for trade
mizzenmast: on a ship with three or more masts, the third mast from the front
mumblety-peg: an old-fashioned game in which players flip a knife and try to stick the blade into the ground
ōkoholā: (Hawaiian) harpoon
papa heé nalu: (Hawaiian) literally, wave-sliding board; surfboard
pilikia: (Hawaiian) trouble
poi: (Hawaiian) a fermented paste made from the tuber of the taro plant
pua'a: (Hawaiian) pig

quadrille: a French square dance popular in the eighteenth and nineteenth centuries

Sandwich Islands: nineteenth-century name for Hawaii

scuppers: drainholes in the bulwarks of a ship that allow water on the deck to flow overboard

sextant: a navigational instrument used to determine latitude and longitude

taffrail: the railing around the stern, or rear, of a ship

taro: (Hawaiian) a plant cultivated in Hawaii for its edible starchy tubers

ti: (Hawaiian) a plant whose leaves were used for such things as thatching roofs and wrapping food for cooking

transship: to transfer goods aboard another ship

try-pot: an enormous cauldron in which oil was boiled out of whale blubber

twitter-pated: lovestruck

wai: (Hawaiian, and general Polynesian) water

Acknowledgments

As always, my deepest thanks go first and foremost to my husband, Steve, without whose unwavering support, keen editorial insights, and cheerful willingness to consume more pizza than has ever before been thought humanly possible, this book would not have been possible. (In all fairness, our sons Ian and Ben also manfully consumed vast quantities of pizza without complaint.)

I owe an ongoing debt of gratitude to Dorothy Boyer Gornick, my wonderful Nantucket cousin, for generously sharing her knowledge of her native island and our family history, and to my dear friend and fairy godsister Cyndi Howard, whose gift of shared studio space rescued me during the "summer of revision." Warmest thanks too, to fellow Voyagers Patty Leeker and Samantha Frishberg, for always being ready with a lifeline.

On Maui, thanks are due to Roz Lightfoot, Gail Burns, and Beryl Bal at the Bailey House Museum for making me feel so welcome, and for unearthing so many valuable tidbits about the Wailuku Female Seminary and the Sandwich Island missionaries. My sister, Stefanie Milligan, was a lively traveling companion throughout that research trip, which took us from Maui's glorious shores through the bustling streets of Lahaina and on to the blistering heat of the 'Iao Valley and more as we sleuthed out the island's history. *Aloha* to you all!

Thanks also to Jim Carmin, John Wilson Room librarian at Multnomah County's Central Library in Portland, Oregon, for a most agreeable afternoon spent plundering a wealth of Victorian etiquette books. Another Central Library treasure, the Sterling Room for Writers, proved a haven, and I am indebted to Donald Sterling Jr., and Sis Hayes for their generous sponsorship of that tranquil space. Half a world away in New Zealand, *kia ora* to Joan Druett, whose splendid books on nineteenth-century women at sea have inspired me over the years—many thanks for all your pioneering efforts in this field (and for luscious kiwi chocolate, too).

And last but by no means least, everlasting gratitude to my agent, Barry Goldblatt, for his tireless efforts on my behalf, and to my stellar editor, Alyssa Eisner, whose boundless enthusiasm for Patience and her adventures is a continual source of encouragement.